SEE THAT
MY GRAVE IS
KEPT CLEAN

Also by Bart Paul

NONFICTION
*Double-Edged Sword: The Many Lives of Hemingway's
Friend, the American Matador Sidney Franklin*

FICTION
Under Tower Peak
Cheatgrass

SEE THAT MY GRAVE IS KEPT CLEAN

A NOVEL

BART PAUL

ARCADE
CRIMEWISE

An Arcade CrimeWise Book

First Edition

This is a work of fiction. Names, places, characters, and incidents are either the products of the author's imagination or are used fictitiously.

Arcade Publishing books may be purchased in bulk at special discounts for sales promotion, corporate gifts, fund-raising, or educational purposes. Special editions can also be created to specifications. For details, contact the Special Sales Department, Arcade Publishing, 307 West 36th Street, 11th Floor, New York, NY 10018 or arcade@skyhorsepublishing.com.

Arcade Publishing® and CrimeWise® are registered trademarks of Skyhorse Publishing, Inc.®, a Delaware corporation.

Visit our website at www.arcadepub.com.

10 9 8 7 6 5 4 3 2 1

Names: Paul, Bart, author.
Title: See that my grave is kept clean / Bart Paul.
Description: New York: Arcade/CrimeWise, 2019. | Series: A Tommy Smith high
    country noir | "An Arcade CrimeWise book." |
Identifiers: LCCN 2019020782 (print) | LCCN 2019021468 (ebook) | ISBN
    9781948924399 (ebook) | ISBN 9781948924375 (hardback)
Subjects: | BISAC: FICTION / Westerns. | FICTION / Thrillers. | GSAFD:
    Western stories. | Suspense fiction.
Classification: LCC PS3616.A92765 (ebook) | LCC PS3616.A92765 S44 2019
    (print) | DDC 813/.6—dc23
LC record available at https://lccn.loc.gov/2019020782

Cover design by Erin Seaward-Hiatt
Cover painting by Denise Klitsie

Printed in the United States of America

To Cal Barksdale

"There's just one kind favor I ask of you . . .
Please see that my grave is kept clean."
—Blind Lemon Jefferson

"Shooting people isn't all fun and games."
—Sam Peckinpah

SEE THAT
MY GRAVE IS
KEPT CLEAN

The first thing I noticed was the girl. I was opening the corral gate just before sunup and watching Sarah's dog bring in the horses and mules. They broke out of the tamarack and splashed through the creek, then crossed the meadow to the corral, running by me fast, the dust they raised hanging in the air. The kid couldn't have been more than ten. Her ratty high-tops with no laces scuffed up dust just like the animals did. Her shorts were small on her, and a dirty Little Mermaid jacket hung too big around her shoulders. She looked like she was headed for a day at some low-rent Disneyland or maybe a haunted carnival, not an early summer hike in the high country.

The dog got the stock penned, and I closed the gate. The girl dropped behind to watch. The man and woman walking ahead of her didn't seem to notice. They were looking at the cabin.

"What place is this?" the man said.

"Aspen Canyon Pack Outfit."

He nodded, looking around at our setup. He and the woman kept moving, talking amongst themselves and still not noticing the child dawdling behind. The dog trotted over to the girl, who squatted down the way kids do and let the dog check her out.

"Hi, mister," she said.

"Hey."

"What's his name?"

"Hoot."

"Hi, Hoot." She looked up. "Can I pet the horses?"

"I dunno. I guess. Sure."

I pulled a handful of hay from the stack outside the fence and gave it to her. I showed her how to keep her hand flat so's not to get bit, and she held it out to one of the mules whose head was first over the top corral pole. The girl squealed when those big mule lips touched her hand, but she seemed to enjoy herself and didn't notice me studying her. She looked sort of grimy and had a sour old-clothes smell to her that cut through the whiff of fresh hay and corral dust. My own little girl was just a couple of months old and had that cool new baby smell, so for the first time in my life I noticed such things.

CHAPTER ONE

"Come on, dammit," the man hollered.

He was hustling back down the trail past my half-finished cabin about forty yards away. Sarah stood in the open front room of the cabin with our baby, Lorena, against her chest, watching. The guy hustled up to the kid and clamped a hand on her arm.

"Quit dragging ass," he said. "We got to hurry. You don't want her to give you the hot sauce, do you?"

The kid shook her head.

When the guy finally talked to me, our eyes didn't meet. "Sorry, sir."

I was looking at his scuffed-up city shoes and all-black clothes that looked like he'd been clubbing in them for a week straight. He had ten years on me, so the "sir" sounded peculiar. The girl wiped the mule slobber on her shorts and yanked her arm from his hand.

"Thanks, mister," she said.

"Sure, kid. Have a nice hike."

"'Bye Hoot."

The sun burned through the tops of the Jeffrey pine down-canyon, and the first rays hit the kid's dirty yellow hair and shined it right up. She looked back at me as she walked away, following the guy along up the trail to where the woman was waiting. Even at a distance, I could see the woman's heavy face, red and weathered, and the scrawny hips of a rummy. I headed back up to the cabin and climbed the temporary plywood steps to the porch. The big front room only had three feet of the log walls in place, snugged up around the base of the rock fireplace with electrical conduit poking out of the logs where the outlets would go. Only the two bedrooms and a bathroom were totally closed in, but I never got tired of looking at it or smelling the fresh-cut pine. Sarah watched the three of them walk up the trail and vanish into the aspen.

"They look like refugees," she said.

"Yeah, but from what?"

I could still hear the seedy looking pair yammering loud out of sight in the trees as Sarah got an extra blanket for Lorena and we walked up the slope through the aspen to Harvey's trailer for breakfast. I thought I heard a motor like from an ATV or dirt bike at the trailhead across the creek, but the sound drifted away and we went inside. Harvey's wife, May, had sausage, eggs, home fries, and coffee waiting. We sat at the dinette all crowded together, and May took Lorena on her lap and hugged on her, then handed her back to Sarah so she could nurse while we ate.

"Sure you don't want me to stay here and work on that kitchen wiring for you newlyweds?" Harvey said.

"Nah, you need a break or you'll sull up on me. A day at the head of a string of mules will do you good, old man."

"I could lead that bunch myself, then," he said. "Give you a day off."

"'A day horseback in this canyon ain't never no hardship.' That's what you used to tell me."

"I guess a junior partner's got no pull in this outfit," he said. He winked at Sarah.

"Don't make Tommy sorry he was so generous," May said. "He's putting everything he has into this place."

"Hell, Mother," he said, "the boy just wants company on those long hours in the saddle."

"That's what he has me for," Sarah said.

"I ain't touchin' that," Harv said.

He poured us all more coffee. I'd worked so many summers for him when I was in high school, it struck us both funny to turn the tables, but he was a pretty famous packer in his day and still had a million friends, even after being out of the business a couple of years. Either way, Harvey was glad to get back to it. Being a poor carpenter and worse electrician, I knew I'd be screwed without his help on the cabin. And Sarah said I was such a grump, if I was starting a business involving actual human beings I'd need all the help I could get.

"Harv just likes watching the way the backpackers grouse when they see the new cabin and trailers where there wasn't anything the year before," May said. She was looking out the trailer window at the winding trail outside. "I heard him tell one guy we were putting in a whole subdivision. Fellow like to soil himself."

Harvey and I worked out some last-minute details of a trip to the Tower Peak country we'd be making in less than a week for two couples from Newport Beach, then we headed down to the corral dragging halters. We started catching fresh horses and mules for that day's trip for the Forest Service. We had sawbucks on six head in no time, and our saddle horses caught. The day before, Harvey'd sorted the loads of tools and supplies we'd be hauling and had them laid out on the pack platforms ready to go. We hoisted the bags and slings and tools up on the animals, tarped them, and lashed them down. Then I went over to the cabin to kiss my girls goodbye. Lorena had dozed off during breakfast, and I watched Sarah set her down in her crib in the bedroom. She took the deputy uniform she'd need that afternoon down from a hook, peeled off the dry-cleaning plastic, and hung the thing in the sun.

"My shift starts at four," she said.

"I'll be back in plenty of time."

"Your mom said she'd be here around two," Sarah said, "so you're good either way."

My mom, Deb Smith, and her boyfriend, Burt, had been living forty miles up the road on Sarah's dad Dave Cathcart's ranch for almost a year, helping him out with his cattle, but this new grandmother thing had Mom hovering close to the baby. She claimed not to mind when she'd have to drive Lorena to the sheriff's office in the middle of Sarah's shift so she could nurse. We'd named the kid for Sarah's mother who'd died when Sarah was eight, and she had a way of looking at that child that got to me every time. I ran my hand over the log wall and the plank door with the iron hinges Harvey had made for us in his shoeing forge, and I had to catch myself. Things were about as good as I'd ever dared hope.

Sarah looked around the half-done cabin like she'd been reading my mind. "We'll remember this," she said.

We stood over the crib together for a last second, then I kissed her and picked up my saddle pockets and my jacket and walked out of the aspen shade into the sun where the horses were tied.

Harvey and I rode past the corrals and followed the dirt track into the trees leading three mules apiece. Harvey wasn't quite right. This was more a two-man job, and I surely did enjoy his company, though I'd never say so.

In a few minutes we were looking down a steep cut into Aspen Creek. A few minutes more and we were in scattered Jeffrey pine, the sound of our hooves muffled by the pine duff and the powdery dust with fresh cattle sign on either side of the trail.

We were heading about seven miles up the canyon to resupply a Forest Service trail crew fixing rockslide damage in the Wilderness Area. We followed the creek as the canyon widened with Harvey out front on his big sorrel mare, him holding the mule's lead with his rope hand resting on his hip, a Winston poking out of the fingers of his rein hand, talking nonstop and never looking back, just like I remembered him doing when I was halfway around the world. I was riding a big common gray gelding I'd just bought, taking him for a test ride before I put customers on him. The morning was warm and blue-skied, and we were seeing the first of Bonner and Tyree's cow-calf pairs in the willows and bogs along the creek.

Then the bankside tamarack thinned down to nothing, and the first big meadow spread out in front of us, descending from right to left with sage and aspen scattered high on the canyon slope. The left side of the canyon was pine-timbered and steep, with boulder slides running between ridges of trees. Beyond the last slide, five glacier-cut granite peaks were set out in a row, looking smaller and smaller off into the distance, only one of them important enough to be named. It was a country of impressive peaks, and you couldn't name them all.

"Did I ever tell you the story of the Spanish Cave?" Harvey said.

"Buncha times."

"'Bout the guy's grave and—"

"Closer to a thousand times, actually."

"So whaddya think?" he said. "You think there could be a hidden cave as big as a boxcar in this canyon with a dead Spanish guy with a box of treasure and a gold-handled sword all laid out like in some church?"

"Sure, except there weren't any Spanish guys exploring this side of the Sierra a couple hundred years ago. It was just mountain men like Walker and Carson."

"Just 'cause nobody's found something yet don't mean it ain't there," he said.

"Then ask Kit Carson about it. You and him are old pals, right? Him and Frémont?"

"You just might be finishing that cabin all by your lonesome," he said. "Smartass. I find that gold sword, I'm keepin' it all to myself."

The trail was far from the creek now, and worn deep

and narrow on the upper edge of the meadow with black mud where it crossed the springs, and gravel fans spilling out on the grass from the snowmelt runoff. We saw more cattle on the meadow grass off to our left. Out ahead the trail disappeared into a line of aspen.

"Some guy wrote about that cave back before World War Two," Harvey said. "His son useta go deer hunting with me every fall, and it was him told me about it."

"Well, if there was such an awesome place, cowboys, loggers, or backpackers would've found it. Besides, not a lot of caves in this granite."

"The guy wouldn't just make up a story like that," he said.

"Why not?"

"You got no sense of imagination," he said.

"I can imagine that old Spaniard must be pretty ripe by now. Pretty damn ripe."

There was a squeaky chirp in the distance, and I scanned the sky until I saw a golden eagle zipping down behind the treetops. I always loved seeing those dark old monsters and remembered missing them when I was overseas. We passed into thick aspen at the top of the meadow, the breeze fluttery in the leaves. I turned back to watch the stock pick their way over the deadfall. I was watching my mules to see how they handled themselves and their loads as they turned back and forth through the winding trail. I'd bought these six the month before from a trader who helped the Marines supply animals for their mountain warfare training base out by Sonora Pass and for overseas deployment. They were out of Belgian-crossed mares and well matched for color and size. They didn't come cheap, but once I'd seen them I had to have them. I'd saddled them and messed with them, but this was the first time they were on the clock. They were all between four and eight years and used to working together, so I was feeling proud of how they handled themselves. I was kind of bursting at how fine the whole string looked, too, but wouldn't say so out loud.

"What the damn hell?" Harvey said.

We heard a commotion ahead and saw flashes of color through the trees. The second mule in Harvey's string sucked back and Harv dallied his lead mule's rope till the scared one settled. Then we heard branches snap and a shout for help. We sat tight until people on foot came toward us all ragged and stumbly. It was the seedy-looking couple who'd passed through the pack station at sunup with the little kid. The guy looked sweaty and frantic.

"Help us," he said.

"What's up?"

"It's our little girl," he said. "She's gone."

He kept coming right up on us, heedless of the animals and what they might do. Almost like Harvey and me weren't there either.

"Whaddya mean, gone?" Harvey said.

"You gotta help us," the woman said. "She's our baby—and now she's gone."

"When'd you last see her?"

The guy pushed down alongside Harvey's string till he got to me, crowding the stock and bumping into the packs. A couple of the mules stepped away sideways, mindful of the idiot in their midst. "I dunno," the guy said. "Hour ago?"

"An hour?" Harvey said. "Jay-sus Chroist."

"It was less than that," the woman said. She pushed through the trees behind the guy and looked at him cross. "We sat down to nap and sorta dozed off. When we woke up, she was gone."

"I bet she's somewhere close. You'll find her."

"Will you help us, mister?" the woman said.

"We got to get this load up the trail another few miles," Harvey said. "Got guys waitin' on it."

"Where'd you take your nap?"

The guy pulled out a cigarette and lit it, watching me. "Back there a ways," he said. He pointed up the canyon.

"Did you pass a fence at the bottom of a meadow?"

"I didn't see no fence," he said.

"You folks still came a long way fast since I saw you this morning. A real long way on foot. Maybe she got tired and laid down."

"We wanted to see the sights," the woman said. "Will you help?" She pulled out a little bottle of Fireball and took a pull. There was sweat on her face. It was maybe nine-thirty in the morning.

I got off my horse and tied him to an aspen, then walked around the mules to Harvey.

"What're you thinking?" he said.

"Maybe you could take the string to the Forest Service camp, and I'll ride back to the pack station, get my pickup, and drive these ginks to the sheriff's office. The trail crew'll help you unload. I don't see any other way."

"I'll keep an eye out for the kid and holler and stuff,"

11

he said. "And I'll keep watch on the crick—you know—just in case."

"Yeah. Just in case." I looked to the woman. "What's her name?"

The man and woman looked at each other.

"Kay . . ." the woman said. "Kay . . . leeana."

"Yeah," the guy said. "Kayleeana."

I told the folks to head down the canyon and always stay on the trail. I told them what Harvey and I would be doing and to look sharp for my truck. I tied my string in behind Harvey's, and he headed off up the trail. I got on my horse and saw the dad flick his cigarette into the saplings.

"Best pick that up."

"Sorry, mister," he said. "I wasn't thinkin'."

"Just stick to the trail and keep shouting her name. I'll be back up before you know it."

"Will you be bringing one of them dogs?" he said.

"I don't think we're there yet."

I broke my horse into a high trot winding through the aspen, listening to the man and woman behind me shouting for a girl they couldn't see, their voices fading as I rode. I didn't dare take a backward look. As scared as they must've been, those two just chapped my hide. I cleared the trees then really busted that horse loose, but I couldn't get that kid out of my mind.

CHAPTER TWO

This was sure as hell not how I wanted to start my first season as a wilderness outfitting tycoon.

"How could they just lose a little girl?" Sarah said. She was sitting in the sun outside the cabin nursing and watching me carry my saddle up from the corral. She looked golden. Lorena looked amped and happy to see me.

"They're a pretty shaky-looking pair." I stood close and let Lorena take my finger for a second, then get back to nursing. "These little rascals are so damn fragile . . ."

"When you get the parents here, I can drive them into town if you want to head back up the canyon and keep looking," Sarah said. "In case they haven't found the child yet."

"I'd feel better doing that. And I gotta catch up with Harvey if I can. Don't want to let him do all the work. I'd never hear the end of it."

She held a hand out and I took it. "It'll be okay, babe. That child can't have gone far."

"Unless she fell into the creek or busted something."

Sarah gave kind of a shudder. I kissed both my beauties and climbed into my pickup and rolled on up the canyon. The Forest Service didn't want motor vehicles past the pack station, so they didn't maintain the old wagon road. Washouts from heavy runoff over the years had me in four-wheel drive pretty quick. Once the road separated from the creek, the track flattened out and was easy traveling for a time, but dusty. Finally, ahead in the distance I could see the couple sitting under some tamarack by the creek at the bottom of the first meadow. They stood up when they heard me. They hadn't come all that far and looked like they didn't know a care in this world. I stopped about twenty feet from them and opened the cab door.

"No sign?"

"No," the woman said, "I'm just beside myself."

The man watched my truck as I turned it around. I'd had that old Dodge Ram almost as long as I'd had a driver's license, but maybe he was expecting something more high-end. The woman climbed in and scooted over close to me, panting. Her breath was hot and rotten, and I moved to give her more room. I obviously hadn't thought this part through. The guy touched a couple of spots on the front panel before he followed her into the cab.

"I'm Tommy Smith."

"Chrystal Dawn," the woman said. She grabbed my hand and shook it. Hers was sticky and damp. "We just can't thank you enough."

"We haven't found her yet—but we will." I turned to the guy. "So, you'd be Mister Dawn?"

He gave me a sour look but stuck out his hand. "Cody

Davis," he said. "Are those bullet holes? Under the bondo and primer it looks like you got some bullet holes."

His hand was skinny and cold.

"Yeah. I need to get it painted."

"Was it somebody shooting at you?" he said.

"Nope."

I wasn't about to explain that my wife's ex-husband had tried to kill me the year before, and had come damn close.

"Probably just some kids or drunks when I left it untended for a couple of days up at the trailhead. It's so beat-up, they probably thought it was abandoned."

The guy asked a lot of questions. Some of them were about the ins-and-outs of the whole search and rescue thing. Some weren't.

"That where you folks parked? The trailhead?"

"We parked by a bridge below the campground," he said.

"You've had a hell of a walk."

The guy only nodded and off we went. I waited a few seconds just to be polite, then fired up the AC and rolled down my window, both.

After a bit the woman gave a big sigh. "Our poor little girl."

"She ever disappear before?"

"Yeah," the guy said. "The kid don't mind real good. And she's got a mouth on her."

"That when you give her the hot sauce?"

The woman laughed. "Yeah," she said. "That stuff shuts her up quick."

We pulled into the pack station in another thirty minutes.

"What's going on?" the guy said.

"What do you mean?"

"What's with the sheriffs?" he said. He leaned his face close to the windshield, watching Sarah trot down the cabin steps toward her truck. She was in uniform.

"That's my wife. She's a Frémont County deputy. She'll be driving you guys into Paiute Meadows, and she'll start the ball with County Search and Rescue. The quicker you do that, the better outcome this thing'll have."

"Is she the one who gets the dog?" he said. "The search dog?"

"Nope."

The woman started sniffling. Sarah gave me a wave as she trotted back up the steps into the cabin. I pulled up next to my mom's Mustang.

"Nice ride," the guy said.

"It's my mother's. She's here to babysit while my wife takes you folks to town."

The woman fiddled with her phone. "I don't get no service. How could she—"

"Sheriff's radio."

"What'll you be doing, then?" the guy said, "when we're at the sheriff's?"

"Looking for your girl, I expect."

I left the pair of them and jogged up to the house to say hi to Mom and brief Sarah about the two drifters standing out by my truck. Mom started to tell me all about her boyfriend, Burt, and Sarah's dad, Dave, and their trip to the stock sale in Fallon the day before, and how content she and Burt were to be living and working on Dave's ranch in Shoshone Valley, and how crazy she was about the whole new grandmother business, and how the turn all our lives had taken in the last year was just meant to be. I broke in to talk about the missing kid.

"I just can't imagine what they must be feeling," Mom said. "Where are the parents from?"

"Hunger."

"*Tommy,*" she said, sharp as could be. "Those people must be going through hell. You be kind."

We stepped back outside, and I introduced the pair to Sarah. The woman asked for a bathroom. Before Sarah could point her to our cabin, I directed her to the outhouse along the corral fence. She came out a couple of minutes later making a face. Sarah piled them into her new Silverado, and off they went through the trees and down the canyon toward town. Mom carried Lorena and some sandwiches and followed me over to the corral while I caught another horse. I picked a young sorrel gelding I'd started for Dave Cathcart before I signed up for my third tour. It'd been Dave's surprise for Sarah. Then she'd given him to me when we got married, and now he was my go-to guy. My saddle pockets were full of sandwiches, jerky, a riflescope, and a flask. I snapped on a cantlebag with a sheriff's radio and a good army flashlight and a first-aid kit, then buckled on my chinks with my skinning knife hanging on the belt. I didn't know what I'd find or how long I'd be.

I broke the sorrel into a long trot over the first rough ground, then hit an easy lope for big stretches when the road was good, raising a fair bit of dust as I went. I was crossing the lower meadow for the fifth time that day, and it was barely past noon. I checked for tracks in the ditch crossings and the seeps from artesian springs. The day was just as pretty as when Harvey and I'd passed earlier, but now when I scanned the green grass and patches of yellow monkey flower it was for something hidden in the low spots that didn't belong.

The trail through the aspen between the meadows was damp and the black earth soft. Before there were years of drought, there were years of floods. The rains came and changed the course of the small streams running off the canyonsides, and the floods they caused took down stands of aspen and left them tangled in the bogs and mud and left the mud impossible to pass. The ranchers and the Forest Service worked to gather the streams and put them back in their beds, but the rocks and brush and downed aspen trunks snarled the trail from meadow to meadow and waited for the shovel and the chainsaw.

Picking my way through the flood debris, I could see the horse tracks and mule tracks Harvey had left that morning after he and I split up. I could see tracks of cheap shoes not made for hiking, heading down-canyon, too, but nothing of the girl until I was almost to the drift fence at the bottom of the second meadow. There, where she must have stepped away from the trail to examine something on the dry ground, I saw a single print from her ratty high-tops. The track was clear and crisp, and I could see every cut and contour of that little shoe in the dust. An afternoon wind would scatter that print soon enough, so for now I was looking at all that the child had left behind.

I got off my horse and hunkered low for a closer look. Then I led the horse through the drift fence gate, got back on, and kept riding. I should be seeing Harvey soon enough.

There's a stand of tamarack that sits like an island in the middle of the upper meadow of Aspen Canyon. I rode to its edge and circled it. I knew from memory that a person could sit under those trees where little grass grew and look out at the meadow and see somebody riding by on the trail but not be seen by the rider if they were still enough and quiet enough. I rode into the trees and looked back out from where I'd come. A bird circled, but this time it was no eagle. It was a buzzard, two of them actually, and they were cruising a spot nearer the creek where it flowed through thick pine along the south side of the canyon. All morning I'd been thinking how a person could get lost in that deep timber. I rode slow out of that island of trees and across the meadow grass to where the buzzards dipped and flapped in the shifting currents. I rode a bit more, then stopped and watched, letting the sorrel stand. I could see a dark patch on the grass, and movement. I let my eyes focus on the spot and could tell pretty soon it was more birds, ravens it looked like, and they were making the buzzards keep their distance. I rode closer, ready for the worst, my eyes on a lone buzzard watching the ravens from the ground, its wings spread motionless, cooling them in the afternoon air. When I got about sixty feet off, I could see the birds were working on a dead calf, one belonging to my parents' old friend Becky Tyree who ran cattle here on a Forest Service permit. I rode close then, shouting the birds away, and checked the brand and ear tag number so I could let Becky and her son, Dan, know which cow had lost this calf. It was the least I could do for that woman. She was the one who'd deeded Sarah and me the forty acres of the pack station site as a wedding present, giving me my past and my future both at once.

I got a whiff of Harvey's cigarette before I saw him coming towards me out of the aspen. I rode past the island of trees and waited for him, relieved as hell I didn't have to tend to the body of a child.

I got off to stretch, looking at something Harvey had draped over his saddle fork. When he got closer, he held it up. It was the girl's jacket, the one with the worn-out Little Mermaid smiling on the back.

"This belong to that kid?" he said.

"Yeah. Where'd you find it?"

"Up past the Roughs in them boggy trees."

He described a place I recognized well, where the trail narrowed close against a vertical granite wall on the right and a scattering of boggy deadfall tamarack on the left, and where a stunted tamarack grew out of a cleft in the granite and hung over the trail.

"How the hell did that little girl get so far so fast?"

"I just don't see it," Harvey said. "The Roughs'd be a bitch for a kid to cross on foot. All that damn loose shale?"

I asked him how the drop went with the Forest Service. I said if he could get down-canyon with our string and wait for Sarah to come back and direct the search and rescue folks, I'd stay up-canyon and poke around looking for the girl. I told myself I knew Aspen Canyon as well as anybody, so the best use of my time would be to stay and search. Truth be told, I didn't much want to be around the parents, as I was already blaming them for being so careless. Harvey held up the kid's jacket.

"What do you want me to do with this?" he said.

"Give it to Sarah and don't let the parents mess with it. If we don't find that girl by dark . . . "

Harvey waited for me to finish. I didn't say anything more.

"You were gonna say you want to let Jack Harney's search dog take a crack at it?" he said.

"I wasn't going to say anything. We'll have done all we can do. It's none of my affair."

I gave Harvey one of my mom's sandwiches, and we went our separate ways.

Above the second meadow but before the Roughs, there was a small stretch of grass, some springs, and a big broken granite outcrop with aspen around the foot. Locals called it the Blue Rock. I got off my horse there and hobbled him to graze while I ate a sandwich and had a pull from my flask. Then I poked around. The creek was close, so I could cover the ground from rock to water pretty carefully but there was no trace of that kid's little high-tops. Beaver dams and drowned trees along the creek below Blue Rock had turned the ground there boggy and pretty much impassable. I didn't figure even a city kid would be crazy enough to wander into all that. What I did see along the trail was the knobby tread of a dirt bike. The tracks probably had nothing to do with the girl vanishing, except that motorized vehicles were supposed to be as scarce in the canyon as missing kids.

I got mounted and rode over that canyon again, somehow knowing I wasn't seeing what I needed to see. I picked my way on the trail that led through the granite scattered at the foot of the slope, then over the Roughs, going slow on the loose shale I'd ridden over a hundred times, the sound those broken sheets of rock make as it shifts and slides under your horse's hooves always a surprise when you haven't heard it for a while. When I was a kid working for Harvey and first led strings of mules over, I was proud of how careful I was and happy to be paid like a grownup doing a man's work. That seemed like a lifetime ago, just prideful bullshit on my part when a scared girl was lost with evening coming on. I rode as far as the narrow trail and the cleft rock, then a bit farther, almost as far as the Forest Service trail camp. Sarah would be radioing them soon about the child if she hadn't already, so they'd be the western perimeter of the search. Without the jacket that Harvey found there, that child would have a bitter night. I told myself again that the spot those drifters got themselves in was their lookout and none of mine. Still, the talk of a search and rescue dog didn't seem so crazy.

The first chopper circled overhead in the midafternoon. I'd heard it down the canyon, probably dropping search crew volunteers. I was riding back down-trail on the Roughs when it passed over. I waved my hat and shook my head. That the searchers were fanning out told me that none of us was having any luck.

I ran into half a dozen folks by the time I got to the meadows, mostly people I recognized—volunteers who knew that canyon well. This early in the hunt they were still optimistic, but we all knew we were racing sundown.

I crossed and recrossed the canyon. Meadow and aspen and tamarack, boulders and willows and creek shallows, they gave me no sign at all. In another hour, my horse and I had picked our way up through rock and sage to a spot high on the north slope. I loosened my cinch, hung my bridle on the saddle horn, and parked myself in the crushed granite. The horse munched the ricegrass tufts that grew amongst the sage, switching his tail at the deer flies while I studied the stretch of canyon bottom, both bare-eyed and through my riflescope. It was an intricate landscape that never looked the same way twice, and it told me nothing. Just sitting there, I could see long stretches of thick brush and timber and tumbles of granite that could hide a thousand kids. It made me think of Harvey's cockamamie story of the dead Spaniard in the cave. If there was such a place, those lonesome brushy stretches could hide it well enough. Cowboys for a hundred fifty years, myself included, had hunted stock through there, but only for a couple dozen days each summer and fall, and usually just nibbling at the edges of the hard-to-get-to places. One way or another, most folks stay close to the trail or in open country.

I heard the far-off four-wheelers of the county search crews. I saw a pair of volunteers, all shorts and water bottles, pushing their way through wild currant bushes and armpit-high aspen saplings and could hear them talking as they passed up-canyon not more than thirty yards below me. These two hadn't found any sign, but then they hadn't noticed me and my big red horse, either. I went back to studying the canyon bottoms one more time.

I got back to the pack station well after dark, riding the last few miles under a setting quarter moon and passing the shouts and flashlights of searchers on foot. I avoided them so I wouldn't have to talk about the child and the odds she had of surviving. Sarah was back from town but still on the county's time. I watched her checking with each of the remaining volunteers, the stragglers passing by the corrals in the dark, her calm face lit by their headlamps. My mom had her hands full quieting a cranky baby. Harvey and May cooked us all a tri-tip with potatoes and onions at the fire pit. Dinner was quiet and glum. Sarah joined us after a bit.

"Jack Harney wondered if you'd help him tomorrow," she said. She sat next to me at the plank table by the fire pit and put her arm around my neck.

"Doing what?" I knew the answer to that well enough.

"If that child isn't found tonight," she said, "he wants to bring up his new dog—and he wants you to go with him."

"Cadaver dog?"

"Let's just call it a search-and-rescue dog for now," she said.

"Can't Jack get somebody else? I can't leave Harvey holding the short end again like I did today."

"Jack asked for you."

I could only nod, then she looked at me the way she did.

"You can ride my mare," she said. "She'd love the work, and I'd love it if you did."

CHAPTER THREE

Next morning, I saddled Sarah's bay mare while I watched Jack Harney unload a rangy palomino gelding from a county trailer. A big mixed Lab sat tethered to the trailer, eager like he knew something was up and curious about Sarah's Aussie. I put Hoot in our cabin and led the mare down past Harvey's place to where Jack was parked. We talked about the missing girl, then about Sarah's father, team roping, and sheriff department politics, which he said were usually worse than tribal politics.

"Gimme dogs and horses," Jack said. "They got no politics except at feeding time."

"What do you call that dog?"

"Spike," he said.

"That's original." I looked his horse over. "This yellow guy new?"

"My nephew's," he said. "He's off the Rez and needs lotsa wet saddle blankets."

"You might want a shod horse where we're going."

"His feet are real tough," Jack said. "Besides, you don't wanna try and get under this bugger."

"Get him sore-footed he's less likely to buck you off?"

"Something like that," he said.

We heard a motor in the distance that got louder fast. Then we heard a rumble and rattle down-canyon coming from the wooden bridge. Jack's dog jumped up and stood real still, just staring in the direction of the noise and whimpering soft. I don't know squat about motorcycles, but I still recognized the pop-*pop* sound of this one. A big Harley zipped out of the aspen then throttled down, and the rider looked around like he wasn't sure which way he wanted to go. The guy stared at the half-done cabin. He was a big sucker, with a mustache and no sleeves. Jack seemed like he was laughing, but I couldn't hear over the pop-*popping*. The guy looked up at us, then revved the bike and blasted by too close to the horses, making Jack's yellow gelding plunge and rear where he was tied. I watched the guy heading up the road that passed the cabin. I hollered that he couldn't ride that thing up the canyon, and he must have heard me 'cause he flipped me off and kept going. I could see Sarah step to the edge of the unfinished porch with the baby in her arms to see what the racket was all about, still in her tee shirt and underpants. She yelled something, but I couldn't hear that over the bike noise either. The guy dropped his inside boot and did a tight three-sixty by the steps, watching my wife and baby and stirring up dust the whole time. It looked like he said something, then wagged his tongue at Sarah and chugged off up the road through the aspen.

I tightened my cinch and swung up on that mare before I knew what I was doing.

"Easy, big guy," Jack said.

I goosed the mare and loosened my rope strap and shook out my loop. The Harley moved steady but not super-fast over unfamiliar ground. My horse got unwound and I was flat flying when I passed the cabin and Sarah shouted my name. I couldn't make out what else she said, but by her tone I could tell she didn't think I was doing something smart. By then the horse was closing the gap. I don't think the guy heard me coming over the motor. I camped on his tail and shouted at him again to stop, just for form's sake. Then I made my throw. The loop whipped over his shoulders and handlebars. I jerked my slack and took my dallies and sat back to see what would happen.

The guy went down hard. I sat there watching him not make a move, that two-banger still roaring in the dirt, the rear wheel racing above the ground, the whole machine sort of twitching under him and dust everywhere. I thought for a second I'd killed him. Then he stirred slow like he was checking himself for serious hurt. He switched off the motor and pulled my loop from around his handlebars and got to his feet. He looked shaky. I could see blood on his head and hand. He rubbed where the poly rope had burned his upper arm, and he moved with a bad limp so I figured he'd done some damage. He looked up at me all crazy-eyed.

"I've killed guys for less," he said.

I coiled my string.

"That your woman?" he said.

"She's her own woman."

"I could call the law on you, shitkicker."

I didn't say anything, just tightened up my rope strap. I'd noticed folks' threats got lamer as they lost their appetite for a fight. The guy and I both looked back at Jack trotting his horse towards us with his dog trailing behind. The horse was still goosey and gave the chopper lots of room. I saw the guy reach down to the bike, and saw the Nevada plate on the rear fender. He pulled a sort of cane that he'd clamped tight across his handlebars. It had a brass rattlesnake head for a knob, and the shaft was machined steel with little dark diamond patterns that stood out over the handlebar's chrome. I was thinking you could beat someone to death with something like that. He used it to walk towards Jack and me, limping bad. He was bulked up on top but looked thin and frail below the waist, so I started to figure he had that limp before I'd roped him.

I watched the guy study Jack and his Frémont County badge and the uniform shirt he wore with his Wranglers, and saw the guy check out the Smith & Wesson .357 Jack carried. He took in everything in an instant—like he'd been in dicey spots before.

"Sign says no motor vehicles beyond this point," Jack said.

"I saw this bastard in a crappy old Dodge driving up there yesterday," the guy said. He looked around at the cabin and the corrals, and Harvey's trailer above us in the trees. "What the hell do you do here that's so damn special?"

"He's a licensed outfitter, so he's allowed, especially in emergencies," Jack said. "You're not."

"You stay out of my way, Tonto," he said, "or next time I see you, I'll notch your ears."

Jack smiled at him pleasant enough in an unpleasant sort of way. He watched the guy drag his Harley upright.

"Be with you in a sec, Jack. Just want a word with Sarah before we go." Right away I was sorry I'd hinted that my pretty wife would be alone at the pack station that morning.

"I'll be right here," Jack said. He never took his eyes off the guy on the bike.

Sarah'd gone inside and slipped on some jeans. She walked back out on the steps barefoot, watching me ride up, the baby on her hip. It was about seven in the morning now.

"I bet you've wanted to do *that* your whole life," she said.

I took the lunch she'd made for me. "Pretty much."

"I know you're worried about that little girl," she said. "Don't let it make you—"

"—a dick?"

She kissed me goodbye. "I was going to say 'reckless.'"

I stowed the lunch in my saddle pockets and looked up as the Harley putt-*putted* by. The guy headed back towards the bridge, not seeing either of us, just looking steamed and sore. Then he turned real sudden and pointed right at me before he disappeared around the curve in the road.

I caught up with Jack on the trail. We rode on, silent for a bit, neither talking about what had just happened. Then Jack started telling me about his dog and how he got interested in having a search-and-rescue dog after he worked with an older deputy from the Mammoth Lakes office who'd trained one and used it on some cases down there. Then the guy trained it up as a cadaver dog to help find avalanche victims and missing hikers and such. That dog was so handy that the deputy was asked by a veterans' group to fly the dog across the Pacific to locate the bodies of some Tokyo-bound island hopping Marines buried in unmarked graves on Okinawa seventy years before. The dog found them quick—like they'd just been killed yesterday.

"I figured that with all the country we have to cover in this jurisdiction," Jack said, "a good dog would be worth his keep."

Jack'd been a friend of my dad's while I was growing up and had been an investigator for the sheriff's office for at least that long. The search-dog thing might've been something new but no surprise to folks who knew him. A pair of buzzards riding a downdraft slid by low in the sky. Jack's face clouded up.

"Did you get a load of that bike?" he said. We were coming out of the tamarack towards the drift fence at the bottom of the second meadow.

"Not really."

"That's a Harley Speedster the guy modified for off-road," he said, "but it's still street-legal, I bet."

"The guy ridin' it didn't seem so street-legal."

"Yeah," Jack said. "I thought he was gonna go all Revenant on your ass." He called for his dog to keep up. "He said he useta be a highway patrolman."

"You believe him?"

"Who knows? Said it was in Southern California," Jack said. "LA. He asked if you knew who he was. He said maybe you knew him."

"Never seen him before."

"He must be a legend in his own mind."

"That happens."

"But I bet you see him again," Jack said.

"He did threaten to kill me, so I just might."

"Don't laugh. Even if the guy pressed charges, that could be a hassle," Jack said.

"I'm sure your boss would like that."

"Sheriff Mitch has plumb mellowed on the subject of Tommy Smith since you and Sarah got married," Jack said.

"That'll be the day. I'm just wondering why that guy was watching me yesterday when I was looking for the kid."

"Who knows," Jack said. "He's a long way from home."

"So's that kid."

I dismounted at the drift fence gate and showed Jack what was left of the girl's single footprint. He got down to look, then I handed him the Little Mermaid jacket for the dog to check out. From then on, that Lab was all business. We got down again at the Blue Rock to let the dog scout around till he was satisfied that the scent continued up-trail. We followed a windy path through timber and water, then broke out of the trees by the start of the Roughs.

"That dog gonna be okay crossing these rocks?"

"Spike's got them big old paws," Jack said. "He should be fine. I had him over worse."

We took our time crossing the shale slide and let the

dog take his. He was game, I'll say that. We couldn't tell if he was following a scent or just happy to be moving, but he was out in front the whole time. Beyond the shale, the trail slipped down into the trees. In a little while on our right was a vertical granite wall close enough to the trail to reach out and touch. To the left the creek had spread out into shallow ponds among the grass and pines in spotty sunlight. Over our heads a single stunted tamarack grew out of a cleft in the rock.

"This is about where Harvey said he found the jacket."

"I can't see how a little kid could get so damn far," Jack said.

"I guess we'll find out one way or the other."

At a wide spot in the trail Jack got off the palomino and handed me his get-down rope. "I'll follow Spike on foot," he said. "That'll give him some room."

I let Jack walk off the trail. Holding the palomino, I watched from a ways back. That horse was sulky and fidgety, but I was keeping my eye on the dog. He was getting focused now and was cool to watch if you forgot the grim chore. I was studying him circle a bog when the palomino jerked back and like to dislocate my shoulder. I yanked the horse and cussed him out. Jack looked over and laughed.

"I always said these Rez horses don't lead for crap."

"'Course not," Jack said. "A guy's supposed to get on a horse and ride 'em, not drag 'em around like some damn farmer."

I got off to piss and let Jack and the dog keep exploring. He'd said these dogs did their best work without distractions. After a minute I got mounted, dallied the yellow horse close, and started dragging him up-trail, riding past Jack and looking for a place to tie up. I was in thick timber, the trail narrow and gently winding and the air cool in constant shade. To my right now, the canyon sloped up with granite and pine, the shady pine duff–covered dirt bare of most growth. To the left of the trail was deadfall and grass and more shallow, boggy ponds. I looked back, catching sight of Jack now and then and hearing him talk to the dog. His voice got excited, which never happened with Jack Harney. Then I heard him shout.

"Get back here, Tommy. We got a body."

CHAPTER FOUR

I rode back and got off my horse. I could see Jack through the tamarack and wild rose, bending low in the shadows, looking at something on the ground. I watched him step down into one of the ponds and heard him sloshing along, talking to the dog that sat on the bank, alert but not moving. Bits of sunlight shone bright on the dog's black hair, and he looked up a second when a Steller's jay flew over him in the branches. Jack scanned the surface, then picked up a stick and reached out into the water with it, pulling out rotting branches and mats of leaves and pine needles. The dog cocked his head, watching. I tried to lead the horses closer, but Jack's gelding was slow to move so I tied them both and waited. I told myself I didn't want to distract the dog while he was working, but I really didn't want to see that body. I'd seen more dead children than I could ever scrub from my nightmares.

"Hey, Tommy," Jack said. "You better c'm'ere."

From where I stood, I could see he'd snagged a bare arm out of the water with the stick. It looked thin and yellow and waxy even at a distance. Jack lost his purchase with the stick and the arm fell back into the water with a little slurp. I walked closer, staying on the trail as long as I could. I moved slow, checking the ground. A few feet from the trail I saw what looked to be a dollar bill in the wet grass. I bent down and picked it up. It was a hundred, faded and crumpled, but a Benjamin all the same.

"You gotta see this," Jack said. He hove an armful of old vegetation on the grass and stared down into the little pond.

I pocketed the bill and walked up behind him. The dog hadn't twitched a hair. I bent down and picked up another bill, a fifty that was torn across President Grant's face. Jack turned back to me, looking just as confused as hell.

In the space Jack opened, there was a small body on its back in clear water, the face just under the surface, the light-colored hair all fanned out and moving back and forth ever so slight. The water was barely two feet deep, and the crushed granite sand under the body almost gold in the shifting sunlight cutting through the tamarack. A couple of pine cones floated on the surface of the freshly turned-up water, moving real slow as if they had all eternity to get downstream.

"The hell?"

"This ain't right," Jack said.

He turned to me and reached out his hand, and I pulled him out of the pond up onto the grass. I put the money I'd found in his hand. He looked down at it then back to the body. The face was sunk in and smooth like the features had been half washed away, and the eyes were bleached white and shrunk if you could even call them eyes anymore. The body looked to be a female, but it wasn't the missing girl. It wasn't Kayleeana. It was a small but full-grown woman, somehow familiar but as vague as a bad dream. Jack reached in his shirt pocket and pulled out two more hundreds.

"This is nuts," he said. "Who the hell *is* this?"

Jack took out his phone and started taking pictures. I stood at the water's edge just looking at the corpse, trying to remember. The dog came up behind me and sat, leaning against my leg enough for me to feel him quiver.

"Ain't this maybe Erika Hornberg?" Jack said.

"The bank manager?"

"Yeah. You knew her, right?"

"I known her my whole life. When Dad ran Allison's, her dad's ranch was just south of us."

"Pruney as this body is, it still kinda looks like her," Jack said. "I recognize them big old gypsy earrings she always wore."

"I haven't seen her since before I signed up. Since the summer I got out of high school."

Jack held up the four bills we'd just found. "All those stories about her getting away with the bank's millions," he said. "I guess they were all true."

"If it's her, how you figure she ended up here?"

Jack put the money and his phone back in his shirt pocket.

"No clue," he said. "Hasn't been a trace of her since last fall when they found her car at the trailhead above the pack station site and folks figured she was going to hide out in the high country, or maybe hike out to Little Meadows or Summers Lake. Like maybe she had another car waiting, or maybe an accomplice. It'd be a helluva hike either way, but Erika was a hiking fool. Real outdoorsy type. Hike, climb, the whole deal. She could hike to Yosemite Valley, she wanted to. Most folks thought she'd left a false trail then skipped down to old Mexico or Costa Rica or some damn place to start a new life."

"Well, she didn't get far."

"It's weird we went looking for one body and found another," he said. "This one looks like a freakin' alien."

"Weird don't begin to describe it."

What I remember next was five quick rifle shots. Maybe six. They seemed like they were coming from above us, across the trail and up the slope in the trees. They zipped and popped, some ripping and snapping branches just over our heads, some pinging against the granite. Jack gave a yelp. I saw him spin and fall into the pond on top of the body, and I heard a branch break and saw that damned yellow horse plunging and tugging, his head shaking back and forth as he pulled until something broke. Then that bugger crashed on out of there heading down the trail at a dead run. Sarah's mare was spooked, and she danced but stayed tied. The dog was watching Jack just still as could be. Being a retriever, gunfire didn't faze him a bit.

I ran over to Jack. He was face down in the water with blood pouring from the side of his head making oil-slick swirls on the ripply surface. I rolled him over and dragged him out of there as another burst of fire from down-trail ripped the trees and chipped the rocks, but not so close. Either the shooter was a sprinter or we had a second gunman. I checked Jack up close and could only see the one wound. A round had sliced his scalp across the side of his temple, taking a bit off the top of the right ear. I looked back for a second and saw the woman's corpse rocking in the shallow water I'd stirred up like she was doing the backstroke. I untied the wildrag from my neck and wrapped it around Jack's head and cinched it down. His ear was red, and he was covered with blood on that side of his head, soaking his shirt. I told myself even superficial wounds to the face and scalp sometimes bleed like crazy.

"What the hell is—" he said.

I dragged him behind a deadfall tamarack and we hugged the ground. I scanned the slope that rose up across the trail where the first shots sounded but the timber was too thick. I reached to my hip on pure instinct, but of course I had no weapon other than my skinning knife. I'd only been looking for a missing kid. I rolled Jack enough to take off his duty belt with the Smith & Wesson. The dog trotted over to us and checked Jack out.

"You gonna tell 'em to quit?" Jack said. He had his hand on the dog's neck.

I shushed him.

"You gotta holler," he said. "Tell 'em they coulda killed us."

"That's probably the plan."

"Then who the hell is 'they'?" he said. He looked bothered and confused.

I figured Jack's duty belt was going to be too big for me

so I just buckled it and slipped it over my shoulder. Then I pulled the .357 and checked the cylinder.

"We gotta get you out of here, pal. We can figure out who 'they' are later."

He raised his head and his color drained. "My goddamn horse run off."

I kept his revolver in my right fist and got my left arm around him and dragged him to his feet. I waited that way for a second, scanning the woods and rocks. The little pond had settled, and just below the surface the corpse of the missing bank manager still stared skyward with those shrunken white eyes. As quiet as I could, I walked Jack toward where the mare was tied, wary about the shots that came from that direction. Jack sort of whispered to the dog and patted his leg and the dog followed, staying close.

I saw something dark moving through the trees down-trail from Sarah's mare. I motioned to Jack. He leaned against a boulder with one hand on the dog, but whoever it was saw us and kept coming. I could see some sort of long gun come up but it didn't fire. Then the uphill gunman squeezed off another few rounds. Jack held up two fingers. I nodded and pulled him down so he could crawl a dozen feet to another deadfall, then collapse.

"Triangulation," he said.

"Yeah."

"They must be pros."

"If they were pros, we'd be dead."

They might be amateurs, but live fire is live fire, though only the one shot that creased Jack seemed to come close. I was worried as hell about Sarah's mare. I thumbed back the hammer of the .357 and peeked over the dead-fall and saw the second gunman walking closer, looking toward the spot we'd just left. He raised the weapon but still didn't fire. Then he swung the barrel until he looked to be pointing right at Jack and squeezed off two rounds. They didn't come close, either. A bit of tree bark drifted down on us. He must've shot six feet over our heads. I shot in front of him once before I even got a good look at him, just to back him off. The shot echoed in the canyon like a damn cannon, and the guy dropped.

"Stay put."

I crawled toward the shooter, stopping behind a tamarack about thirty feet away to wait and watch for any movement. There was no way I could've hit the guy. I turned back toward Jack to look for anyone coming up behind him. All I heard was the rush of the creek just out of sight and the nice breeze in the pines. I stood up and walked to the shooter. He was on his back with one foot bent under him. His dirty black shirt looked shiny in the sunlight slanting through the tree canopy. It was Kayleeana's dad. Or the gink who'd said he was. He had a head wound soaking down into his shirt and the wet grass. He wasn't moving. I checked for a hint of a pulse, but he was gone. I kept my fingers on the artery for a bit longer than I needed to, just to be sure, then wiped my hand on my jeans. He'd been hit by a clean shot. It was a shot I'd have made—if I'd been trying to kill him.

His rifle was a beat-up Ruger Mini-14. The magazine only had two .223 rounds left so I tossed that toward the creek. For two rounds, the rifle wasn't worth the weight of the carry.

I walked back to Jack.

"Gimme your radio. I'll get us some help."

"The radio was on my horse," Jack said. "Who the hell is the guy you shot?"

"Cody Davis. Father of the missing girl."

"Tommy, that makes *no* goddamn sense. We were trying to help him, for chrissakes."

There was no phone service so deep in the canyon, so with no radio we were on our own. I walked up the trail another dozen feet and stopped, standing quiet, watching and listening for some sign of the original shooter. When I didn't catch a trace, I hustled to where Sarah's mare was tied and led her to Jack and got him mounted. He was mostly dead weight so that wasn't as easy as it sounds.

"What's the plan?" he said when he was aboard. He leaned forward with his left hand on the horn and his right hand clamped around my coiled rope on the saddle-fork, his feet dangling loose in my stirrups.

"We cross the creek and pick our way down the canyon, keeping off-trail through the tall timber in places you wouldn't ride if you didn't have to. Stick to terrain a four-wheeler can't go."

Jack whistled for the dog and I started leading the mare. We passed the gink I'd tried to miss, twisted on the ground. I watched Jack looking down at the guy's town shoes. The dog checked out the fake dad, too. That probably wasn't what the guy had in mind when he asked for a dog the day before.

"You steady up there?"

"So far," Jack said. He reached up and touched the

41

wildrag wrapped around his head. His fingers came away sticky from blood.

"I must look like a damn pirate," he said.

"You look like Keith Richards."

In twenty minutes I'd led the mare across the crotch-high, hard-flowing, slippery-bouldered creek. I only fell twice, but the mare stopped with better footing than me and let me lean on her till I got upright. I reached the shallows wet to my armpits, and cold from the snowmelt creek even in the warm morning. Jack would've laughed if he wasn't so groggy. A few minutes more and I'd stranded us in aspen thickets and deadfall. We waited there, listening for anyone on our trail. After a minute or two I could just make out the faint buzz of a motor. The dog had liked swimming the creek, but when he whined once Jack spoke sharp and he was quiet.

"If the dog gives us away, you can kill him," Jack said. "That's how the Comanche useta do it so the dogs didn't give away the location of the people."

"Whatever you say, pal."

The motor had sounded closer for a second then began to fade. It could have just been county search and rescue. I pulled my riflescope and scanned the far side of the creek. I thought I saw movement but couldn't be sure. Could've just been the wind. We heard a voice shout way off in the distance, then the whinny of a horse. The voice sounded high-pitched, almost like a woman's voice or somebody singing or yodeling.

"Sounds like somebody calling your name," Jack said.

"You're loopy."

We got moving again until I managed to high-center the mare on an avalanche-downed aspen. I thought she'd have a come-apart with Jack on her, but she managed to jump her hind-end over the trunk once she calmed down. I'd never been on this side of the creek so far back in the canyon. If Jack was in better shape, I'd have led him back to the trail and let him make a run for the pack station by himself. After another forty-five minutes we came to some beaver dams and I knew we were opposite Blue Rock, so we were making tolerable time even with bad terrain. I stopped and pulled Jack down from the horse to check his wound and let him rest. I dabbed his head and ear with betadine from my drugstore first-aid kit and could see the bone of his skull exposed by the bullet furrow.

"You look half scalped."

"I feel like a bad hangover," he said. "I know you. I bet you got whiskey in your saddlebag. Gimme some whiskey."

I pulled my flask, and he sipped a little. I was stowing it in my saddle pockets when I heard another far-off motor that almost sounded like the putt-*putt* of a Harley, but I figured I must have Harleys on my mind since that morning. I listened and it faded out. Then we got moving again. I didn't want to say so, but Jack was right. The voice we'd heard did sound like it was calling my name, kind of faint and eerie, and it sounded like the voice of a woman.

CHAPTER FIVE

I found a game trail through tamarack and willow against the south canyon slope. The trail passed too close to the big trees, and I had to lead the mare into the mud more than once to keep her from scraping Jack out of the saddle or sticking him with dead and jaggedy branch stubs.

"There's more to this than meets the eye," Jack said.

"No foolin'."

"I mean the parents of that missing kid," he said. "They weren't playing straight with you."

"True."

"Question is, why?" Jack said.

"The question is, where the hell's that little girl?"

"I thought you told Harvey this was none of your affair."

Jack was so smeared with blood I couldn't tell if he was joshing me or not.

We slogged down-canyon through bogs and timber for another hour or more. We finally got opposite the second meadow, and I started to lead the horse back toward the creek. Then something half hid by the trees caught my eye. I swung the horse around and waded through mud-holes and pushed through willows until I got to a camo-patterned dome tent hidden deep in the Jeffrey pine at the foot of a steep slope. The entrance of the tent faced the slope, not the meadow.

"What the hell?" Jack said.

"Just sit tight and quiet. I'm gonna tie the mare with you on her."

I found a spot where Jack wouldn't be buried in branches, then I poked around the tent. It was good-sized, about shoulder-high on me, and pitched tight, so I didn't figure it was abandoned. And it hadn't gone through a winter in the Sierra. Not even close. I found a fire ring set up against the hill so the tent would block the view of the flame. I unzipped the flap. Inside was a mummy-bag and some freeze-dried food packages and yogurt and cooking stuff, but no clothes or personal gear except hiking socks. Everything was tidy, even the ground, which was nothing but pine duff. You could see where it had been disturbed, but pine duff doesn't hold footprints, so the person left no trail. I hustled back to Jack and untied the mare.

"Some damn poachers, you think?" he said.

"Yeah. Maybe. It's a pretty snug little setup, but if someone's hung some meat here, I didn't catch a trace."

"If we run across the owner," he said, "we should ask 'em if they seen that kid."

"Right."

I got the mare turned around and headed towards the creek, but I couldn't quite figure that tent. It was meant to be hidden, so I guess Jack's suspicion that it was poachers made the most sense.

I kept to the tree line when we got to the edge of the meadow so we could make better time on the solid ground and still not be super visible. Plus, we'd be able to see or hear anyone out on the trail. We got to the drift fence where I'd seen the little girl's footprint, and I stopped to look at it again, like maybe it could tell me something. I could see our tracks from earlier in the day and my tracks from the day before, both sets careful to step around the girl's footprint. There were the deep-running prints of a barefoot horse that was hauling ass. That would be Jack's palomino. But now there was a last set of hoofprints, the even, clear impression of a horse at a calm walk. A lone horse with a set of hand-clipped front shoes. The new prints covered both mine and Jacks, and stepped right in the high-top print I'd tried not to disturb. The new tracks were heading down-canyon, so they might've been made by whoever shot at us. Maybe the first shooter that we never got a look at. I snapped out of it when the dog whined. He was watching something coming at us from down-canyon. I led the mare into some young pine right at the edge of the creek and pulled Jack's revolver. Through the branches I could see a rider coming a few hundred yards off leading a horse. Before I could see her hat or the sunglasses she wore riding into the afternoon sun, I could tell it was Sarah from the way she moved and how she held herself. When she got closer, I could see that the horse she led was saddled and yellow, and though she wasn't in uniform she'd armed herself. I stepped out of the trees and waited for her. I was always happy to see that beauty, now maybe more than usual. She hopped off and kissed me quick, then took a fast look at Jack's oozing bandage and my wet boots and muddy clothes. I briefed her about the shooting while she tended to Jack. Then I showed her the new set of tracks.

"I figured something was up when Jack's horse came blasting in by the corrals," she said. She pulled her radio from her belt. "I've got a county ambulance standing by." She put a hand on Jack's knee. "Hey, old friend. Are you going to need a chopper ride to Reno?"

"Hell no," he said. "Just a clean bandage and another shot of whiskey."

We left him up on Sarah's mare so he wouldn't have to get off and back on again. I lowered the stirrups and tightened the cinch and got on the Rez horse. We headed on down the trail as easy as we could so as not to jostle Jack too much. It was too breezy to talk, but when we got into the first meadow we rode abreast and I told Sarah about finding the woman's body, the getting shot at and shooting back, and about the shape the body was in.

"What about the little girl?" she said.

"No trace. But one of the shooters was her dad."

"My god, honey," she said. "Which one?"

"The dead one," Jack said.

The ambulance was waiting in front of our cabin when the three of us rode into the pack station an hour later. The EMTs wouldn't let the dog ride with Jack to the Emergency Ward in Mammoth Lakes, so Harvey said he'd watch him while Jack got his wound tended and his ear sewn up. It was late afternoon when Harvey and I unsaddled and Sarah and I drove down into Paiute Meadows.

Mitch Mendenhall was waiting for us in his office behind the county court house. He was the Frémont County sheriff and no fan of mine. No matter what Jack had said, me marrying his best deputy hadn't smoothed things between us any. The three of us sat down at a table, and Mitch closed the door.

"Are you certain you saw Erika Hornberg's body?" he said. "How the heck can you be sure? That woman's been missing the better part of a year."

"Didn't say it was her. But it looks like her, and both Jack and I think it sorta fits the facts."

"What facts?" Mitch said.

"Size is about right. Clothes kinda similar. Body wasn't fresh. And I knew her. She was my neighbor. I used to shoe her horses when I was in high school."

"We can bring in her brother," Sarah said. "Buddy Hornberg can ID her for us."

"Well, if he can," Mitch said, "that'll save the department beaucoup bucks."

"I'll call him," Sarah said. "And you should call Becky Tyree."

"Jeezo," Mitch said. "That old hide is a pain in the butt."

"It's a courtesy," Sarah said. "She was Erika's friend and was ready to put up bail for her when she disappeared."

"You're just sucking up to Becky 'cause she gave you forty acres in the canyon," Mitch said.

I was halfway out of my chair when Sarah stopped me with a glance.

Mitch laughed. "Old Becky is always throwin' her money away on some hard case," he said. "Remember that old husband of hers?"

"The ranchers around here support each other," Sarah said, "to keep the valley viable and developers at bay. So yeah, Becky was the one who engineered a land swap with the Dominion partners to get back the pack station site. She hated it when outsiders put Harvey out of business. Now everybody wins."

"'Specially you two," Mitch said.

Sarah pretty much ignored him and got back to it. "When Kurt Hornberg died," she said, "his kids struggled. Buddy wasn't the rancher his dad was, everyone knows that. Erika helped all she could with a banking job in town."

"And helped herself to their money," Mitch said. "Talk about a bank job."

"That may turn out to be the case," she said. "But for now Erika's only a person of interest—and a missing person."

Mitch glared at her across the table. "Well, we gotta get the body out of there," he said. "No matter who the hell it is." Then he glared at me. "And the body of the guy you shot."

"He was the one who claimed to be the missing girl's father, and he called himself Cody Davis. I didn't say it was me who shot him."

"What—you shot so many guys here the last couple of years you can't keep track?"

"I generally hit what I aim at. If I say I didn't hit him, I didn't hit him."

He ignored me and turned to Sarah. "I'm going up by chopper," he said. "I bet I can get pretty close."

"Oh for christ's sake, Mitch," Sarah said. "From what Jack said, in that rough country you won't get within a mile of the bodies. I thought you wanted to save money."

She was using that tone on him she used on me when I wanted to buy a new spade bit and the bill for conduit on the cabin hadn't been paid.

"I can't let this guy ride roughshod over his own crime scene," Mitch said.

"Bank embezzlement is a federal beef," Sarah said. "Call Aaron Fuchs at the South Lake Tahoe FBI office. He headed the Erika investigation. Let the Feds handle the crime scene and move the body out for us."

"Okay," Mitch said. "Then contacting Fuchs should be our first priority."

"Your first priority oughta be a little girl back in that canyon with some killer."

"What's it to you?" Mitch said.

"Not a damn thing. You're the sheriff. Do your job."

The sun was a low glare when we walked around the corner from the sheriff's office towards the side door of the Sierra Peaks. Sarah stopped at the curb and radioed Mom to let her know where we were headed, then we went inside and took a booth against the rear wall. Sarah used to tease me about keeping my back against the wall, but that would only make me more fixed on doing that exact thing, so she quit. After a couple minutes, Judy Burmeister came over. Instead of taking our order she started talking about Jack getting shot a few hours before and me killing one of the gunmen with Jack's revolver. I kind of grunted, wishing she'd just get to it. Sarah interrupted her and asked for some rib eyes with iced tea for herself and a Jack on the rocks for me. And she told Judy that I hadn't shot anybody. While Judy wrote on her pad, I scanned the room. A big shaved-headed county deputy named Sorenson was sitting at a table near the bar with a Paiute Meadows mechanic and some folks we didn't know. We could hear bits of talk from them about the shooting, too, including that it was my shot that killed the guy.

"Some of my colleagues are idiots," she said. "Ignore them."

"Small town. Folks like to talk."

Judy brought drinks and garlic bread. Sarah tried to distract me from the deputy and the other diners who were looking at us and talking about the shooting. She told me her plans for a branding at her dad's ranch in a couple of days and said she wanted me to be there. She skooched over next to me in the booth and took my mind off of all the jerks. We were digging into our steaks and talking cattle when somebody in the other room called my name. I turned to look. It was the guy I'd roped off his Harley that morning. He was sitting at the bar with a girl.

"Ignore him," Sarah said.

I got up. "I'll just be a sec. I don't want him coming over here."

I went into the bar before Sarah could tell me not to again.

"Hey, young dude," he said, "I hear you've had a hell of a day since the last time I saw you. You and that wagon-burner deputy. Heard somebody notched his ear. Just sorry they beat me to it."

The girl on the barstool next to him stuck her tongue out at me. I recognized her as one of the high school kids who flipped burgers at the Sno-Cone down the street. The bartender avoided looking at either of them.

The biker nuzzled the underage girl. "Busy day. I'd say you're lucky to get out of that alive."

"And this would be your business, how?"

"I'm just one of the concerned citizens who was looking for that missing kid, same as you. I heard about it last night out at Summers Lake Resort. It's all the guys at the bar could talk about. Poor little girl lost in the mountains like that." He tried to look real concerned. "I wanted to do my part."

"Good for you."

This was the first chance I had to look at the guy up close. He was still in the leathers he'd had on when I roped him, and he had a raw spot on the side of his forehead from hitting the dirt. He was maybe in his mid- or late forties, so he had about twenty years on me. He looked pretty weathered—like he'd had a lot of pain from whatever wreck he'd had that crippled him up. I know pain can age you pretty quick.

"Name's Sonny VanOwen." He reached past the girl and held his hand out. "And you'd be Sergeant Tommy

Smith, recently hot-shit sniper of the United States Army."
He wore those fingerless gloves like a jerk in an old biker
movie. "A real-life rifleman."

I didn't shake his hand. "What do you want?"

He slid off the barstool and stood in front of me leaning on his steel walking stick. He looked to be about six-
four, so he had a couple inches on me and wanted me to
notice. Instead, I noticed the stick. The shaft was steel like
the one he had strapped to his handlebars that morning, but
the machining pattern was different somehow. And instead
of the brass rattlesnake head, it had a grinning skull at the
top. I looked back at him. He was looking at me looking.

"I'm from LA," he said. When he got tired of holding
his hand out for me to shake, he hooked a thumb in his
belt. The buckle had a skull and crossbones on it. Real sub-
tle. "Not the same as here, where everybody knows everybody's business."

"They only think they do."

"I bet you know a lot of folks' business," he said.

"What're you gettin' at?"

He ran the back of his hand along the bare arm of
the girl from the Sno-Cone. "The missing kid up in those
spooky woods? Pretty little girl. Be a shame if the big bad
wolf took a bite of her. I got a couple of little girls of my
own." He smiled under his Fu Manchu. "All cute, blond,
and not a day over fifteen." He laughed. "I'm just trying to
help find the kid—same as you."

I started to walk out of the bar. The guy looked past me
into the dining room. He was looking at Sarah. Sorenson
turned to watch the guy.

"Just find that girl . . . *Tommy.*" VanOwen said, loud enough for me to hear. He smiled over at Sarah. "Find that little girl."

My mom caught up with us to hand off Lorena. She asked how I was handling what had happened that day and tried to be cheerful, but I could tell she was in a hurry to get out of Paiute Meadows and drive back to her place on Dave Cathcart's ranch. The news I might've shot some guy had made her sad and distracted.

When we got back to the pack station, the stock was out on the meadow and Harvey and May were off to Carson City, so we had the place to ourselves for a few hours. The bumpy truck ride up the logging road from Paiute Meadows had Lorena sleeping hard. Sarah tucked her in her crib, then we just stood over her and stared for a few minutes. I was wondering what her life would be like when she was as big as the missing kid. I built a fire outside in the pit, then we showered up and sat on the porch to enjoy the evening together, our feet dangling, making out like teenagers. Sarah's dog slept nearby. Sarah kept her arm around my shoulders, and we didn't talk for a bit.

"Did Mitch's crack about the forty acres get to you?" she said. "You seem bummed."

"More bummed than I'd be for shooting somebody today and not meaning to?"

"Okay," she said. "That was a dumb question."

"I quit worrying about what that idiot boss of yours says when I was in high school. I was thinking about being lied to about that kid."

Sarah made a serious face and lowered her voice. "'That's none of my affair.'"

"You been talking to Jack."

She kinda smirked.

"Do you figure she's alive?" she said.

"Who knows."

"What does your gut say those shooters wanted?"

"Jack's been a deputy for a lot of years. Maybe he made an enemy he didn't know he had."

"I'm just glad he's okay," she said.

"He's a tough old bird."

Sarah squeezed me and looked glum. "Maybe it was somebody after you, babe."

"Could be."

I went inside and brought a coat out for Sarah, then threw big chunks of pine on the fire.

"I hate to think of any child being raised by that horrible pair," Sarah said. "Maybe the dead guy was up to something funny and he forgot to keep an eye on the girl."

"And on top of that, he just happened to be in the same spot as a body that's been missing nine months?"

"I'd rather wrap my head around all that coincidence," she said, "than think someone was targeting you." She kissed me like that would make the craziness go away. "And what's with the guy on the Harley showing up at the Sierra Peaks?"

"What I wonder is, how he knew to call the kid a pretty little girl if he'd never seen her, and how come he knew I'd been in the Army if he'd never seen me before?"

The pine blazed up in the fire pit and put a flickery

glow on her face. The flames lit up our half-done cabin, bouncing shadows high off the open rafters. I held her close. I was hoping that this whole new life—the marriage and the baby and the pack station—wasn't just me spitting in the eye of fate to see what fate would do to knock me down a peg.

"So yesterday—what did the Harley guy say to you?"

"Nothing," she said.

"Come on. I saw him do that thing with his tongue."

"If I'd told you," she said, "you'd have shot him. Then where would I be? I'd have two husbands in the penitentiary, not just one."

I could see out past the corral to the dark shapes of the animals moving as they grazed and the moving shadows of the aspen in the night breeze that got cooler as we sat there. The dirt road curved and disappeared into the trees on its way up-canyon to where Erika Hornberg or her double still floated in the shallow water and the seedy father in his cheap shirt was probably getting his first visits from the ravens and magpies. The flies had surely paid their respects already.

In the pit, a pine knot flared. Looking up the road I saw a pair of eyes glow greenish-orange in the firelight. The eyes faded just as fast, but I could make out a dark shape against the night like maybe a small bear or a big dog, and for a second I thought maybe Jack's dog had got away from Harvey somehow. There was no sound coming from whatever it was, but Hoot growled and Sarah put a hand out to quiet him. The shape moved like it was shambling our way. We sat shoulder to shoulder, watching. There was still no sound, then the firelight caught bits of color, raggedy and indistinct.

"Hey, mister."

It was the girl. She was wrapped in a ratty kid's sleeping bag. She stepped closer, and I could see she was dirty as hell and barefoot.

"Can I come in?" She stopped on the rocky dirt like she couldn't take another step.

"Oh, my god," Sarah said.

We scrambled up the road, and I reached to scoop the kid up before she fell. She put her arms around my neck and was asleep before her feet left the ground.

CHAPTER SIX

We set her down on our bed. She was grimy and sour and out like a light. Sarah got a wet cloth and wiped the girl's face, hands, arms, and legs, talking to the child as she did it. When the girl stirred a bit Sarah got some Gatorade down her so she'd get hydration and electrolytes. The kid drank like a champ, then passed out again. Sarah pulled an EMT kit from the closet and checked the girl's vitals.

"We need to Care Flight her out of here?"

"I don't think so," she said. "I'm kind of amazed. She's in great shape, all things considered." She started rubbing the girl's feet to keep the circulation going. The kid frowned in her sleep and made sounds like it hurt.

"So what do we do now?"

"We can take her to town, and the deputy on duty will call county Child Services since her family situation is sketchy," she said.

"That sounds best."

"Mitch will want to be notified. He'll keep her sitting in a plastic chair under bright lights while he takes some of the credit for the department 'rescuing' the kid. Then one of us deputies will have to take her down to Mammoth tonight, and it'll likely be sunup before they turn her over to a bunch of strangers—probably in some nasty group home."

"Aren't we strangers, too?"

"Yeah," she said, "but she seemed pretty taken with you. I just feel so bad for her. What was she doing up in that canyon for almost two nights?"

"So what do you want to do?"

"Protocol would dictate at least notifying the parents, but you already shot one of them." She gave me a sly look. I hoped it meant she was kidding.

"The guy wasn't exactly father of the year."

Sarah sat on the bed and looked down at the girl. "Since her vitals are good, I think the first thing the poor child needs is a good night's sleep in a warm bed."

"Not exactly protocol, babe."

"Since when has that ever bothered you? With what happened to you and Jack, she could be in real danger." She stroked the kid's hair. "Don't be in such a hurry to get rid of her."

I got Sarah's bedroll from the saddle shed and unrolled it on the floor on Sarah's side of our bed and watched as she tucked the kid in with the same care she used with Lorena. She left a little battery light on so if the girl woke in the night she could see us right next to her and not be spooked.

I heard the girl rustling around a couple of hours later. I looked outside and guessed it was just before midnight. I lay there and watched her staring at the two of us in the bed and the baby in the crib. She wrapped herself in her dirty sleeping bag and walked out across the unfinished front room. For a minute I thought she was going to light out on us. She stood there watching the trees and corrals and sheds in the quarter-moonlight. She came back into the bedroom and stood on my side of the bed.

"Hungry?"

She nodded, and I got up and pulled on my jeans. We went out to the kitchen, and I held up a box of Honey Nut Cheerios. She nodded again. I got her squared away and sat with her while she ate. When she was finished she put her bowl in the sink and took my hand, and we walked back to the bedroll on the floor. I tucked her in and let Hoot sleep on the floor next to her. The kid wrapped one arm around her bunched-up sleeping bag and reached the other arm out to the dog. Neither made another move for hours.

Sarah had the girl in the shower by dawn and scrubbed her up. She wouldn't let her put her rank clothes back on so we went over to Harvey and May's for breakfast with her wrapped in a clean blanket. The girl ate pancakes and bacon and drank orange juice nonstop for a bit while May rooted around in the back of their trailer. She came out with a pair of Wranglers she was mending for her thirteen-year-old grandson. Harvey cut a piece of baling twine and showed the kid how to make a poverty belt by tying two belt loops close together. The twine cinched the jeans enough so they wouldn't fall off. May gave her a new tee shirt she'd bought for the grandson with the name of a fishing resort and a jumping trout on the front. It hung to the girl's knees.

She looked pretty Okie, but now she was clean and fed. She thanked May for the breakfast and the clothes.

"No problem, Kayleeana," May said.

"That's not my name," the kid said.

"That's what your mom and dad called you."

"They're not my mom and dad," she said. "And Kayleeana's one of them made-up names—like Chrystal Dawn."

"Then what is your name, sweetie?" Sarah said.

"Audie Ravenswood."

"That's a nice name, darlin'," May said. "Were you adopted?"

She shook her head no.

"Where are your parents, then?"

"My mom died last year, mister," she said.

"Why then, who takes care of you?" May said.

"Sonny," Audie said. "He's got a motorcycle." She didn't look very happy.

Sarah and I swapped a look.

"Are you gonna bring the horses over, mister?" she said.

"It's about that time. And you don't need to call me mister. Name's Tommy."

"Okay. Can I watch? Can Hoot come?"

I said yeah, and we went outside. She was still sore-footed, so I carried her across the corral and she waited with me while the Aussie blasted across the meadow toward the creek. That was the cue for the stock to haul ass up to the corral for the morning. We watched the forty-odd head running towards us, hooves slapping the wet grass and lips motorboating with every exhale. When they were corralled, I showed Audie how to close the gate. She was about the most serious, unsmiling little human being I ever met, but she seemed to be enjoying herself. We walked back slow to the cabin because of the rocks, and she took my hand in her hand like we were old pals.

Sarah radioed my mom and explained things. Mom said she'd run up to Gardnerville and buy the kid some clothes, then meet us back at the sheriff's office. Sarah left a message for Child Services, but nobody was in their office that early.

I helped Harvey load a stout pack horse with salt blocks that he'd be hauling up the canyon for Becky Tyree's cattle. I'd figured on going with him, but this thing with the kid seemed more important. May saddled herself a horse and packed lunches to go help Harvey instead. She was a pretty handy woman who'd helped her first husband run a ranch in Oregon before he died, so she jumped at any chance to get into the back country. Sarah and I were loading both girls into Sarah's truck to drive down to Paiute Meadows, and May said we looked like one of those dorky family vacation movies.

The sheriff's office was a zoo. Mitch was on the radio with the California Highway Patrol chopper crew who'd scanned Aspen Canyon from the air but were clueless about where exactly to land, and once they'd landed, exactly where to look. A pair of whipped Search and Rescue folks who Mitch said had spent the last two days looking for Audie sat on hard chairs staring at their phones. From the way one of them talked, though, it sounded like he'd been searching for a stash of bank cash up in the canyon instead. The guy acted like he had a bunch of friends, and every one of them had their own theory about Erika Hornberg and her missing money.

FBI Supervisory Special Agent Aaron Fuchs stood in the doorway of the conference room drinking coffee and looking like he wished he was somewhere else. Sarah went over with Lorena on her hip and gave him a hug with her free arm.

"Hey, Sarah," he said. Then he looked at me. "More trouble in paradise, Tommy?"

Aaron had been the Bureau's liaison with the Frémont County Sheriff's office when Sarah's dad, Dave, was kidnapped and almost killed by her first husband the year before.

"I guess Erika Hornberg's your headache again, pal."

That got Mitch's attention. He put down his phone.

"You absolutely sure it's that bank manager?" Mitch said. "She must be picked clean as a whistle after all this time."

"Actually, she's sorta pickled—like a brisket of beef."

Mitch shifted his look from me to Audie. She was still dragging the raggedy-assed sleeping bag.

"Dang," he said. "Is this the kid everybody's been looking for?" He looked her up and down in her borrowed clothes. "You got some explaining to do, young lady."

"This is the child," Sarah said. "She's been through hell, so knock it off." She told him Audie's name, and that the losers we'd seen her with at the pack station two mornings ago weren't her parents.

"Then who the hell were they?" Mitch said. "And what was their deal?"

"We've been looking for a kid who was supposed to be lost, and instead we find a dead body that's been buried for months. No telling what the deal is."

Mitch looked around the big room like his brain had already moved on. "It looks like a danged daycare in here." He fixed on Sarah. "So what's the bottom line?"

"If we find the fake mother," Sarah said, "maybe we can get some answers." Deputy Sorenson handed her a piece of paper. She read it and looked up at Mitch. "The Reno address the woman who calls herself Chrystal Dawn gave us two days ago is bogus."

They didn't get very far into that before Mom came in with plastic shopping bags full of clothes and shoe boxes and toys for Audie.

"You're his mom?" Audie said. She seemed semi-amazed at the whole idea of that.

"Yeah," Mom said, "but don't tell anybody." The two of them started opening the bags. Mom pulled out a doll and handed it to Audie. She looked at it like she'd never seen one and dropped it on a chair.

Right behind Mom was the lady from county Child Services down in Mammoth Lakes. Mom and Sarah huddled with the woman for a minute, then came back to the kid and me.

"I can't make any guarantees," the county woman said.

"We understand," Sarah said. She sat on a chair and took Audie's hands in hers. "If these people let us, how'd you like to spend a few days with Tommy's mom while we try to find your real family?"

"I don't know if that's such a great idea."

"This doesn't concern you, Tommy," Mom said.

"Will folks mess with me there?" Audie said. The kid looked pretty wary.

"Mom's boyfriend is a big old Marine. Anybody messes with you, he'll shoot their ass."

"*Tommy*," Mom said. "Burt will do no such thing."

"He better," Audie said. "What kind of gun does he have?"

"Let's not talk that way," the county lady said. "I might change my mind."

She and Sarah took Audie and Mom in the conference room and closed the door. Mitch followed, but they made him wait outside.

"Hey, Mitch."

"What now, Tommy?" he said.

"Was that the highway patrol on the phone?"

"What if it was?"

"Can you have them check if in the last few years they had any renegades or grifters in their motor units named VanOwen?"

"It would help if I had a first name."

"If I knew that I wouldn't need you."

I ignored him when Aaron came over. We sat, and I told him about the guy on the Harley and how he might be tied in to Audie and her bogus parents. He said he'd get on it, since he and Mitch would be dealing with the CHP a lot that morning.

"They're not making fast progress retrieving those two bodies," he said. "Any chance you could take me up there tomorrow along with an Evidence Response Team?"

"Heck yeah."

"I want to leave a two-man crew to secure the site," he said, "then they can pick a landing spot for a chopper and give us coordinates. I want to pack out the guy you shot as early as we can tomorrow so we can get started on him. Can you do that on a packhorse?"

"Sure—if you stop sayin' I shot the guy."

"If Erika Hornberg's been pickled in a pond like you say, an extra day won't matter. Our medical examiners will want to supervise the body removal in case nobody can ID her and we need to do a full-on exam later. Meanwhile, I'd like to get an ID on the dead guy ASAP." He semi-smiled. "Your dead guy."

"Thanks so much. How 'bout you bring a body bag for the sake of the mule."

He thought about that a second then looked grossed out. "You sure you don't want to take Mitch along with us?"

I must've looked sour, and that made him laugh.

"The guy we ought to take is Erika's brother, Buddy. He can let us know right away if it's her. Sarah's gonna contact him."

"We worked him over pretty good last year when the embezzlement first came to light," he said, "so he might not want to go. We were looking to see if he was involved. The guy had financial issues. Dug the old homestead into debt."

"I can talk to him about riding up with us if you want."

"That'd be good."

"Was he involved in the embezzlement?"

"Nothing concrete."

"I wouldn't think old Buddy was that smart."

"Your words," Aaron said, "not mine. And don't worry. The Bureau will pay for the trip."

"Damn right they will."

Aaron took a call, and I looked at the dirty sleeping bag on a chair. It had the name of some kid's cartoon show on it from back when I was little. It looked like the safest thing to do with it would be to burn it. I was pretty sure neither Audie or the fake parents were dragging that with them the first morning I saw them walking through the pack station. Sarah and Mom walked out of the conference room with the county lady. Audie followed them. She had on new shorts and a new tee shirt and shoes. She looked like a totally different kid.

The Hornberg Ranch sat three miles south of Paiute Meadows on the Reno Highway. It was one of the oldest in the valley but smaller than either Becky Tyree's place or the big Dominion outfit that bought out the Allison ranch where I'd grown up when my dad was manager. And Hornberg's looked way more rundown, some of the outbuildings old and not well maintained. The two-story house was even older, and smallish, sitting under some poplars with a screened front porch that sat right on the grass, and smoke pouring from the chimney even at mid-day. I turned down into the ranchyard from the pavement and saw the only new thing on the place, a big Ford F-350 extended cab with the dealer sticker still on the window. Buddy must've been doing better than the look of the place would let on, financial issues or not. Or maybe he was just one of those guys who always got their spending priorities back-asswards. Maybe Fuchs's team should've worked him over harder.

A guy in a tee shirt walked over to my truck from the house.

"Yeah?" he said.

"Buddy Hornberg?" He'd gained a bunch of weight since I'd seen him last, and I didn't recognize him.

"Who wants to know?"

I got out of my truck, and he stepped back like I was going to bite him. "It's Tommy Smith. How the hell are you?"

"Well, I'll be a sonofabitch," he said. We shook, but he didn't break a smile. "I thought you were still in the Army in some godforsaken hellhole takin' down the towelheads."

"Been back a while. Married Sarah Cathcart. Got a baby girl, and we're re-opening the pack station in Aspen Canyon with Harvey and May Linderman."

"I guess maybe I did hear something about that," he said. "I heard Becky Tyree got the pack station site from Dominion in a land swap. Something about highway access for shipping their steers. Then she just gave it to you for nothing." He looked like that pissed him off.

"Yeah, sure, Buddy. That's exactly what happened. But I didn't come here to talk about the pack station."

"So this must be about my sister, then." He said it slow, more nervous than nice.

I told him about searching for a missing child with Jack Harney, and how, when the cadaver dog found a corpse, it wasn't a child at all but a grown woman who looked like it could be his sister, Erika. He didn't turn a hair when I told him we got shot at almost as soon as we stepped off our horses. He just stared off into space till I was done.

"You saying somebody was following you guys?" he said.

"Either that or they were waiting for us. Or we mighta just had the bad luck to surprise 'em at something extra-legal."

"No offense, Tommy, but this all has jack shit to do with me."

"The FBI'd like you to ride up the canyon to ID the body."

"Screw that." He finally looked at me. "Why?"

"They want a positive ID to know what they're dealing with. Might take a cloud off of you."

"Then why don't they ask me?" He sounded tense.

"'Cause you and me were neighbors."

"And when did these Feds want to do this?" he said.

"Dawn tomorrow."

He fussed about all the things he needed to do before he could even think of going anywhere, but quit objecting soon enough. He quit so soon that it seemed like quitting was something he'd perfected over the years. I followed him into the house, and we talked about nothing, then I waited in the living room while he disappeared upstairs. The furniture was old and cheap, but the plasma TV was new and Judge Judy was scowling at somebody with the sound off. The place was hot from a woodstove in the corner and close with the smell of the way other folks lived. I wondered why I'd even come inside. There was a bookshelf with a bunch of pictures and doo-dads, but no books. Two of the pictures were of Erika when she was younger, about twenty. In one she was standing at the edge of a cliff in hiking clothes wearing shades with a big mountain behind her. She was smiling and looked the way I remembered her, kind of pretty and sandy-haired, but compact and athletic as hell. In the second picture she was out past her dad's barn, posing in a shooter's stance with earmuffs, holding a tiny automatic pistol and blasting away at something. In a minute, Buddy came downstairs and we went outside. He said he wanted to take his own horse in the morning but wanted me to check it out to see if it was up to the trip.

I waited in the yard while he got a halter and walked out into an irrigated pasture to try to catch the horse. It was pleasant enough on the grass outside of the screened porch in the shade of the poplars. Something at the far edge of the yard caught my eye. In the shade under a single aspen I saw a tiny enclosure made of white picket fence, about four feet by three. I walked up to it and looked inside the fence and saw it was only a cast-iron well-head. From a distance it looked like the grave of a small child.

I took a closer look at the ranchyard. It was actually a semi-functional place, and the corrals and chute and an empty feedlot weren't as decrepit as they looked from the highway. The brick slaughterhouse was still standing. Buddy's dad and grandfather before him had run a commercial meat business for years until grandpa Fritz got cranky and wouldn't make the upgrades the state health folks had wanted. I stuck my head in while I waited. On one side of the center aisle, the door to the refrigerated meat locker was open, and the locker was stuffed with old furniture and crap and the fridge motor was silent. On the other side of the aisle, the concrete killing floor was empty, but the gambrel hung high from the ceiling pulleys like it did when my dad taught me to butcher a steer in that place and hoist it by slipping the curved tips of the gambrel under the tendons above the hock. Then the carcass would be sawed in half along the spine. Each hind leg would be swapped from the gambrel tips onto a single hook hanging from a steel wheel that ran along a ceiling rail, then the two halves of the carcass were pushed across the center aisle to the refrigerated room to cure.

Back outside, the bunkhouse door hung open, and a broken front window was covered in plywood. The equipment shed was empty except for two motorcycles. A pretty beat-up looking dirt bike and a tricked-out Harley street bike under a clear plastic sheet. Next to them sat stacks of motorcycle parts, some still in boxes. I saw that the Harley packed Nevada plates. I dug out my phone and took a picture of the tags.

I walked out to the barbed wire and looked over some cattle. I saw longhorns, maybe thirty head, in an under-irrigated over-grazed field near the barn, and saw the Hornberg brand on them. Some folks like to keep a few around, but dad always thought of longhorns as a vanity project. In the big field that stretched out across the valley toward the Summers Lake Road, I could see a good bunch of Angus heifers. On the ones close enough to read, I could make out Becky Tyree's brand on their sides. So other than the handful of longhorns, Buddy Hornberg wasn't even running his own stock on the family ground.

He came back wet to the knees leading a shaggy gelding he said hadn't been ridden in a while. A couple more horses had followed him to the gate. One of them didn't look much better than the horse he caught. The other was a zebra dun that at least looked like it wouldn't fall over after an hour under saddle. The feet of the gelding Buddy led were crap and would never make the ride up the canyon. I told him to turn the horse loose, and in the morning I'd get him mounted at the pack station. He asked what time he should meet me there. I said not to worry, I'd pick him up at six. I didn't trust him not to flake on me.

"So you gonna rent me a horse then?" he said.

"Something like that."

"Am I gonna hafta pay?"

"No."

"Your department should pay," he said.

"I don't have a department. I'm no sheriff."

"You act like one," he said. "And I heard about you tangling with drug dealers and killing some guys. Last year, then the year before that, too."

"You said you thought I was still in the Army and still deployed."

"Look," he said. "This crap with my sister has made my life a steaming shit pile."

"The embezzling?"

"Everything. Everybody thinks I must know what she did with the money."

"Do you?"

"No, goddammit," he said. "And it's not just the money. Since Dad died, she was always hard-assing me about the ranch and how it was run and why didn't we cash out and live like kings. It was always all about her."

I snuck a look. He was so mad he was almost crying.

"I don't care what anybody says. I'm glad she's dead."

CHAPTER SEVEN

I had to wait about twenty minutes for him the next morning. I knew I would. I'd brought a Thermos and a month-old issue of *The Progressive Rancher* and sat in the truck cab in his yard with the diesel idling, drinking coffee and reading and enjoying the morning until Buddy shuffled out. He got into the truck and slammed the door. I looked at him. He was still wearing just a tee shirt and jeans. It was a cool morning like all mountain mornings even in summer, and the smoke was still pouring out of his chimney. We'd be riding a long way, maybe well into the darkness, and he hadn't as much as brought a jacket or a damn granola bar. And he was one of those guys that never wear a hat unless it's snowing. He didn't say a word all the way to town and out across the meadows and up the logging road to the pack station.

Sarah dragged a saddle and a pad from the shed and set them up on the back of one of the horses tied to the hitching rack. She had three more already saddled and two mules rigged out and set to go. She was wearing her deputy uniform, ready for work, but she still made me catch my breath. I parked the truck, and Buddy and I got out.

Aaron sat on one of the pack platforms talking to a man and a woman in FBI windbreakers and ballcaps. Stuff sacks of camping and cooking gear and what I figured was their forensic kits were already stowed in sets of panniers on the platforms, the pack tarps and lash ropes laid out next to each pair. Sarah'd had herself a busy morning. Buddy looked around at the work we'd done on the pack station and walked over for a close look at the cabin.

"Is that Erika Hornberg's brother?" Sarah said.

"Yeah. Glad he's not my brother."

"I wouldn't have recognized him," she said.

"I'll go catch him a horse. Where's Audie?"

"Shoshone Valley. Still at your mom's. I'll see them both in a couple of hours."

"Still, huh?"

"Child Services went for it . . . for Audie to stay with Deb a few days more while they try to find her legal guardian."

"Ain't that a bit loosey-goosey?"

"Don't be so grumpy. Deb's daughter-in-law is a county deputy," she said. She pulled her blond hair over the back strap of a Frémont County ballcap and shook it out real slow then squared the cap. She turned and smiled at me. "In case you hadn't noticed. That's how we bureaucrats look at things."

"And the kid is cool with that?"

"She doesn't seem in a hurry to go back to wherever she lives."

"With some guy named Sonny who ain't her dad."

"Audie said she'd stay with Deb if she could take Hoot back to the ranch with them," Sarah said.

"Terrific."

She started off towards her truck with an armload of Lorena's stuff.

"Hey, babe?"

"Yeah," she said.

"She shouldn't get too comfortable with this deal."

"Who shouldn't get comfortable?" she said.

"Either of 'em."

In another half hour Aaron and I were heading back up the canyon with our livestock and passengers. I drove the gooseneck with five saddle horses and two pack mules to a small meadow on the south side of the creek, figuring to shave off an hour or so of horseback time for my non-riders. We unloaded and got the gear lashed down and everyone mounted. Agent Fuchs didn't look super comfortable on a horse, but he seemed pretty athletic in a hoops-shooting, bike-racing, downhill-skiing sort of way and was relaxed enough I didn't worry about him. In spite of looking like a couch left out on a curb, Buddy Hornberg rode my gray gelding like the rancher he was. Still and all, it was slow going. We could finally see the buzzards circling above the timber from below the Roughs, and they were still loitering overhead when we got to the shooting scene. Old dad in the black shirt was already reduced a fair amount by the time we swung off our horses, his polyester holding up better than the rest of him.

We got the animals secured and the packs unloaded. The two FBI folks gave the dead guy and Erika a quick look then picked a semi-dry spot and set to work making camp with down bags, bivy sacks, and bear-proof food storage. I could see why they got assigned this job. It was just another day at the office for those two.

I walked with Aaron over to the pond. Buddy hung back. The woman was floating just like I'd left her, but even a couple of days in the oxygen and half-sun had begun to restart the decomposition and alter her look.

"How the hell do people end up like this," Aaron said. He put on latex gloves and bent down to pick up a crumpled twenty. "I've been with the Bureau twelve years and never came up with a good answer."

"Greed?"

"Kind of simplistic for a student of human depravity such as yourself," Aaron said. "Mister Hornberg, can you come up here please?"

Buddy slopped through the bogs and wet grass not really watching where he was walking. He hung back, stopping before he got too close.

"Is this your sister?" Aaron said. "Is this Erika Hornberg?"

Buddy just nodded. The lady agent walked past him. She took off her windbreaker and squatted down, looking at the body. She was dark-haired and olive-skinned and thirtyish, and in a tee shirt looked strong as hell. Buddy watched her put on her gloves. She introduced herself as agent Alicia Castile and gave him a latex hand to shake.

"So what's the drill?" he said.

"You ID the body," Aaron said, "and our team secures the site. People are curious, and we can't have treasure hunters and sightseers disturbing the evidence looking for a missing fortune that may or may not exist."

"Well, sure it exists," Buddy said. "You just got some. I saw you."

"Maybe," Aaron said, "maybe not."

"Why'd you drag me up here, anyway?" Buddy said. "I coulda done this once you'd choppered her back to town."

Agent Castile stood up. "Because this is the last time your sister is going to look anything like your sister."

"I don't get it," he said.

"This water is more stagnant than you'd expect," she said. "It's cold and acidic and lacks the oxygen to aid in decomposition. So your sister's corpse has been somewhat preserved. Until now."

"Yeah, yeah, I know," he said. "When I was a kid I fished the beaver ponds here. I found a totally intact marmot in these bogs when I was digging for night crawlers. Big deal."

"So you're familiar with the process," Aaron said.

"It's kinda cool, actually." The woman was cheerful as could be.

"Now it's like she's frozen in time. Like Joaquin Murrieta's head in a bottle of alcohol back in the gold rush days. They pull her out of the drink, she'll fall apart and start decomposing fast."

"Sergeant Smith is exactly right," Alicia said. "The visual identification would be harder for you tomorrow. In more ways than one."

Buddy walked back toward the horses. "Like I give a shit," he said.

She watched him go. "What a dick," she said. She said it like he wasn't even there.

Buddy turned when she said that and sized her up. Then he kept walking like he didn't want to tangle with her. Aaron laughed, but not loud enough for Buddy to hear.

"We'll start with our gunshot guy," the other FBI man said, "then you gentlemen can pack him out of here." I saw him pick up the dead guy's Mini-14. He looked it over, noticing the missing magazine. Then he tagged it and bagged it.

I looked at Aaron. "So, Fuchs—do you tell everybody about my military career?"

"Pretty much," he said.

We were in the long afternoon shadows by the time Aaron's team had given the guy and the death site the once-over, the sun dropping towards the head of the canyon. He and I watched the two wrestle the dead man into a body bag and zip it up.

"The jostling on the mule won't mess up your evidence?"

"Nah," the guy said. He was closer to Buddy Hornberg's age than he was to his partner's, but real fit, just like the woman. She called him Vinnie, but I never caught his last name. "We got what we need till the lab refrigerates him. You're good to go."

"What happens later?" Buddy said.

"We'll either recommend a full autopsy for your sister, or not," Vinnie said, "then the powers that be will decide."

Buddy started to say something, then didn't.

I led a mule over and checked its rigging. The two agents picked up the body bag and carried it over to me and set it down. I knew Buddy to be a hunting fool, so I motioned to him to give me a hand. We hoisted the body and set it across the sawbuck just where it needed to be. I started to lash it down.

"This sonofabitch was light as a feather."

"He's been on that buzzard-coyote-raccoon weight-loss program, Sergeant," Alicia said. "Guaranteed to reduce ugly belly fat."

"Gutted like a deer," Buddy said. Hearing his own voice seemed to surprise him, and he didn't say anything else.

I finished securing the body bag on the mule while he watched. It actually *was* a lot like packing a dressed-out buck.

The FBI folks wanted another full day to examine the scene and Erika's body, so I didn't want them to have to deal with horses in camp for a couple of nights if they weren't used to it. I checked Aaron's cinch for him, and we got mounted and headed back down the trail with me leading the two mules and one of the saddle horses. I had Buddy lead the other horse. I figured he was still hunter and rancher enough to handle that little chore. I could've led all four easy enough, but I wanted to make that contrary bugger work, even a little bit. After all, it was his sister down there in the bog. When I looked back, the two agents stood in their waders, working in that icy water on either side of the body. Just two pros getting to it. I saw Buddy sneak a look backwards, too. Then he straightened around in the saddle, eyes forward.

"He didn't exist, y'know," he said. "Joaquin Murrieta? That was just a folk legend. There was no such guy."

Three days in a row of riding back in the twilight or dark, the setting moon always a bit later, a bit brighter. Tonight it shined on the FBI forensic van waiting to receive the first body. Sarah was off duty by then, but always busy as usual, chatting up the FBI crew, working on a dinner of backstrap venison she'd thawed, and helping me unsaddle as fourth generation Paiute Meadows cattleman, Buddy Hornberg, just stood there like a tourist with his hands in his pockets. She told Aaron he was having dinner with us or else, and told me to hurry up and drive Buddy back to his ranch. She said she'd run off with Agent Fuchs if I wasn't back in an hour.

I could see the cookfire burning and smell the venison as I walked up from my truck fifty-five minutes later.

". . . he took the army money he'd saved for college and put it into this place. New mules, new packs, a new home for his new baby where there was nothing left standing just a year ago. That's when I knew he'd finally figured it out. That he didn't have to take the same road I'd taken for us to—"

"For us to what? You spillin' my inner-most secrets to the Man?"

Sarah turned and looked at me. "For us to grow old and cranky together," Sarah said. "And hey—you're halfway there, baby." She got up and kissed me and handed me an enameled cup from the jug of Basco red she and Aaron Fuchs were drinking around the fire as they dug into venison, fire-baked potatoes, garlic bread, and roasted corn on the cob. Lorena sat bundled in her baby seat next to Sarah. It was cooler than usual and felt like rain coming. Sarah handed me a plate. We were quiet for a few minutes while we ate.

"I never had venison before," Aaron said. "It's really good. Different, but good."

"It's freezer meat from last fall."

"You like to hunt?" he said.

"I was a hunting fool when I was a kid. This was my first buck in half a dozen years."

"Probably nice to shoot at something that doesn't shoot back," he said.

"*Aaron*," Sarah said.

"If you didn't shoot the guy in the canyon," Aaron said, "then why not? And if he wasn't a threat, why did someone else take him out with such a well-placed shot?"

He stared at me like he expected an answer.

"Okay," Sarah said. "I'm changing the subject. What did you mean when you said the embezzled money might not exist?"

He didn't answer for a second. I put my plate down and picked Lorena up and set her on my left knee, wrapped up in my arms.

"I mean we don't have the solid evidence people around here assume we have," Aaron said. "We've got a huge discrepancy of funds according to bank examiners and my forensic financial guys. We've got cranky bank customers who say they were shorted. We've got lax administration at a rural branch not prepared for an accounting shit-storm. And we've got a missing bank manager. But if Erika Hornberg was alive, we might not have quite enough to base an indictment on. Until we sort it out, it's all circumstantial—coincidence and conjecture."

"So this dead woman's name is trashed for good with no proof yet."

Lorena was wide awake and full of beans after I picked her up, chattering and waving her arms. Aaron stopped talking a sec to watch her.

"Pretty much, Thomas," he said. "She looks good for this, all right, but the cybercrime guys are still working to present concrete evidence of an illegal funds transfer into a secret account that they can tie to her. Maybe she's just super-crafty. Or maybe she took that info to her grave."

"Meanwhile, everyone around here thinks there is a huge stash of cash just waiting to be found," Sarah said.

"Those bills scattered near the body'll clinch that."

"It's a little too pat," Aaron said. "People don't steal over a million by dipping into the till anymore."

"So how was the whole theft pulled off?" Sarah said.

"Let's assume it's Erika. She did her stealing in two phases," he said. "The first was a lot of small stuff that didn't get caught right away—about thirty-eight thou and change. Then a few months later, just as the bank got hip to the small stuff, she went for a big haul—over a million."

"How the hell does that work?"

"It looks like she started shorting deposits from local

businesses," he said. "Motels and fishing cabins and travel trailers here get rented by advance reservation, lots of times by checks from older customers who come every year. Opening day of fishing season, Memorial Day, Fourth of July, hunting season—all those. Merchants deposit bundles of checks all at once. A bank employee pulls out one or two smallish checks, maybe a few grand worth from different customers and deposits them in dummy accounts. If anyone notices or complains, the thief transfers the money back where it belongs. No biggie, just a clerical error. But during a busy season, sometimes the business owner thinks maybe it's their goof—a case of crappy record keeping. They look for the short. They blame their customers and tell them to look in their pants pockets. But if it's two or more checks from different customers and the amounts don't jibe, then it gets confusing as hell."

"How do you set up a dummy account?"

"A lot of times they're under the name of an existing customer," he said, "except the customer has no clue. Hey, Tommy, big New York banks just got caught doing the exact same thing. Millions of fake accounts."

"Then?" Sarah said.

"Then from the dummy account, the thief sends a little cash offshore to some account we can't trace so easily. So the bank doesn't get wise, they use another transaction from the offshore account *back* to Paiute Meadows, but the amounts are never what might be missing from any individual depositor. It's like a puzzle game to a smart thief. What we think Erika did was to lay low for a while after that first thirty-eight grand. The bank was getting the picture, and she was definitely in their sights, but they still were trying to figure the details. We even hauled her in to question her, but she was super smart and asked questions right back at us. She had it wired." Aaron looked beat. "Then one day last fall—bam. The million-plus gets transferred from a dummy account here to a new dummy account, then to an offshore account, and Erika Hornberg is gone like a cool breeze."

"And you can't track her?"

"If there's no further transactions, it's hard." he said.

"Damn smart."

"Then my department finds her car at the trailhead," Sarah said.

"Yeah," Aaron said. "So everything pointed to her."

"Why would someone who had access to that much money go hide in the back-country—if that's what she did?"

He shrugged. "No clue as to why. You get away with stuff once, you get reckless or greedy."

"With Erika dead, the bank will write it off and you Feds will lose interest and wrap this up. The trail will be too cold."

He held his arms out and I handed Lorena to him. He looked pretty awkward. "Harsh but true. The case will stay open, but that's pretty much how this will go. New cases will move to the head of the line. And like Sarah knows, there's always new cases."

"Guilty or not, her remains'll get buried and her reputation with it."

"Why do you sound like you think she's innocent, babe?" Sarah said.

"I have no goddamn idea. I'm just asking questions."

After Aaron left, Sarah took Lorena into the cabin, and I walked down to the tack shed to lay out what Sarah and I'd be taking to a branding at her dad's the next day. I reached into my saddle pockets hanging behind the cantle of my rig looking for my whetstone. Instead, I got my hand around a fistful of paper. It was slicker than newspaper but not as slick as a catalogue. I pulled it out and put my phone light on it. There was about eight hundred dollars in new twenties, all wrapped up with a new rubber band.

CHAPTER EIGHT

I shoved the cash back into my saddle pockets and went up to the cabin. Sarah was in bed but awake, and I didn't mention the money. I didn't know what to think of it or who left it there, and didn't want to waste the night talking about it.

The next morning early, the four of us saddled a horse apiece and loaded them into the gooseneck. Then we piled into the Silverado—Harvey and May and me—while Sarah and the baby followed us down the mountain in her sheriff's SUV. Watching them in my rearview, I thought of my daughter lashed down in her car seat behind the steel screen that kept the deputies safe from the perps, the kid only three feet behind the 12 gauge locked upright between the front seats. That's just how our life was then.

We had no trips that day, and Sarah's dad had sixty head of calves to brand. The two of us helping him on the ranch was part of our plan when Sarah and I got married. Her dad had heart problems but wanted to keep the family place productive. Besides, Sarah had always been his good right hand since she was a kid, and sheriff's department or no sheriff's department, she wouldn't have it any other way. We left the SUV in town. Sarah cinched down Lorena in the pickup for the rest of the forty-mile drive up the Reno Highway to the Cathcart ranch in Shoshone Valley, about six miles south of the Nevada line.

Sarah wanted her dad to take it easy, so she divided the rest of us into two bunches of three each, one bunch to rope, the other to do the groundwork. After a bit we'd switch off.

"It'll be you boys against us girls," she said.

I worked with May every day at the pack station and knew how tough she was, but since Dad died and Mom had to move off the Allison ranch, I'd forgot what a hand Mom could be with a rope, catching her share of heels and razzing us guys when we missed, a ranch woman from top to bottom. She'd had her arm operated on after a propane explosion the year before, but looking at her take her dallies you'd hardly notice. Harvey and I were teamed with Mom's boyfriend, Burt, who was a Marine packer. He wasn't as good a roper as Harv, but he was a big guy and a working machine on the ground. Lorena was in her baby seat in the shade outside the corral and Audie tended her like the kid was there just for her amusement.

Dave left the branding fire and spelled her, holding his granddaughter so Audie could watch the action up close. Jack Harney showed up with a bandage over his ear and a sheriff's ballcap tilted to fit plus a cooler of Genuine Draft. He sat with Dave and took a turn bouncing Lorena on his lap as they hard-assed each other.

"Since the goddamn accountants made the Flying W

sell all their damn Santa Gertrudis," Jack said, "you're the only one left in this country contrary enough to run these rank old cows."

"The day some accountant knows shit about the cattle business," Dave said, "is one day too many." He spit. "'Sides, in hard country I'm a guy that likes to see a cow with a little ear on 'em."

Even fifty feet off, Sarah kind of laughed. She'd heard it all before.

After a bit, the girls took their turn doing the ground-work. Mom steered Audie to the branding fire and explained the drill, so when I roped and dragged a bull calf to the hot irons, Audie was right there next to Mom with the bawling cattle and smell of burning hair, the antiseptic spray in one hand and the nut bucket in the other.

Before noon Becky Tyree drove into the yard with her half-Paiute son Dan. He built a mesquite fire in Dave's barbecue to broil flank steak, then borrowed my gelding to rope and drag a couple of calves to the fire while the coals burned down. He was a stout guy, so when he took a turn on the ground our pace picked right up. Becky handled the iron on a few, then I helped her set out the tortillas and guacamole and watermelon and such. She and her late husband had been big friends of my folks, and at sixty she was still slim as a kid and could out-work most men. I asked her about her heifers pastured at Hornberg's.

"Buddy liquidated a lot of his herd to clear up some debt," she said, "and I wanted to expand." She gave me a quirky look. "Worked out for everybody."

It was what I'd figured. She'd helped Buddy just like she'd helped Sarah and me.

"You need to ride up sometime and see how the cabin's coming."

"Invite me," she said. "May says that log house is perfect for the canyon." She squeezed my hand. "And you running a new pack outfit up there is just what our valley needs—even if to get it started you're working yourself like a rented mule."

"Harvey's doing most of the work."

"Yeah, right," she said.

"You haven't asked me about Erika."

For a minute the only sound was bellowing cattle. "I don't dare," she said. "If it is her you found, I only hope she's finally at peace."

In another hour we all sat at a long table in the cottonwood shade and ate the asada burritos and beans Dan had cooked. A wind was kicking up, so we ate fast. When I was a kid, I never missed a branding. Not ours, not our neighbors. It was always one of the best things a kid could do on a ranch, working right along with the grownups, polishing your skills. I tried not to think about this being my first branding in years, or to wonder why that old feeling was gone.

I went back to the barbeque for seconds.

"Hear you took a trip with Buddy Hornberg yesterday," Dan said.

"Yeap."

"Me and him went to school together," he said. He cut me another slice of beef. "Even then, I thought he was useless as tits on a boar."

"Didn't you used to date Erika?"

"You know how it is in a small town," he said. He looked kind of muley. "Sooner or later, everybody dates everybody."

Audie sat by herself in the stiff wind with Hoot, chewing on a burrito and watching the cows and calves while Hoot chewed on scrotum sacks scattered by the branding fire. She inhaled food like Burt and seemed happy to be away from folks, even the ones who were kind to her. She looked suspicious when I came over and sat cross-legged next to her in the dirt.

"What'd I do?" she said.

"Nothin' yet."

"Can I have a sip of your beer?"

"Hell no."

She went back to eating and didn't pay me any mind. When I glanced over at the other folks, I saw Sarah and Becky looking my way and talking amongst themselves. They stopped when they saw I'd noticed.

The doll Mom got for Audie was lying in the dirt already looking trashed.

"You don't like the doll?"

"What am I supposed to do with it?" Audie said.

I didn't know how to make small talk with a kid, so I got right down to it. "You need to tell me what the deal was with those two drifty characters. Who were they and why were they pretending to be your parents, and why were they sayin' you were lost?"

She got scowly and ignored me.

"You gotta tell me."

"You'll be mad at me. You'll make me go away."

"Hell I will."

She finished her last bite of tortilla, and I finished my beer. Then she told me how we all got sent on a bullshit errand that morning by the guy named Sonny. The dead guy called Cody worked for Sonny in Reno. Doing what, Audie didn't rightly know. The one called Chrystal Dawn was really named Myrna Jenks, and Audie hated her. She'd been living with her since her own mother died.

"She a relative?"

"Uh-uh," Audie said. "They useta work together."

"Doing what?"

"Dancing for Sonny."

That was a sight I didn't want to conjure.

"Where?"

"The Pink Corral."

"Do I want to know what that is?"

"It's a titty bar."

She told me things that painted a damn grim picture of life for a kid at a place called 4th Street in Reno. It was no world for a little girl, or for a big girl either.

"Why were they pretending you were lost?"

"They wanted you to find something they'd hid. Sonny said people would find it when they was looking for me."

"What was it they hid?"

"A dead person."

"Who was supposed to find the dead person?"

"People like you," she said. "Shitkickers."

I gave her a look. "How the hell would that work?"

"Sonny said he'd let all you guys chase your tails 'cause you were rubes and chumps and stuff."

"Sounds like a pretty lame plan."

"They're all totally lame," she said. "I hate 'em. They left me up in the trees, and I was scared as crap."

"Scared of ghosts?"

"Of guys with guns. Sonny had guys watching you. They had guns. I wasn't supposed to see 'em, but I did."

"They damn near killed Jack and me."

She picked up the doll and looked at it, then tossed it back in the dirt.

"Why were Sonny's guys trying to kill us? They didn't even know us."

"I don't know. Sonny was hella mad about what you did to him. And he was mad at that guy over there." She pointed at Jack. "He don't let people diss him like that and live to tell the tale."

"What was supposed to happen when we found the dead person?"

"I dunno," she said. "I was up in the mountains freezing my buns off, remember?"

The kid made me laugh.

"Who was the dead person we were supposed to find?"

She looked at me like I was an idiot. "How would I know?"

I turned and saw Sarah studying us again. I thought about that cash in my saddle pockets that I still hadn't told her about and wondered why I hadn't.

"Where were you while I was looking for you?"

"Hiding in the trees."

"Do you remember where?"

She shook her head no. "I saw you once. On a pretty horse with the Indian guy and a big dog. You seemed nice and I wanted to holler at you, but Cody said if I tried to get away he'd make it bad for me."

"Did you have food?"

"Couple energy bars."

"Cody give them to you?"

"No," she said, "the spirit lady. At first I thought it was my mom come down from heaven to see me, but when she got close I could tell it wasn't. Then I was afraid it was the dead person's ghost, but she was real nice. The spirit lady, I mean."

I started to ask her more about that, but the kid was wiping away tears so I let it be.

"Those energy bars musta tasted good if you were hungry."

"They tasted like dirt."

"Were you cold?"

"It was cold as balls. Chrystal and Cody took my jacket."

"Where'd you get the sleeping bag?"

"The spirit lady give it to me. She said it was hers when she was little."

"Were you alone the whole time?"

She gave a shrug. "Mostly. I heard stuff. I was scared they might be bears or ghosts. Or Cody. He scared me too. Asshole."

I told her Cody was dead. She didn't react a bit. No fake sorrow or fret. Not like the thing about the spirit lady. That seemed to make her sad.

I asked her where Chrystal, or Myrna, or whatever she called herself, was now.

"We were staying in that town near your place," she said. "In Paiute Meadows?"

"Whereabouts?"

"Some motel. It was crummy, and it stunk. Partly 'cause Myrna drank so much. When she drank she'd whup me and make me drink the hot sauce if I sassed her."

"You remember the name of the motel?"

"No. But it had a big cow out front. A cow and a guy with a beard and an axe. I remember that. I wanted to sit on it. The cow, I mean."

Midafternoon we loaded up to haul the horses back to the pack station. I got behind the wheel, and Audie ran over.

"You won't make me go back to Sonny, will you?"

"No. You're safe with my mom. For now." I felt like I was lying to her.

"Sonny made me do—." She stopped talking but looked me right in the eye. "I know you shot Cody."

"I did *not* shoot Cody."

"The sheriff said you did. Look, you can shoot Sonny too if you want. I wouldn't mind at all. Just sayin.'"

CHAPTER NINE

The rain started as we topped out at Hell Gate Pass, a gusty summer storm that dumped buckets on us then cleared, then poured even harder as we took sheets of water on the windshield from the big trucks ahead of us on the two-lane road. Our rig drenched the smaller cars that we passed. Ten miles farther on, in Paiute Meadows, the pavement was wet but the storm had stopped and the sky in the west was clear.

I pulled over behind Sarah's department SUV. After me pestering on her for a year or two, she'd picked up my paranoid parking protocol—always park on a side street so you're as inconspicuous as possible, and never park with someone in front of you in case you've got to rattle on out of there quick. It may not have made a damn bit of difference but it made me feel a whole lot better.

She and I got out, and Harvey and May took Lorena and the rig back to the pack station. We were eating in town—sort of like a date—and would follow in about an hour. The Mansion House Hotel had the nicest dining room in town, so we washed up, then we took a table by the window. The sunset with the rainclouds was a big mess of purple and pink and gray. Sarah was still enjoying the newness of being the married lady and the mom, so she hadn't got indifferent to us doing the couple thing in public. I kept to my old habits, sitting sideways across from her so I could watch the dining room and the entrance. The whole front of the room was windows, so I could keep my eyes on the street, too. Sarah was in her dirty branding clothes but looked so strong and pretty I forgot my paranoia for a while. I'd no intention of ever getting indifferent to anything about her. She ordered salmon for herself and prime rib for me. She asked me once if I minded when she ordered for us both. She said she did it to save time. I'd laughed. I thought it was cute, but I wouldn't say so to her face. We both sat quiet a minute. The last three days was just a tangle of loose ends.

"Do you think this guy Sonny is some relative?" Sarah said.

"I guess we'll find out soon enough."

The waitress put down some salads, and we got started. We were hungry enough not to talk for a bit.

"Somebody left a wad of cash for me to find at the pack station."

"I know," she said. "In your saddle pockets."

"How the hell did you know?"

"I'm married to a guy who taught me that a sharp knife is a good knife," she said. "I was looking for your whetstone."

"How come you didn't let on you saw it?"

"I knew you'd tell me when you were ready. I know you probably wanted to sort it out in your own mind."

"Yeah, but I'm coming up empty."

"It does make the whole dead embezzler story a lot less clear-cut," she said.

"No foolin'. Hate to think somebody's setting us up."

Sarah tensed when I said that. "Or trying to send us a message."

"I don't know what else it could be. It all seems related somehow."

The owner of the Sporting Goods, Nick, and his wife, Sonia, stopped by the table, and we talked for a few minutes about the weather, the fishing so far this year, and dead embezzlers. Nick was one of the local business folks whose check deposits for fishing guides got screwed up by the bank. I studied Sarah after they left.

"So what were you and Becky talking about at lunch?"

"You, of course," she said. "You're our favorite person."

"Yeah, right."

"She's sorry the whole forty-acre thing makes you uncomfortable," she said.

"I'da felt better if she'd taken payments or something."

"She knows that. But you're missing her point." She looked like she was getting up the nerve for a touchy subject, but it wasn't what I guessed.

"If your dad hadn't got sick, he'd still be running Allison's. The Allisons wouldn't have sold out, and there would be no Dominion Land and Cattle here in the valley. You and your mom would still be living on that ranch whether you married me or not, and Harvey would still have his pack station in Aspen Canyon on leased Allison land. When you and your mom had to move off after your dad died, there was nothing to hold you here. You just vanished on us all."

"Like you noticed."

"You were eighteen," she said. "Of course I noticed."

"I was in the Army pretty soon after."

"Yeah. And as far away from here as you could get." She reached across the table and took my hand. "Becky wanted that pack outfit for the whole valley's economy, not to mention tradition. But more than that, she wanted to give you something to hold you here. To— I don't know— to root you to this place."

"I got you. I'd live with you in a trailer park in Fernley if it came to that."

That made her laugh.

"I get Becky's point, I guess."

"Okay," she said. "Now you share with me what else you and Audie were whispering about."

I told Sarah more about the things I'd learned from Audie about VanOwen and his crazy plan to have folks find a corpse in the canyon. And how he had the notion that I somehow knew about that. I tried to keep it jokey, but the idea of a low-rent thug putting me in his sights scared Sarah, I could tell. I finished with Audie's story of the motel with the cow and the guy with the axe.

"The Paul Bunyan Motel," she said.

"Yeah. Why would someone name a motel in gold rush and ranching country after a folk legend from Wisconsin?"

"People are idiots?"

"So . . . after dinner?"

"Yeah," she said. "After dinner. We should check it out."

Our dinner came, and we tried to talk about other things like how cool our log house would be when it was finished. That didn't last long.

She gave me one of her looks. "What else is gnawing at you? And don't say 'nothin.'"

"I'm thinking Mom is getting too attached to Audie."

"Are you sure it's your mother you're worried about?"

After dinner we walked without talking into the evening still damp from the rain. We passed under the streetlights and turned up the side street to the SUV. I hung back on the curb as Sarah unlocked it with her clicker and pulled out her duty belt with the 9mm. She got back to me, and we started the two blocks to the Paul Bunyan. She buckled on the 9mm over her Wranglers and walked like she was Wyatt Earp. When I was young and my dad felt the need to smarten me up about women, he said that with the right one it was more than just tight jeans and pretty faces. He tried to hint that it could be like an add-on to yourself, like the right person could let you find out just who the hell you were supposed to be. I'd already decided when I was maybe twelve and Sarah was in high school that if I couldn't have her somehow I'd never want anyone else, but it was just then with her buckling on that pistol and both of us wondering what we were going to find that I thought about Dad and knew in my bones what he meant. The tight jeans and pretty face still got me, but us guys are shallow that way.

The Paul Bunyan Motel was the oldest one in town, built maybe in the fifties, and small. Babe the Blue Ox stood about seven feet at the shoulder. The blue paint was chipped and the plaster hooves weren't cloven like a bovine but rounded like a horse or mule. It wasn't the only thing the first owners hadn't thought out. Old Babe was a long way from Wisconsin, stuck in the wrong legend there on Main Street.

The motel rooms were set in an L, less than a dozen of them, and only three cars were parked in the slots in front of the rooms. It wasn't full dark, and the light was on in the office under the red neon vacancy sign, but we couldn't see any movement inside. We stood watching for a couple of minutes, then crossed into the parking lot, staying in the shadows where we'd be hard to spot. There was a newish Toyota parked next to the office and a Ford F-150 close by a room with a light shining through the curtains. In front of the room farthest from the street was a beater 280-Z that somebody must've thought was a hot car sometime during the first Reagan administration. It was parked in shadow, and there were no lights on in the room. We walked along a block wall that separated the parking lot from a Shell station. When we were just a step from the door, we stopped to listen. A semi rolled west on the wet asphalt of Main Street, so for a minute it was hard to hear. I glanced at Sarah, and she half smiled as I put a hand on the door. Unsaid was that a deal like this could always go sideways. The door wasn't latched and swung open with the littlest push. We stood on either side of it, letting our eyes focus on the gloom. I saw Sarah had drawn her piece.

The woman had been dead for at least a day, maybe more, and the room stunk. There was blood and a broken bottle of Fireball on the carpet. Sarah flipped the switch to the bedside lamp lying on the floor and we gave the place a look-over in the jaggedy shadows. She stepped outside and radioed her office, and I took a close look at some of the bruising on the woman's head and arms. I saw small diamond shaped marks on her skin, but that didn't surprise me much. The machined steel walking stick lashed to the Harley a few mornings ago was made to be a weapon. The woman looked like she'd taken a hell of a beating, hard with no let-up. Where the force of the steel hit bare skin, the row of diamond-shaped bruises made a snakeskin pattern—like a rattler. Like it was supposed to send a message from the dead to the living.

We waited until some on-duty deputies got there and took control of the crime scene. They huddled with Sarah a while, and she told them about the ex-highway patrol guy VanOwen and his possible knowledge of the corpse in the canyon and the corpse's connection to this woman called Chrystal Dawn. Sorenson, the deputy who'd been talking about me in the Sierra Peaks a couple of nights before, took me outside and questioned me in the flashing blue and red lights. I told him what Audie had said about the dead woman and her role in the bogus search, and that the woman's partner had been killed three days before by a bullet between the eyes.

"That's the guy you shot, right?" Sorenson said. The big doofus smirked like he was being funny.

I told him my notions about the walking stick and its owner.

"You're saying this VanOwen guy still has the murder weapon?" he said.

"Isn't that what I just said?"

The deputies were done with us in another fifteen minutes. They secured the murder scene, and we walked back to the SUV.

"They don't have a handle on how this woman might tie in to Jack finding Erika's body," Sarah said.

"Neither do we, babe. Except for her partner getting shot dead a hundred feet from the body in the bog."

"You can tell Mitch how you think this all is connected," she said. "He wants to brainstorm tomorrow morning."

"That shouldn't take long."

She gave me her long-suffering look, then put a hand to her chest. "Let's get home. My boobs ache."

We climbed into the SUV. Sarah had me drive us back to the pack station—to *our* pack station—while she snoozed.

We pulled into the yard and stopped below Harvey's trailer. The place was dark, and I left the headlights on so we could gather Lorena and her gear from May, who'd been sleeping in a chair with the baby in her arms. We piled back in the SUV, and Lorena nursed while we drove the last hundred feet to the cabin.

We could see right away that something was wrong. Storage boxes from the second bedroom were opened and tossed out on to the dirt. When we got closer, we saw our half-finished kitchen was ransacked and our bedroom was a mess. Even the baby's stuff was tossed around. It looked like there'd been a SWAT raid.

"Who the hell?" Sarah said. "Who would do this?" She sat down on our bed. I heard the half-asleep murmur of the nursing child. Normally the sound would've been nice and reassuring.

"I got a couple guesses."

"But how could they do this without rousting Harvey and May?"

I fired up the generator and got some lights on. Sarah watched me come back inside and go to the back of our bedroom. The closet I kept locked had been kicked in, the doorframe splintered and a shotgun of my grandfather's was missing. It was a cool old Winchester lever-action from the 1880s, and I'd never seen another like it. I'd used it as a kid, but now no kid of mine would have that chance. In the night breeze I caught a whiff of cigarette that could've come from Harvey, and a mix of sweat and some other smell that couldn't. A city sort of stench that always reminded me of beer joints and strip clubs around Fort Benning.

I heard Sarah fighting back a sob. I turned around. Lorena's crib had been flipped over, the bedding tossed. I set it back up and could see the top rail was smashed so the thing would never be safe to use again. It was a mad cry, and I knew the sound. The crib had been Sarah's when she was a baby, and her mother had tended her in it. I watched her face get hard. She held the baby in her left arm and rested her right hand on her pistol butt.

"What do you think they wanted?" she said.

"Something we ain't got."

"Do you think this was the same person who left the money?"

"No. I don't know. The money was new. Like from a bank."

She looked around at the mess. "Well, we can't stay here tonight."

"We can't leave. We've got to secure this. We gotta make sure there's someone here all the time—that this place is always safe. For Lorena."

"It's not safe now," she said. "Even with Harvey asleep close by, it wasn't safe."

"I know that, okay?"

Sarah looked at me, surprised as hell. I'd never spoke a cross word to her as long as I'd known her.

"I'm sorry, baby. I shoulda been on this."

I leaned down, and she grabbed the back of my neck and squeezed it and I put my arm around her. We were both quiet for a minute, then I stood up.

"Okay," she said, "what are you thinking?"

"We've got Jack shot across the ear, we got two grifters posing as Audie's parents shot and beat to death, an embezzler who may or may not have been found, and fistfuls of money that may or may not have been part of the embezzlement."

"And now this," Sarah said.

"And the lost kid who wasn't lost."

"And that ex-CHP biker who's way too interested in it all," she said.

Lorena was dozing off now that she had something in her belly. Sarah handed her to me and walked over to the fridge and pulled out a couple of beers. She opened them and handed me one then slumped down on a chair next to the bed.

"This would be the best place in the world if it weren't for a few sons-of-bitches," she said.

"More than a few. So much for a romantic night with my hot, overworked deputy."

She leaned over and kissed my cheek. "Go get your dad's rifle," she said, "then we can clean up this mess and rig a place to sleep for Lorena." She kissed me again. "And then, who knows?" She didn't look real positive.

Folks always look behind locked doors, but doors can be smashed so I kept dad's Remington .270 in the rafters of the outhouse. I thought I caught the bad smell of the dead woman who'd used it four days before, but hoped I was just imagining it. Sarah telling me to get the rifle was like her saying that we were about to cross a line. We'd crossed that line twice together in as many years. I reached over my head and felt the rifle right where I stashed it, running my hand over the walnut stock. I didn't take it down. I wasn't ready to cross that line again.

CHAPTER TEN

I was walking back to the cabin and saw May coming through the trees from Harvey's trailer in her bathrobe. She'd seen the yard lights come on and stay on and came over to see if everything was okay. Harvey was still sleeping.

I told her about the vandalized cabin, and she walked back with me. When she saw the mess, she offered to help us straighten things up enough so we could get some sleep.

"Any idea who did this?" she said.

"No, but whoever it was has been watching us."

"You think they're watching us now?" Sarah said.

"Maybe."

I got up and stood in the open front room. Sarah was quiet as I studied the shadows.

"What are you going to do?" she said.

"Just have a look around."

"I could go with you," she said. "May can watch the baby."

"No need. I just need to know all my babies are gonna be safe tonight." I kissed her cheek.

The road leading away from the pack station back down-canyon wound through aspen, then turned right and crossed a wooden bridge over the creek, then climbed alongside the fence that marked the boundary of our forty acres. As the road topped out at the trailhead, I could just make out a hole cut in the fence about thirty feet below the locked gate. The gate was a twelve-foot Powder River steel outfit meant to keep vehicles from going any farther up-canyon or cattle from straying back down. Ten feet beyond that, a four-foot gate hinged to a Jeffrey pine was kept unlocked so horses and hikers could come and go. I guess whoever cut the wire in the dark didn't have a clue that gate existed.

I dug out my phone. By the light I could see that every strand of the barbwire had been cut and peeled back. I studied the ground. I had to walk out of the pine duff and onto the road to sort out the tire tracks, but after a bit they told me what I needed to know. I could make out two sets of knobby dirt-bike tires and what looked to be one set of wider motorcycle tracks. In the faint light they looked more like a street bike pattern, but maybe that was what I wanted to see. There was no way to tell if the tracks had been heading up-canyon or down.

I walked below the road among young tamarack and sugar pine until I was opposite our cabin across the creek below me. I was wishing Hoot wasn't still up at my Mom's. I started studying that ground. It was pretty much more pine duff over crushed granite so tracks would be hard to see even if the trees weren't blocking the moonlight. A little farther on, and I was at the edge of a long break in the timber around a big depression. Fifty years back some genius thought he'd make a fortune in the tourist business by clearing the trees and bulldozing a hundred-fifty-yard-long man-made pond high above the creek where no water flowed. The guy ran out of money before he got the first cabin built or the first water diverted, but he did excavate down about thirty feet. Now as part of our forty acres Sarah and I owned a big hole in the ground.

I found a spot on the berm where the pine duff had been cleared away by someone bored and squirming as they waited and watched. It was pretty much what I expected—Coors and Red Bull cans, burger and fry wrappers, a Copenhagen tin—all scattered about. The trash and disturbed ground made it clear this was a watching spot. I waited there for a bit, staying quiet and listening, trying to tell whether I was alone or not. Down through the trees I could see our yard lights between the corral and the cabin. Our new generator was so quiet there was no noise from it over the distant creek and the wind in the trees.

I started up toward the road I'd driven the day before with Aaron's crew. I'd be packing their gear the following day after the two of them choppered out with Erika's body. I caught another whiff of cigarette and sweat in the night air, then a single hi-beam lit me up from the trees.

"Why, howdy stranger." It was a familiar voice, faraway, but deep and rumbly.

I walked across the empty lakebed and climbed the bank.

He straddled the bike and the night hid his face. I held an arm over my eyes to block the glare. It was a minute until he spoke.

"Well if it ain't the rifleman," he said. "You look like you seen a ghost."

"I see ghosts every night."

"And they don't scare you one little bit, right?"

"Not the ones who like to scare little girls."

"Funny thing," he said. "You're a famous rifleman, but I don't see you with a rifle. You lose it, or somethin'?"

"I'm retired."

"Yeah, right. Let's skip the bullshit, then," he said. He turned the Harley's front wheel so's not to blind me. "You got something of mine, son. You better not've lost that."

"Which would be what?"

"You got my money—or you know how to get it."

"The money that dead banker stole?"

"See? Now *that's* what I'm talking about, young man. The very same. About a million plus."

"So that's what all this is about."

"Yeah. And a little birdy told me you knew how to get to it."

I just laughed.

"And since I missed a real lucrative rendezvous a few days ago, I figure that birdy was talking straight." He pulled what looked like an automatic from under his vest. "Well, rifleman, am I right?"

"You're the one talkin' to birds."

He turned the forks of the bike so his headlight blinded me again. Now all that was left of him was his voice.

"That banker lady and me had an arrangement, see." He was working up a pretty good mad. "We had a *deal*."

"Got nothin' to do with me. Besides, I thought that woman was long dead."

His voice got low and rumbly again like he was trying to sound in control. "The only thing changed since her and me made our little arrangement is *you* in this damn canyon messing in my shit."

"How so?"

"You know about that banker, son. I think that's why you showed up here."

"I been coming here since I was a kid."

He started to say something else, and I cut him off.

"I do know that I saw your leavin's at a motel tonight."

I couldn't make out his reaction in the glare.

"Killin' off your weak links?"

He just laughed like it was none of his affair and turned the headlight away from me a second time.

"Say, that's a nice big cabin you're building."

"It was until some honyocker trashed it."

"It wasn't here last fall." He spit. "First time I saw this place, wasn't nothin' here at all."

"That's a fact."

"You know, I always thought it'd be nice to have a cabin in the mountains. If I don't end up blowing your head off, you could give me some good ideas. Maybe even sell me yours."

I just let him talk.

"That banker money was gonna be my last big score. A new start. Sell my strip joint, move back down south away from you shitkickers, dump the hookers. You got no idea what a needy pain in the ass those bitches are."

"Guess I wouldn't."

"Trust me, you never want to find out. I could go legit. Use that money for a classy custom shop. Be like American Chopper." He laughed. "Can you see me with my own cable show? 'Sonny's Cycles from Sparks, Nevada.'"

He turned the headlight back into my eyes. The back-and-forth was giving me a headache. I guess we weren't sharing our plans and dreams any more.

"Now, you know how important that money is. Clock's ticking, rifleman. Otherwise there's no place you and that cute little family of yours can go that'll—"

"First thing, *Sonny*, I don't have any money except what I earn. Second, it's the Feds poking around missing bank accounts, not me. Maybe some computer hacker ripped off the bank and is sitting in the Caymans right now laughing at chumps like you."

"So is there a third thing?" he said. "You know so damn much. There's always a third thing."

"Yeah. *Never* threaten me or my family again."

"Brave talk from a guy who don't even carry a weapon."

"You think I need a weapon?"

He kept his eyes on me then. Even from a distance I could hear him breathe, though in the glare it was hard to make out his expression. He pocketed the automatic, then raised one hand and made a little movement. An engine fired up from the road behind him with a steady whine, and a headlight lit him up from the back and lit me up, too. Then he shouted.

"*Tiny.*"

He brought his hand down and a shotgun blasted

from the road and kicked up dust and pine needles and tree bark about eight feet to my left.

I just stood there and watched the new headlight wobble down in my direction and stop a few feet behind VanOwen.

"Where's Flaco?" he said. In the second headlight he was nothing more than a big shape rimmed by flickering yellow.

"He ain't coming," the guy called Tiny said.

In that light I could make out that Tiny was about as wide as VanOwen was tall. VanOwen turned back to the guy. He tried to talk soft, but he was just too pissed.

"What the hell?" he said.

"Flaco ain't coming. We found out the—"

"Shut *up*," VanOwen said.

He started to raise his hand again when Sarah's 9mm made a double click as she racked it in the dark not more than thirty feet away.

"You'll want to lower your hand slowly," she said. "Very slowly."

I turned and could just make out Sarah on her mare coming up the slope from the pack station. She stopped a bit behind me in deep shadows. It was good positioning if shooting started, but I wasn't too concerned. If these clowns were gonna shoot me, they'd have shot me.

VanOwen did like she said. He turned to his guy. "Get on outta here."

Nobody said anything. All three of us followed the headlight with our eyes as the dirt bike picked up speed. I'd turned back to VanOwen when I heard the metallic wire-screeching sound every ranch kid knows from when an animal or vehicle hits a barbwire fence hard and stretches the twisted steel strands and pops the stays and staples as whatever it was that hit it plows through that fence, snapping wood posts and bending steel ones until the fence finally wins, and whatever hit it stops cold. The headlight disappeared for a second, then looked to be pointing straight up, lighting the tree canopy near the trailhead gate.

"Ohh . . ." Tiny said in the dark. "Ohhh, *shiit*."

The guy had forgot where they'd cut the fence and missed the hole as he blasted on out of there. As tense as things were just then, Sarah and I both laughed.

"Well, for chrissakes," VanOwen said.

He revved his bike and turned it again so his light was on both Sarah and me. I could see Sarah had put on a Cal Poly hoodie. Her duty belt was still buckled around her hips.

We watched the light on the dirt bike go from vertical to level, and heard Tiny moan and whimper. We saw his headlight arc away from us and saw it lighting up the wire and posts as he finally found the hole in the fence. Then it picked up speed, and his light shone on the Jeffrey pines as it wobbled down the canyon road, flickers of red taillight bobbing behind it.

"So how come you're going to all this trouble for a lousy million bucks?"

"Hey, I'm not greedy." VanOwen laughed. "Just remember, I'm on to you, shitkicker. I'd say you and that banker-bitch been plottin' this little rip-off for quite a while."

"Get over yourself. I never knew you existed till four days ago."

He revved the Harley a couple of times, starting off. Then he circled and stopped opposite Sarah and leaned forward.

"Good to see you, blondie," he said.

He revved the bike a last time and chugged off till his taillights kinda blended in with Tiny's.

Sarah rode up on the mare, bareback with just a halter. She holstered her weapon as she rode closer, then waited for me to finish hiking over. I got to the top of the bank and she slipped off the horse. She gripped my arms up and down like she was making sure all the pieces were there. Then she looked off down-canyon into the shadows.

"We okay?" she said. "I saw the headlight and knew something was wrong."

"We're okay for now. I don't know what those ginks were doing lurking around up there in the dark, but I guess we'll find out soon enough."

I got out my phone and showed her the spot on the berm where the person watching us had hunkered down. She examined the human sign and gave a disgusted little shiver, then swung back up on the mare. "Hop on. I'll ride you double. I want to get back so May can go to bed. We can clean up the mess in the morning."

I swung up behind her, then we watched the last lights disappear far down-canyon.

"I told you you should have taken your rifle," she said.

I patted her hip next to the holster. "That's what I got you for."

I was saddling mules with Harvey at the hitching rack the next morning to pack out the forensic team's gear. Sarah walked out of the cabin with her sheriff's radio in her hand, and Lorena on her hip. She had to step around the busted crib and didn't look happy.

"It's Jack," she said, "calling from the office. A guy named Sebastian VanOwen just met with Mitch. He showed Mitch a court order from last fall saying that he is the temporary legal guardian of Audie Ravenswood. My god, Tommy, that creep's heading for your mom's right now. He's taking Audie."

CHAPTER ELEVEN

It didn't take me long to get on the road.

"What are you going to do?" Sarah said.

"Get her back."

"But if he's got some sort of legal justification, there's really nothing you—"

"Look. All I know is, where he's taking her ain't no place for a kid."

"You said she was none of your affair."

She had me there. She didn't say it mean, but she had me.

"Things change."

We walked over to the corral.

"I should know better than to try and talk you out of this," she said.

I tried to act normal but probably looked as lame as I felt. I walked over to Harvey.

"I hate to do this to you again, Harv."

"Hey, Tommy," he said. "This guy's dickin' with you. That bullshit lost kid business, trashin' your cabin, then this. You go do what you need to do. You want me to tag along, just say the word."

"If you and May could just pack out the Feds' gear. That'd be great. I'm sorry."

I fired up my old truck. I let the diesel warm up, ran into the cabin, grabbed a water bottle and a jacket. I didn't know how long this idiocy would take or where it would lead. Sarah and Lorena were waiting for me at the bottom of the steps.

"Go see Mitch first," she said.

"I will."

I kissed her goodbye, and she held me hard. I thanked Harvey again and walked down the corral fence line to the outhouse. I opened the door and just stood there. Leaning in with my hands on the plank doorframe, I could feel them all watching me, waiting like it was forever. I turned back without the rifle and let the spring on the door slam it behind me. From across the yard, I could almost hear the air come out of Sarah in a long sigh.

I don't know what I was thinking about when I drove down the logging road to the valley except what Harvey said about the guy dicking with me and wondering where VanOwen got the idea I had that damn money. I tried not to think about the kid being a hostage to fortune in this. I knew I was crazy to stick my nose into this guy's business and let him force my hand, but I was across the meadows and turning down Main Street before I had an answer. Mitch was sitting at his desk when I walked in. He looked up like he was expecting me and held up a Xerox of a document, just cozy as hell in his own little cloud of smug.

"Looks like we solved the mystery of who that kid's guardian is," he said.

I yanked the paper out of his hand and only halfway read it before I tossed it back. It granted the guy temporary custody if his employee was incapacitated or dead. Or at least until there was a hearing.

"I had a good talk with that VanOwen fella," he said. "He's pure by-the-book law enforcement. Had a dandy career till he crashed in the line of duty and crippled himself up." He picked the paper off the floor. "Looks good to me."

"Did you ask him why he staged that search-and-rescue bullshit?"

Mitch gave me a look. "Who says it was bullshit?"

"Did you hold him for questioning in the murder of the woman at the Paul Bunyan? The woman that lied about the kid being hers and lied about her being missing?"

He just glared at me.

"Afraid to tangle with him, Mitch?"

"Look," he said. "When it comes to that little girl, he's holding all the cards. Maybe this trouble between you two started when a disabled cop got attacked for no good reason by a goddamn cowboy what thinks he's above the law."

"Those fake parents that ended up dead were his people."

"Says who?"

"The little girl he's grabbin' right now while I'm wasting time talking to you."

"He's got friends in Reno law enforcement," Mitch said. "You got no play up there."

I was heading for the door. "Somebody beat that woman to death with that guy's steel cane. I'll bet my life on that."

I rattled on out of there and barely heard Mitch's shout behind me.

"Well, you may have to do just that, hotshot."

I didn't want to waste any more of my life talking to that jerk than I already had. Jack was waiting by my truck when I got outside.

"This whole deal kinda pissed me off," he said. "That big crippled bastard kinda smirkin' my way when he was talking to Mitch." Jack handed me some notes he'd written on a pad.

"I tried to check the guy out but couldn't find squat that applies," he said. "No arrest records here or in Nevada. He was a person of interest in an arson for insurance deal in the torching of a motorcycle shop up near Bordertown, but the policy and business was under another guy's name."

"Whose?"

"A guy named Carroll Gopnik."

"Should that mean anything to me?"

"He sometimes used an alias—Cody Davis." Jack reached up to touch the top of his bandaged ear. "One of the guys shooting at us in the canyon. The guy Mitch says you clipped with my pistol."

I took a minute to ponder all that.

"Where's VanOwen live?"

"No known residence," Jack said. "His California disability checks are sent to another custom motorcycle shop in Sparks called Vicious Cycles. That's a totally different jurisdiction, but he ain't the owner of record there either. I got the address for you if you want to check it out."

I looked at the notes and got in my truck. "Thanks, Jack."

"You going to Reno?"

"I'm going to Sarah's dad's first. Talk to my mom. See what happened when the guy took Audie."

I flew out of town and made good time for a bit. Then ten miles from Dave's ranch I hit road construction with a flag-man, a pilot car, the works—fifteen minutes at a dead stop. That gave me time to think about what I was doing, and it wasn't pretty. And it sure wasn't smart. I thought about the forensic team we had to pack out and wondered what VanOwen's guys were doing in the canyon. There had to be some connection, but I couldn't imagine what. I thought about the cut fence I needed to mend and the crib I needed to rebuild. I couldn't fix on a subject that didn't piss me off. I got up to Dave's by mid-morning, half furious, half burned. Mom and Burt and Dave were all waiting in the kitchen for me, looking like death. I knew my thinking on my own child and the missing child was getting all mixed up, and that just pissed me off more. Sarah had told Mom over the radio not to argue with VanOwen or interfere, as that might make things worse.

"It was hard," Mom said. "Audie was crying, and . . . oh, Tommy, it was just real hard."

"That kid's a trouper," Dave said. "She sure didn't want to go. She kicked the big bastard a couple of times."

"What're you going to do, son?" Mom said.

"Go to Reno. Bring her back."

"He's got the law on his side," she said.

"I could really give a shit right now, Mom. The guy beat a woman to death a couple nights ago right in Paiute Meadows. Audie knows stuff about him that could put her life in danger. I don't want that girl anywhere near him."

"How could a man like that be granted custody?" she said.

"Audie said her mother used to work for VanOwen before she died. She was a stripper in Reno. Maybe she named him as guardian or something in case something happened to her. I'm gonna try and find out."

"Good heavens," Mom said.

"Lemme get my AR," Burt said, "I'll go with you." Mom's boyfriend Burt had been with the Corps in the first Gulf War. I'd seen him use that AR to take down a drug peddler who had pistols in both fists the year before, not two miles from where we stood.

"Appreciate it, Burt. But, you know, gunfire breeds gunfire, and I got these girls to think about, now."

Mom gave me one of her teary smiles when I said "girls."

"However you want to play it," Burt said.

I took a deep breath and headed back outside to the truck.

I drove slow as the highway left the pastures and cottonwoods of Shoshone Valley and crossed into the sagebrush and piñon of Nevada, trying to keep my head clear. I hadn't gone to Reno much since high school when I went there looking for girls and trouble. When I was younger,

Dad had taken me to the Snaffle Bit Futurity there a bunch of Septembers. Reno had a great Western store we'd stop in at from time to time, and it was smack in the crappy 4th Street neighborhood where I was headed. At least I remembered that I needed to take the Wells off-ramp off the I-80 Westbound.

Fourth Street was wide and depressing, with block after block of low one- and two-story buildings, lots of them brick like old Reno, some new and industrial, some bars and Lysol-stink motels. I found the Pink Corral pretty quick. Inside, the walls were painted black, and the only lights were on the stage and behind the bar. Girls dancing naked before noon in front of boozy men isn't so uncommon if you figure that when guys work a night shift at a casino or hotel or a mine, they get off work at six or seven in the morning and this is their happy hour. Not that anybody in the joint looked very happy.

A semi-naked middle-aged woman sat at a table by the door. She told me what the cover charge was. She pointed at the cashbox with a flashlight pen.

"I'm looking for Sonny VanOwen."

The woman told me what the cover charge was again. I walked past her scanning the room. A bouncer was right on me. Sucker was huge—all black tee-shirt and bench-pressed like crazy. I asked him for Sonny. He looked me up and down. I was the only guy in the place in a big hat and spurs. It was like I could hear the guy thinking.

"He usually comes in midafternoon."

"Thanks. He the boss?"

"Well, *yeah*. Ain't that why you want to see him?" he said. He looked like he'd already talked too much.

"Any idea where he'd be now?"

"No clue. You might wanna check Vicious Cycles in Sparks. Right across the tracks from the Nugget."

He walked away without bothering me, so I figured he was telling the truth.

I got back in my truck and drove east. I passed the Western store like it represented normal life in a sea of pus. I had the thought that what I was doing was crazy, and I should just go inside and buy a saddle pad or new hat or something. But I didn't. I cruised further on, slowing down opposite a brick corner bar with a sign that said The Nogales over the entrance. A half dozen bikers in their leathers and shades with bandanas around their greasy heads watched me creep by. I made eye contact with a fat one and he flipped me off. He was shaped kind of like the guy on the dirt bike the night before, so big you could barely see the Harley under him. I slammed on the brakes in the middle of the street and got out, leaving the engine running and the door open behind me. I was right in the middle of that bunch before they knew it. Actually before I knew it either. I walked up close to the one who'd flipped me off. He was most definitely the fattest. The black biker chaps he wore looked all muddy and had some fresh tears. From the waist up he was filthy with dust. The rest of him was just normal filthy. His arms and face had fresh cuts, too. He looked like he'd wrestled a badger. I knew he was the guy from the trailhead fence.

"I'm looking for Sonny VanOwen, *Tiny.*"

"Never heard of him . . . *Tex.*" He said it real slow. Then he laughed. He had some broken teeth. Guys behind him laughed. A car zipped by, and its horn honked at my truck.

"Don't dick with me." I grabbed him by the throat with just my left hand and squeezed.

It's a funny thing that if folks think you are batshit out-of-your-mind-crazy mad and ready to take them down or die right there, it makes 'em cautious. Kind of a rabid dog thing. If you actually are that mad, it helps. Still, a couple sonsabitches straddling their hogs closest to the bar entrance fired them up and revved them so loud that if this pig had squealed I would've had a hard time hearing. Just as fast as I grabbed the guy, I let him go. The revving got less loud.

"Try Mama's," he said. He was panting and his face was stone white under his beard. Cutting off the blood supply to somebody's brain is quick work.

"What's Mama's?"

"An Italian joint," he said. "Snake eats there every day. Damn near lives there."

I must've given him a funny look.

"Snake," Tiny said. "That's what his friends call him."

"I ain't his friend. Where is it?"

He told me. I walked out into the street through traffic to my truck without looking back. A couple more cars honked at me.

"May wanna watch yourself, Tex," Tiny semi-shouted loud enough for me to hear. "Joint's full of cops." He tried to laugh, then he put a dirty hand to his throat and started to gag. I flipped a U turn and headed back the way I'd come.

Mama's was an old house a few blocks west. It sat right on the sidewalk edge like it was left over from an older time. I saw a little parking lot behind. I figured that would be too cramped for a quick getaway in a pickup, so I left my truck at the curb under a No Parking sign. Before I went inside, I gave the lot a quick walk-through. I saw two sedans side by side. One was definitely unmarked law enforcement with radio, laptop, shotgun, the works. I saw a couple of motorcycles up against the back wall. One of those looked semi-familiar. I looked at the plate and remembered to check my phone for the picture I took of the chopper in Buddy Hornberg's equipment shed. The plate was a match.

Inside looked like any old frame house except for all the heads that turned when I walked in. Somebody must've noticed me leave my truck under the No Parking sign then disappear around back for a couple minutes, because when I stopped to scan the place the chatter quieted for a second. The rooms were small and crammed with tables. The place was getting busy with lunch trade, and I could see a couple of obvious plainclothes cops at the tables in what had been the front room. One of them, a heavy red-headed guy in a Hawaiian shirt, checked me out, then went back to eating. I stood there a minute studying the place, checking exits and wondering where the ball bats and shotguns might be stashed. There was a kitchen in a back room and a bar along one wall by the entrance with a big goofy-looking guy in a ponytail tending it. I put down a ten. The guy asked what my pleasure was, and I pointed past him to a bottle on the back bar. He held up the Jack Daniel's and I nodded, holding my thumb and forefinger about two inches apart. He poured me a shot with water back and I tossed them down. He set my change on the bar. I could see the one cop watching me from across the front room. The Hawaiian shirt probably hid a pistol. He was just starting to get up when I heard VanOwen's voice loud in the back room. I left my change and headed in that direction. I was looking in the doorway at VanOwen by the time that cop got halfway to the bar. He took a seat on a barstool fifteen feet behind me.

VanOwen was sitting at a table against the rear wall with a couple of guys. And with Audie. He had parked her close on his left, wrapped in her ratty sleeping bag. She started to say something when she saw me, but he shut her up with a look. A druggy-looking loser, dressed more like the fake dad who got shot back in the canyon than the bikers I'd seen at The Nogales, sat across from VanOwen. The guy turned in his chair to check me out. The third guy at the table was a surprise. It was another big hat—a dirty palm-leaf—and the guy looked as out of place as I felt. He was sunburned and wore a wildrag tight under his chin and stared at me like I'd just kicked his dog. He never so much as blinked.

VanOwen watched me, too, fiddling with his steel walking stick. I noticed this was the one with the brass skull for a nob, not the rattlesnake head I'd seen the day I roped him—the one I figured he'd beat the woman to death with. He must've stashed or scrapped that one.

"Hey there, rifleman," he said. "Where's your rifle?" He turned to the guy with the wildrag and laughed, then turned back to me. "You know, I was right about you last night. I was right that I'd be seeing you again. I just didn't think it'd be so quick."

I let him talk.

"I figure you're here to deliver something that's mine or to tell me where I can find it." He smiled pretty nasty-like. "So which is it, dude? Door number one or door number two?"

I caught Audie's eye.

VanOwen's laugh sounded pretty faked. His eyes moved just so. "Tiny?" he said.

I could hear and smell the fat biker as he shuffled in from the street and sidled up close to me. He must've just rolled in from The Nogales to warn the boss. This time I grabbed his throat with my right hand and pinned him to the doorjamb with my thumb deep in the artery. Fifteen minutes before, he was pretty slow from the rough night he'd had. Now he was even slower. I glanced at him just a second and could see the red of broken blood vessels spreading across the flesh of his neck from the first squeezing he got.

VanOwen watched the guy squirming and turning white. "You're outliving your usefulness, Tiny," he said.

Tiny made a little gaggy sound in his throat, and bubbles popped out of his nose. I heard a clatter on the floor like the guy had dropped something. I glanced quick. A Winchester Model 12 pump lay there between his boots, but I didn't linger on it. I could hear more snot bubbles and I let him go before he passed out.

VanOwen straightened up in his chair. He clamped a big hand on Audie's leg and just looked at me.

"It's time you tell me what I want to know." He squeezed Audie's leg till she squealed.

I heard a wooden barstool squeak on the wooden floor and heard the cop in the Hawaiian shirt moving up behind me slow. I half-squatted and scooped up the 12 gauge with my left hand. When I did, I caught a quick look at the bartender coming, too. Once he got out in front of the bar I could see an automatic on his belt. I got up slow and careful. I turned sideways so I could see both rooms and gripped the fore-end of the shotgun and jerked it skyward, jacking a shell into the chamber. Then I turned to the two guys coming up on me.

"Easy, Carl," VanOwen said.

The cop stopped. The bartender faded to the side out of my line of sight.

VanOwen nodded to the cop he called Carl, then turned to me again. "You look tweaked, dude," he said. "Like you're about to have a freakin' aneurism."

I looked at Audie and jerked my head just so. She squirmed away from VanOwen and scampered across the room to me, keeping scared eyes on the guy in the palm-leaf hat the whole time. I put an arm out and pushed her behind me.

"You ain't takin' the kid," VanOwen said. He looked mad as hell all of a sudden, then tried to make light of it. "Why, that'd be kidnapping—a no-shit *federal* crime."

I took a step back, the shotgun still in my left hand, my right on Audie's shoulder.

VanOwen kept looking at me like I was crazy. "How the hell do you think you're gonna get out of here alive?"

The bartender was right behind me then. I turned and pushed Audie out of the way and pointed the 12 gauge at the ceiling and squeezed. It sounded like a grenade going off in such close quarters, and left about as big a hole. Folks dove for cover. Dust and splinters and bits of cardboard and mattress floated down from the attic in a puff of plaster dust. Then I brought the shotgun to port arms and held it there like I was on the parade ground, not in this dump. The bartender's eyes followed the shotgun. I lowered my left hand and raised my right till the weapon was horizontal across my chest. Then I snapped my right arm straight out and drove the stock into the bartender's face. He dropped without a word, slipping on his own blood as the cop behind me took a step closer, but real careful-like now. I gripped the barrel like a ball bat and smashed the stock as hard as I could against the doorjamb—hard enough that the stock cracked. The cop flinched and ducked. I stepped in tight enough to jab him in the chest with the splintered stock and smell the lasagna on his breath. VanOwen started up from his chair. The guy in the palm-leaf kept staring at me but never moved. I dropped the 12 gauge and grabbed Audie. We walked on out of that place, and nobody tried to stop us.

I shoved her in the truck cab and fired up the diesel. She jumped up with her knees on the bench seat so she could watch the front door of the restaurant through my back window as I hauled ass on out of there. In my rearview I could see Carl and the oily guy who'd been sitting across from VanOwen step out to the sidewalk, then into the street. They didn't look like they had much appetite to follow me. Tiny stumbled out last like he had even less appetite. Audie turned back to me when I'd headed down a side street and she couldn't see Mama's anymore.

"That was hella scary," she said. "At first I thought you were mad at me. How come you didn't say nothin'?"

I just shrugged. I didn't have an answer myself. I looked down and tapped the buckle on her seat belt. She buckled herself in and kind of smiled. She reached over and touched some of the bartender's blood on my shirt.

"I knew you'd come and get me," she said.

CHAPTER TWELVE

A fast couple of hours later I cruised along the reservoir in sight of Paiute Meadows. When I had service, I tried to reach Jack at his desk at the sheriff's office but only got his voicemail. A half hour before he'd texted me to keep rolling and stay out of Mitch's way. When I pulled into the pack station, I saw agent Aaron Fuchs's US government Chevy sitting under the lone Jeffrey pine along the corral next to Sarah's Silverado. Sarah sat on the cabin porch with Lorena, watching Aaron cutting and nailing 1-by-4s to replace the closet doorframe trim. It was hot in the canyon, and he was sweating and coated with sawdust from Harvey's table saw, but he seemed to be enjoying himself. When they heard Audie and me, Aaron turned off the saw and took off his safety glasses.

"Nothin' better to do, Aaron?"

"Just trying to keep my mind off the mess you've made," he said.

We both watched Audie run up the steps and wrap her arms around Sarah and Lorena. Things got teary and quiet for a minute. Even Aaron looked pretty relieved. He walked over to me as he brushed the sawdust off.

"You're a difficult guy to be friends with, friend. Mitch thinks you crossed the line and I ought to haul you in." He looked up at Audie on the porch. "You okay, young lady?"

She nodded and looked to me to see if she should answer.

"Did Tommy hurt anybody in Reno?"

"Oh, totally," Audie said. "You never seen nobody so freakin' mad." She laughed and turned to Sarah. "His face was all stony, and he smashed a guy's nose with a humongous gun butt then broke the gun all to crap almost in another guy's face, then we walked out of that place just as chill—like we'd ordered takeout. It was awesome."

"Terrific," Sarah said.

I looked at the carpentry. "Nice work."

"My grandfather had a furniture shop in Boyle Heights," Aaron said. "East LA. But don't change the subject. Tell me what you thought you were doing with a possible kidnapping of this girl and assault on a Reno vice cop. I know you're certain VanOwen is responsible for killing the woman in the motel, but this morning you kind of muddied the waters."

"Hadn't thought that far."

"That would be apparent."

"But we did run into VanOwen last night after we found the woman's body."

"Where?" he said.

"Here. Just up the road. Two of his bunch were riding

dirt bikes up the canyon and only one came back. VanOwen was waiting for them at the gate."

"Maybe the other one got stuck or ran out of gas," he said. "Did your partner, Harvey, see the other guy?"

"Couldn't say. I was too busy muddying the waters."

"What do you figure they were up to?" he said. He looked worried.

"I know what he's up to."

"How, babe?" Sarah said.

"He told me. He said he'd been plotting with Erika Hornberg. That she was getting that million bucks for him."

They both just stared at me.

"Now he thinks I got it. And if I don't, that I can get it."

"Oh, shit," Aaron said. "You better know what you're dealing with."

I went inside and got us two beers and a couple of Gatorades and we sat out on pack platforms in the shade. Audie curled up on her sleeping bag next to Sarah, her eyes on Lorena. Aaron fiddled with his tablet.

"His name is Sebastian VanOwen, but you probably know that, and that he goes by Sonny or sometimes Snake. Like he told Jack, he was a CHP motor officer for eight years, and a pretty good one," Aaron said, "at least in the beginning."

"From what I just saw, the guy still seems to have law enforcement friends."

"Yeah," he said. "And now one of them is your sheriff."

Audie's eyes were on Aaron now. His were on his tablet. "After a couple of years VanOwen's CHP file started to fill up with accusations of sexual harassment, shakedowns, bad companions," Aaron said, "but nothing actionable because folks were afraid to testify against him. Then he got in a hellacious motorcycle wreck one night out on Coast Highway by the Ventura county line and almost didn't make it." He fiddled with his screen. "CHP thinks his wreck might be crime-motivated. A turf war between officers on the take. After he was disabled, the LAPD picks up his story."

"Doing what?"

Fuchs scrolled down. "Once he's back on his feet, VanOwen surfaces down by LAX, running a string of girls out of a bowling alley on Century Boulevard called the Alabama Lanes, specializing in black prostitutes for out-of-town business dweebs. Plus loan sharking, stolen goods—anything where intimidation and muscle can help you score. Folks were afraid of the guy, and big city law gave him a wide berth. Apparently worried he'd rat out some higher-ups. Even to the bad actors down there, VanOwen was unique—a truly scary guy—like something out of the old west. You cross him, then one night a crew of big dudes with ski masks and baseball bats and blowtorches visits your family. Word gets around."

"How'd he end up in our nightmare?" Sarah said. The color had just drained out of her.

"So-Cal bad guys had enough. Somebody tried to cheap-shot him at his house in Tujunga in the hills outside LA," Aaron said. "Filled it with a ton of lead one night. Sonny got away without a scratch, but somebody torched the place. It went up like a rocket with his wife inside. Or at least they thought it was his wife."

I looked at Fuchs. He looked at me.

"LAPD just thought a bad cop crossed one guy too many. So he decides on a change of scene and shows up in Reno," Aaron said. "Then a year later, some hikers find the real wife with a bullet in her head in a shallow grave out at Joshua Tree. VanOwen's a guy who covers his tracks."

"Who got shot in the burned house?" Sarah said.

"I don't know if they ever found that out," he said.

"Same MO up in Reno?" Sarah said.

"Similar," Aaron said. "Now he's added underage girls right off the bus from little towns in Idaho and Utah."

Audie sat up and pulled the sleeping bag over her head.

"It's okay, sweet pea," Sarah said.

"And the usual ancillary stuff," Aaron said, "like stolen car-parts. He seems to operate a custom chopper shop in Sparks."

"That's what Jack told me."

"Any arrests?" Sarah said.

"Zip," Aaron said. "A hardnose Sparks homicide detective heard about him and paid him a visit when he first settled in. Told VanOwen he'd checked him out and didn't like what he'd found. The detective must have put a scare in him. Out there he behaves like a model citizen."

"Because he doesn't have to look over his shoulder?"

"And because he doesn't have the allies he did down south," Aaron said. "Now it's like he doesn't exist anymore. Besides no known residence, no cars or bikes or property or taxes in his name. Burner phones. It's like he's a total phantom."

"Until now. He keeps one of his Harleys in Buddy Hornberg's equipment shed with a lot of chopper parts." I showed him the picture of the license plate on my phone. "So those two clowns are connected."

"And somehow connected to this child's faked disappearance," Sarah said.

I watched Audie's head poke out from under the sleeping bag.

"Which makes Audie a material witness."

"And a target," Sarah said.

"So you're not going to arrest me for kidnapping her?"

"Not today," Aaron said. "The guy could still bring charges. Sarah said you weren't armed. I just wonder why VanOwen let you take her?"

"'Cause Tommy looked like he wanted to cut 'im a new one," Audie said.

"*Audie!*" Sarah said.

"Maybe since VanOwen thinks I have this connection to Erika Hornberg, he needs to keep me alive."

Aaron held out his tablet for us to look at something. "Agents Castile and D'Angelico, the forensic pair we left in the canyon? They found a couple of intriguing—"

He stopped talking to watch a car pull out of the aspen from the bridge. We could see it was another FBI Chevy. It pulled up next to the saddle shed. We could see right away that Aaron wasn't expecting any of his people. He put down his tablet and stood up.

"Gimme a sec," he said. "He may be here to arrest you, Tommy."

I sipped my beer and watched him walk across the

dirt out of the trees. The guy in the car hadn't got out, but he handed Aaron a piece of paper. I couldn't see Aaron's face as he leaned down and talked to him. Audie mumbled and stirred and moved my way. I tried to scoot over but she curled herself around my knee, half asleep. Aaron and the agent talked for a long time, then the guy circled his car and drove off the way he came. Audie raised her head and opened her eyes. We watched Aaron just stare at the ground. After a minute he walked over to the pack platform and sat down next to Sarah.

He was staring out at the pasture, sweat on his forehead. He kept staring when he started to talk.

"Evidence Response Team Special Agent Vincent D'Angelico. Age thirty-seven," he said. "Shot dead last night." He didn't say anything for another minute. But he looked down at the paper in his hand.

"Vinnie and Alicia were eating dinner around the campfire. Their work all done. Not dark yet. Crime scene photographed and logged. Body of the bog lady bagged and tagged. They hear motors way in the distance. They're on alert, but then it's quiet for a long time, so it's probably nothing. They go back to eating. Later they hear rustling close by in the brush and panting like a bear or something. Vinnie grabs a flash and scouts the perimeter—which he shouldn't have done, because he's basically a lab and crime scene guy, not a field agent. He stumbles on a couple of guys hiding in the trees spying on them. Alicia tells Vinnie to stand down, but he's nervous and orders the guys to show themselves. One is a huge fat guy in biker leathers holding a shotgun. He was so close they could hear him wheeze, then he crashed off through the trees. Alicia pulls her weapon and tries to control the situation, but all hell breaks loose. The fat guy fires the shotgun from somewhere in the dark and Vinnie is hit in the leg. Just a couple of pellets. A second guy pops up close. Vinnie thinks he's unarmed and tells him to step into the light. The flashlight makes Vinnie an easy target. The guy has some kind of small caliber pistol, and he puts a round in Vinnie's chest. He drops. Alicia runs for the light and grabs it and Vinnie's pistol, too. She dives for cover in the dark, firing with both weapons. The shotgun fires a second time, but even farther away this time and misses her. The pistol shooter disappears in the dark, but Alicia lights him up with the flash. He raises his arm to shoot again. She drops him. Three or four rounds. She doesn't remember. He's a skinny guy in biker leathers, too. Not very handy with the pistol but still good enough to . . ." Aaron looked at me, unable to get the words out. "Anyway, does this sound like the guys you told me about from last night?"

"Yeah. I saw the fat one with VanOwen this morning in Reno. And he had a Winchester Model twelve."

Aaron just nodded like he was trying to reconcile the thinking part with the talking part. He'd taken it hard.

"When I debrief Alicia, I'll know more," he said.

"VanOwen sends two of his guys back into the canyon to spy on your crew and only one of them came out. Wonder what they thought they'd find out?"

"It must have been pretty important to kill a federal agent," Sarah said.

"It doesn't seem like a firefight was part of the plan," Aaron said. "This sounds like a screw-up on all sides."

"Where's your lady agent now?" Sarah said. "Where's Alicia?"

"Still up there securing the area," Aaron said. He held up the paper. "This rundown is all second hand info from the chopper crew. She hunkered down against a granite wall all night and sat there watching the shadows. If anybody showed . . ." He was quiet a minute. "Alicia's fierce." He said it so soft we could barely hear him. Then he told us the rest.

Agent Castile was out of communication range, so she waited there till morning, her back against the rock with a pistol in each fist just a few feet from her dead partner as the fire died down. It was just coals by dawn and another two hours until she heard the chopper. There wasn't room for her and what was now three bodies—the one from the bog, Vinnie, and the guy who killed him. She was too much of a hard case to fly out leaving an unsecured crime scene. She told the chopper crew to take the dead and she'd fix herself breakfast while she waited.

Harvey and May would've got to the campsite with the mules before the chopper came back. Knowing her, Aaron said, Agent Castile would have coffee ready. Knowing Harvey, he and May would wait with her until she could finally fly out, which is why we hadn't seen any sign of them yet. Aaron stood up. Audie stood up too, never taking her eyes off him. She took Sarah's free hand, and we all walked back up to the cabin.

"Alicia and D'Angelico found more cash scattered in the area," Aaron said, "but it only added up to another couple hundred. No sequential bills, which is consistent with just glomming the occasional fifty from the teller's drawer.

Alicia said it seemed bogus since some of the bills were hardly weathered at all."

"And the bog lady?"

"No surprise. They found a gunshot wound." He looked back at me again to see how I'd react. "A twenty-five caliber round to the temple."

"Who uses something like that, anymore?" Sarah said.

"When we interviewed him last fall," Aaron said, "Buddy Hornberg told us his dad collected old pistols. Since folks launder money buying and selling collectibles, we asked for an inventory. He had a little vest-pocket 1908 Colt twenty-five cal."

"Don't tell me," Sarah said. "It's missing, right?"

"That would be correct," he said. "Anyway, after months in the drink, the body isn't telling us much more without a more thorough exam, and with a positive ID from the brother, that notion doesn't seem warranted to your department. But based on what happened last night, I can't leave anything else to chance. I've authorized my people to go ahead with a full autopsy. I can't dink around with Mitch anymore."

"He'll be so pleased," Sarah said.

"Yeah. Anyway, the wound to the temple is consistent with the note."

"The note?"

"A suicide note," Aaron said.

"Is a handwriting expert looking at it?" Sarah said.

"It was written on a computer and printed out then folded in a ziplock sandwich bag and stuffed in her shirt pocket."

"Who the hell?"

"Someone who wants it readable after a whole winter underwater in the Sierra," Aaron said.

"So what did it say?"

Aaron read it off the tablet. "'My luck has run out. I'm sorry for letting you down.' Some locals said she had a gambling problem."

"There was talk in town," Sarah said, "that Erika liked video poker, playing the horses, that sort of thing, but mostly just talk."

"So who's the 'you' she's writing to in the note?"

"Could be her brother," Aaron said.

"Or her bosses at the bank," Sarah said.

"It's obvious the note's bullshit. Planted like this." I pulled out my own ziplock with the cash I'd found in my saddle pockets. I handed it to Aaron and told him where I'd found it, and when.

"If she committed suicide, how did this get in my saddle pockets?"

We all just sat there for a minute. This was taking all the life out of Aaron.

"This is all on me," he said. "I shouldn't have left them alone up there. My fault." He stood up and took off the shades he was wearing and pinched the bridge of his nose. "In my twelve years I've never lost an agent."

Sarah reached out and squeezed his arm.

"There's no way you could've seen this coming," she said.

"That what you think, Tommy?" he said.

"We know the dead woman didn't die in a fall or

from exposure. And she didn't scatter ratty fifty dollar bills around then lay down in that water, cover herself with leaves and branches, and blow her own brains out. Someone killed her and dumped her in that water or found her dead and stashed her there. Someone placed her where Jack's dog would find her a few days ago. A place Jack and I'd be looking because in this whole big canyon that's exactly where somebody planted Audie's jacket. Now, almost a year after Erika disappears, that same somebody wanted her found real public-like and used this bullshit story of a missing child to do just that."

"The brother says the body's Erika," Aaron said.

"Buddy's lying."

Sarah's sheriff radio crackled and buzzed. She handed me Lorena and stepped away a few paces and talked, then got quiet and listened. In a minute she walked back to us and sat down.

"That was Jack," she said. "Alicia Castile finally was flown out, and she's okay. Your lab guys started right in on the first chopper load, starting with ballistics." She looked at me. "Cody Davis, the fake dad you packed out? He was killed by a single shot to the forehead. The round was a polymer-tipped thirty-thirty."

"Not Jack's three-fifty-seven that Tommy was carrying?" Aaron said.

"Correct," Sarah said. She looked at me kind of relieved. "And the shot that killed Agent D'Angelico? A twenty-five caliber. Alicia recovered the weapon. The same gun that killed the woman in the bog almost a year ago was used on your agent last night."

CHAPTER THIRTEEN

We lay under light blankets letting the night breeze cool us. Lorena was asleep in the next room in a crib Sarah borrowed from May's sister, and Audie was tucked in Sarah's bedroll right beside her. I watched the stars through the aspen outside the cabin and watched the tree shadow skitter across the curve of Sarah's bare back in the last of the moonlight.

"The one bright spot"—she spoke in almost a whisper—"you got this child back safe."

She turned her head towards the open door, then rolled back until we were laying nose to nose.

"Yeah. that's the only thing that makes sense. I'm sure as hell missing the rest of the picture."

"The money. The body. The missing girl," she said. She nuzzled closer. "How does it all fit?"

"I know. I thought we were for sure supposed to find that body but couldn't figure why. Now we got four more bodies and nobody's got any answers. Maybe it just—"

"Go to sleep, honey."

I crawled out in the early dawn chill without waking her.
Even before I ran the stock in from the creek I put on my
jacket and hiked back up to the trailhead in the near dark,
going through the cut in the fence. I saw the turned up dirt
and pine needles where Tiny had found his way through
the cut wire before he headed down-canyon. I followed the
fenceline up towards the road and saw the scraps of oily
blue jean and black leather where he misjudged the hole in
the fence in the dark and sproinged hard on taut barbwire.
There was a bunch of blood, too, and a bit of motor oil from
the flipped dirt bike. I started studying the ground by the
light on my phone. There'd been so much traffic I could
barely see traces of my own truck and trailer from a few
days before when I hauled Aaron up-canyon. I made out
VanOwen's crew's motorcycle tracks, but there was nothing new to learn from any of them. I walked a few hundred yards up the canyon as the sky lightened, and I put my
phone away. I wasn't looking for motorized tracks anymore.
I was just seeing what the canyon had to show me. I was following the uphill side of the old excavation for the fishing
lake when I stepped into another disturbed spot in the dirt
and pine debris. Instead of beer cans and Copenhagen tins,
I found a neat little cache of Greek yogurt cups, an empty
sea-salted almond bag folded up neat, and a half-torn tab
off a teabag. It made me wonder just who the hell I was
dealing with. Some tough gunsel who shopped at Whole
Foods, maybe. I looked across the excavation and could see

right about where I'd found the first mess. It looked like we had one watcher watching the other. I took it all in, then kept walking.

In the dawning light I spied something new where a stock trail from up in Ox Bow Canyon curved down to join the dirt road. I saw a single a set of horse tracks that came along that trail and mixed with the dirt bike traces. The shod prints had stepped in the tire tracks so they were newer. The front shoes had hand-drawn clips like the tracks I'd seen the day Jack got shot. The clips made little irregular indentations at ten and two on the curved steel of the toe that were real distinctive. I took off my jacket and hunkered down for a second look. With all the traffic, I couldn't tell if the hoofprints belonged to the first watcher, or the second. Or maybe neither. By now the sun was up, and it was already getting warm.

A Newport Beach couple in a Land Rover drove up with their gear. I'd just started pulling the shoes off my sorrel gelding. Sarah sat on the porch in her uniform looking serene and pretty, eating a ham and cheese omelet I'd made for her and talking with Mitch on her radio. Audie ate a bowl of Frosted Mini-Wheats while she stared down at Lorena dozing in her car seat. I dropped my pull-offs in my shoeing box after only getting the fronts yanked, and went to greet the customers. I caught Sarah watching the man and woman get out of the Land Rover with that blank Comanchero stare she sized up strangers with when they weren't looking, a look that no one could ever measure up to—like she already knew all she wanted to know about them. She signed off with Mitch, and, all smiling and charming, came down the steps to the tree where I'd tied the horse.

"Mitch is meeting with Aaron about VanOwen in about an hour," she said. "You should probably be there."

"When I get our party and their goods squared away."

"Okay, babe. I'll tell them you're on your way."

She gave the Newport Beachers a little wave, kissed me goodbye, fired up her truck, and headed out of the canyon with the baby and Audie. A big lanky woman waved at Sarah, then called over to me.

"Well, you certainly are on intimate terms with the local authorities," the woman said.

I walked over, and the woman shook my hand just as cheerful as hell and said her name was Scottie and she was in real estate and her husband's name was Drew and he was a lawyer. Her hand when I shook it was smooth, and the rings she wore were hard and cold. I told her that the deputy I just kissed was my wife. She said she was just teasing, and that her friends had researched us on the website Mom and Sarah had set up that winter and seemed to know all about us even before she first phoned. In their boat shoes and rugby shirts, they didn't look like they were ready to line out behind a string of mules, but the guy spoke about streams he'd fished and peaks he'd climbed in this part of the Sierra like he knew what he was doing, so I was hoping for a good trip.

I'd be packing these two plus a second couple up to Little Meadows the next day. They'd brought their own food and wall tent, but they wanted both me and the stock to stay with them in camp the whole three nights while they climbed Hawksbeak and Tower Peaks and did some fly fishing in the high lakes. A month earlier Sarah had walked in the cabin when I was trying to give them cheaper options over the phone. She made a throat-cutting gesture and tried not to laugh out loud at my foolishness.

I unbuckled my shoeing chaps and draped them over the anvil stump and started to help the guy unload their stuff, sorting it all on the pack platforms as we went. They had a lot of stuff. It was turning into one of those hot summer mornings where the flies buzzed around the pressure valve of the propane tank. We hadn't got very far when he started messing with his phone, and I let him discover that he'd get no service in the canyon. I finished emptying his gear except for the bags they said they'd leave at their motel. Then he got in the Land Rover and drove off without a word.

"He's running up to the airport to pick up our friends," Scottie said. She had been taking pictures of the stock in the corral.

"In Reno? You're going to be stuck here for hours."

"No, silly," she said, "the airport here—by the reservoir. Our friend Bill is a pilot."

I already knew from their reservation that the other guy was a beach club friend of theirs. There was a strip of asphalt that stuck out into the reservoir north of town, but there was no tower and no landing lights so you wouldn't exactly call it an airport.

The woman shielded her eyes as she watched the Range Rover grind up the hill across the creek. "Would that be so bad?" she said. "You being stuck here with me for a few hours?"

It was going to be a long couple of days.

Down in Paiute Meadows Aaron briefed Mitch about the dead agent and about VanOwen's history and about the money I'd found in my saddle pockets. Mitch interrupted every few minutes, and Aaron tried to keep him semi-focused. I put in my two cents about the machined steel beat-marks from VanOwen's cane on the flesh of the woman in the motel.

"I had a guy from Sparks PD stop into Vicious Cycles where Sonny hangs out," Mitch said, "and he asked him about that custom steel stick you say he carries. The pattern on the shaft is maybe similar to the untrained eye to the marks on the skin on the dead woman, but to a professional, it's not even close to being a match."

"Ask Jack. The guy had two of them. Steel canes."

"Well, shit," Mitch said.

Aaron looked like his life was draining away in absolute bullshit.

"And the guy who was shot in the canyon you called Cody Davis?" Mitch said. "Jack says his real name's Carroll Gopnik."

When Mitch looked down at his notes, Jack reached around and gave himself an imaginary pat on the back.

"He's done hard time in Lovelock for grand theft. Seemed to be kinda an all-purpose thug and errand boy for some Reno loan shark and pimp."

"Yeah," Aaron said. "Sonny VanOwen."

Mitch looked up at Aaron. "What kind of name is Carroll for a dude?"

"Last questions," Aaron said.

"Okay," Mitch said. "Your team found the guy's rifle in the trees near the bog lady, but there was no magazine." He just sort of smiled to himself then looked up at me. "I wondered how come?"

"I threw the magazine in the creek."

"That was evidence," he said.

"Jesus Christ, Mitch, have you ever been shot at?" Aaron said. "We've got a BOLO out on VanOwen, and my team will do a full autopsy on our possible Erika Hornberg. I think we're done here." He stood up and thanked us. He looked rocky and stretched thin. By now it was about eleven in the morning. I noticed Aaron hadn't bothered to tell Mitch about VanOwen's story of me and the million bucks.

I hadn't got my sorrel shod before I'd headed to town, so I was glad to get out of there quick and get back to work. Plus, I had the hole in the fence to fix and my own gear to square away before morning. All I knew was that it looked like VanOwen had faded into the woodwork. Killing his loser flunkies was one thing. Just tying up loose ends. Putting them in a position to swap shots with a federal was way past stupid. But as long as he thought I had his money, I'd be sleeping light.

I could see Dan Tyree's new dually Ram and gooseneck parked alongside the trailhead gate and a saddled horse tied to the side of the trailer. Dan was walking down the fence line to the hole that VanOwen's guys cut carrying a light coil of used barbwire and wire-pliers. I pulled over and got out.

"Forget where your gate was?" he said.

"Not exactly. You gonna fix it for me?"

"Not exactly," he said.

The fence was more-or-less Sarah's and mine and the Forest Service's, but the cattle up-canyon were Dan's and his mom's. I told him what had happened up there the night before.

"This whole Erika thing is crazy," he said. He cut some short lengths of wire and handed me a couple. I took a hammer and gloves out of my toolbox. "Guys gettin' shot almost a year after she flies the coop."

"Where you headin'?"

"Check a couple of drift-fence gates," he said, "Harvey thought the search-and-rescue folks mighta left some open gates closed and closed ones open, so I figured I'd best check for myself."

We spliced in lengths of barbwire at the cut spots and stretched them tight. Dan tucked his head, concentrating on the splice but looking pissed. "You think Erika did all the things they said she did?"

"Nope."

"How come?"

"'Cause I knew her. Same as you."

A guy with a straight-clawed hammer can hook a barb in the claw then wind the slack around the hammerhead until the strand is tight at the splice if he knows what he's doing. Sort of a mini wire-stretcher. The trick is bending the wire back on itself once you wind it taut. Dan and I took turns.

"Tommy?"

It was my turn, and I'd been woolgathering.

"What's eatin' you?" he said.

"I saw a guy in Reno when I brought the girl home. I'd never seen him before, but he seemed kinda familiar." I described the super-intense guy in the palm-leaf hat I'd seen sitting next to VanOwen at the Italian place.

"Hell, I know him," Dan said. "That sounds like Twister Creed. Or that's what he calls himself, anyway."

"Where's he from?"

"All over," Dan said. "Originally from a ranch in Doyle, north of Reno. He's one of those guys who always finds something wrong with every job he takes, then ships his freight and moves on to the next one. He's a decent hand but a total jerk. Thinks he's a badass."

"How do you know him?"

"Well, he worked right here," he said, kind of nodding down the hill, "packing for Harvey when you were in Iraq. He worked a couple of deer seasons but Harv shit-canned him for stealing cash and a pack saddle. Guy was a real good hunter and an awesome shot, though."

He clipped a spliced strand on to a steel post.

"Seen him recently?"

"Nah," Dan said. He handed me another length of wire. "Don't want to, either. Got a bad temper. Folks say he killed a guy down at McGee Creek."

We got back to it.

"This whole thing with missing bodies and missing

money feels like it's gonna end bad," Dan said after another little bit.

"It's making Sarah nuts, I can tell you that."

"Isolated as you are, you guys think you're in harm's way up here?" he said.

"Yeah, I kinda do." I told him about the trip I'd be taking in the morning and how antsy being gone for three nights made me. "That's why Harv isn't going with me."

"You want me to help?" he said. "Maybe put a bedroll down in the trees where I can't be seen? Rotate standing watch with Harvey?"

"I'd be obliged. The more the merrier."

The second trick is paying attention. Dan turned away to cut the last length of wire. I looked over to say something and the straight strand I was tightening snapped out of the loop-end and tore my shirt and cut my forearm. I always hated fixing fence.

Sarah had invited the Newport Beachers to dinner that night and told me to be on my best behavior. The two of us talked about our eating options while I nailed new front shoes on my sorrel. I told her my choice.

"Why are you so hot to go out to the Summers Lake Lodge?" she said. "The Mansion House would be so much more these folks' style."

"Just in the mood for a chicken-fried steak, I guess."

"You are so contrary sometimes. Fried batter, grease, and gravy? For this bunch?" She checked the time on her phone. "You better wrap this up and get in the shower, or we're going to be late."

We dropped the baby at Becky Tyree's. Besides being cranky and fearless and armed, Becky was unknown to VanOwen—at least for now.

At the end of her lane I turned left onto the Summers Lake Road. A mile west, the pavement crossed the tip of a sage-covered moraine. To the left, the moraine rose fifteen hundred feet, treeless sand and sagebrush pouring out from the mountain wall. The ice that dug Summers Lake and carved the twelve-thousand-foot-high Sawtooth range behind it had ground the granite, pushing it miles out into the meadow, the ridge as clear to see as a row of fresh dirt turned by a plow.

Random granite chunks as big as horse trailers parked on the meadow grass where the glacier left them when it had melted twelve thousand years before, rocks inching into the valley then settling as the world changed. There was a horse trail that climbed to the top of the ridge through sage and mahogany. You could turn in your saddle and see Becky's ranch a thousand feet below like a village out on the grass, and see the Hornberg place at the far side of the valley, a scar against a yellow cutbank. At the crest you could look down the backside of the ridge to the blue of Summers Lake. It would take a while for a rider to climb to that altitude, but then it took a few hundred thousand years for the glacier to push all that dirt.

The paved road bore left through the sagebrush to the far side of the moraine and followed a line of tamarack along Summers Creek, all that was left of that big ice flow.

"What the hell are you thinking?" Sarah said. "You look demented."

"Just thinking how this canyon gets narrower and narrower."

"Well . . . yeah."

"Like a mustang trap."

"What do you mean?"

"One way in, no way out."

"Baby," she said, "it's a good thing I'm crazy about you."

CHAPTER FOURTEEN

I was thinking about VanOwen and wondering who'd be trapping who. I drove the last couple of miles to the resort, vacation cabins in the trees on the right, moonlight on the dark water to the left, with that big timbered ridge rising up black over the far shore.

We got to the café before our customers. It was just a diner with a bar attached. This was the place where VanOwen said he was drinking the night before I'd dropped a loop on him at the pack station. A place he knew. There were booths in the front room and windows looking across a dirt lot to the lake a hundred feet away. We told the guy there would be six of us and he had to push another table next to the booth. The Newport Beachers got there about fifteen minutes later. They looked around like folks whose flight had just landed on the wrong continent.

Sarah and I knew the menu, so we let our customers negotiate with the waitress on the changes they wanted— if they could have the dressing on the side, what kind of bottled water was stocked, what kind of lettuce was in the salad, where the wine list was, and such. Sarah and I had a side bet about kale. I lost, and she called me a cynic. The second couple were the folks who'd flown in that morning. There was a nice looking dark-haired woman who said she was the first guy's law partner. Her name was Tess. She had an older husband who was an air-conditioning tycoon. That would be Bill, the pilot. He ordered a vodka rocks and talked about his house on a place called the Back Bay, and about his sailboat and his tennis game. He definitely had the best tan at the table—if you didn't count the back of my hands. When the waitress left, he asked about pack trips and what to expect. I tried to do what Sarah asked—be entertaining. I told them about the first party of fishermen I'd helped Harvey take up to Boundary Lake when I was twelve or so. Harv was old-school, from the days when packers supplied everything including food and the customers were tough and thought it was bad form to whine. I told how the three doctors we'd packed in reacted when they saw that the only food he'd brought was a sack of potatoes, a sack of onions, a side of bacon and a can of Folger's. Anything else they wanted to eat they'd have to catch. I laughed. Sarah sort of grimaced. Dead silence from Newport Beach. Then Bill laughed real loud.

"Folger's!" he said, like it was the funniest thing he'd heard in a week.

Bill had just asked for the check when I saw a single headlight reflected in the glass behind us. It came across the lot past the cars then circled down by the boat dock and looped past the cars again, slower this time. I stopped in the middle of another Harvey Linderman story to turn and stare out the window. It was a motorcycle headlight, and the bike came to a dead stop behind Sarah's Silverado, then revved and blasted off towards the campgrounds.

"Tommy . . ." Sarah said.

I nodded to the folks. I was already half out of the booth. "Sorry. Back in a sec."

When I got out the door, there was no trace of the headlight and no one walking among the parked trucks and cars and campers. A couple of boys shot hoops on a patch of pavement next to the café, and a girl stood under a pine tree staring at her phone, her face glowing from the screen—city kids not happy with the whole car-camping thing. I walked away from the café and away from the lake, out of the yard lights and into the dark. Through the trees I could see the flickering blue-white of television and computer screens in the campgrounds, then I turned back to the lake. It was pretty easy to see a couple of guys talking, hugging the shadows along the fake log wall of the boat rental building. I circled around the campground's check-in kiosk and was up against them fast. One of them reached for something on his belt, and I shoved him back against the wall. He was wearing one of those baggy shirt jackets over his tee shirt and I could just see the pistol-butt on his waist. It was a revolver, maybe a Colt, in a scuffed leather holster. No nylon for this old rancher. I yanked the pistol out and almost took his pants with it.

"Lookin' for me, Buddy?"

The pistol was a Colt .38 Police Positive with a four-inch barrel and fake gutta-percha grips, a gun like every cop in America carried from the end of the old six-shooter days to the eighties, when 9mms became the thing. A collectible.

"What the hell?" Buddy said. "You got no right."

"Shut up. Tell me why you're riding VanOwen's Harley, or he's riding yours."

He just stared up at me, sullen as hell. The other guy moved in the shadows. It was the big red-headed cop called Carl from the Reno Italian place.

"Kinda outta your jurisdiction, Slim."

"Watch it," he said. "It's a free country."

"Not for a shady vice cop. You need to be bought and paid for."

His look told me I'd guessed right. "Run along now, Slim, but keep your hands where I can see 'em."

Carl looked at Buddy, and Buddy nodded. The guy started to walk across the dirt over towards the boat rental. Then he stopped after he'd gone twenty feet.

"I better never catch you in Reno," the guy said.

He hustled over to a little German convertible he had trouble squeezing into.

"I could tell Carl to phone Sonny," Buddy said. "I could have a dozen guys from The Nogales down here in two hours. They'd kick your ass." He gave me a strange look. "You think that's funny?"

"Yeah. I do. It's a pretty sorry-assed pecking order if you're calling the shots."

"Screw you, Tommy," Buddy said.

"C'mon."

I grabbed his arm and walked him towards the lake. There was some stoutness there under the fat—like he still had some muscles that remembered what work was—but he went where he was dragged, just passive as hell. We came to the water's edge. I watched the convertible bounce over the broken pavement under the log arch, it's silver-blue beams marking the road along the shore of the lake. I walked Buddy towards the rental docks where twelve-foot aluminum outboards were tied in rows. We walked out on a man-made breakwater that paralleled the docks. It was covered with grass so kids could play on it during the day and jump off its vertical sides into where the water was shallow and the lake bottom sandy. When I was little, my mom used to take Lester and me swimming there if the day was really hot and we pestered her enough. Now, it was just Buddy and me.

I let go of his arm and looked at him. I scoped out his pistol, rocking the cylinder of the .38 open to check the rounds—old Western factory loads. When I played with the ejector rod just a bit I could feel a couple of the waxy casings drag in the cylinder like they'd been parked there for a long time. He took care of that pistol the way he took care of his family's ranch. I snapped it closed.

"You gonna let me go?" he said.

"I'm not keeping you. You came here looking for me, remember? Sonny send you?"

"No." Buddy looked around all antsy, like we weren't the only two people for a hundred yards. "Look, Tommy, I thought maybe you and me could work something out."

"Like?"

"Like maybe I know where my sister hid the money she stole."

"Yeah? How'd all that happen? How'd Erika get herself in such a mess?"

He just slumped and didn't answer right away. "I borrowed some money. From Sonny. Couple times, actually."

"How much?"

"A few thou."

"Like maybe thirty-eight thousand?"

"How the hell did you—? Oh, yeah. That FBI guy told you. Your big friend. Yeah, VanOwen was all friendly, too, when I was up against it. But he . . . I signed a note. He made me. A recorded deal all filed and legal with the ranch as collateral. Then he wasn't so helpful. Said I better pay."

"And you told your little sister that he had you by the balls and she went apeshit."

"Something like that. Nothing I ever did was good enough for her. But she said she'd get me the money to pay Sonny if it meant stopping foreclosure. Plus a couple thou extra to make it a nice round number, an easy mistake. From the bank. She said she could sell some jewelry and stuff over time and replace the cash before the bank found out." He looked like a surly kid. "She said taking the money would be easy. Like she'd thought about doing it before."

"And the rest? The big hit?"

"Sonny was surprised I could pay him back. He hadn't figured on that. He wanted to know where I got the cash. I wasn't gonna tell, but up in Reno he and some of his guys—"

"Don't tell me. They didn't hurt you. They just scared you, right?"

"Not everybody's you, you prick."

"And?"

"Let's just say Sonny went after Erika. He threatened her, and I don't know what-all. It was just when the bank was figuring they had some screwed up bookkeeping—money they couldn't account for—stuff like that. Sonny wanted a big payday or he'd rat her out for the thirty-eight thou before she could replace it and she'd go to prison. She didn't tell me the details but I—"

"But you guessed it was pretty grim."

"At first he hid her out at his strip joint," Buddy said. "She said it was worse than grim. Let's just say Sonny knows how to sniff out folks' weak spots."

"What was Erika's weakness? Besides her lame-ass brother."

He kind of shrugged. "The ranch, I guess. She said she'd do whatever it took keep the ranch in the family."

"You told me she was the one wanted to sell."

"I might have shaded that a bit," he said. "But it didn't start that way. Before Sonny got wind, she thought she could pull it off. Then when he leaned on her, she told me she couldn't take it anymore. She'd have to disappear—at least for a while. That's when I think she decided to double-cross Sonny. She told me the money was parked in a dummy account she set up that only she could get her hands on. Something about access codes. When Erika . . ." He stopped himself from saying whatever it was he was going to say. "Look, she's dead, and the money is gone but getable, but I can't get it by myself."

"What you mean is, you can get it but you need somebody to keep VanOwen from killing you when you do."

"Okay. Yeah. I wouldn't cross that guy without somebody watching my back. He's not a guy you cross."

"What was the point of the fake search for the kid?

What difference did it make if your sister was already dead?"

"I don't know squat about that. He said it was something about letting the trail get cold. Making it look like she'd taken the cash into the high country."

"So people'd think the money was gone for good."

He kinda shrugged like that seemed like bullshit, even to him.

"You'd have to ask Sonny."

"So Sonny killed Erika, then found out he couldn't access the account?"

"You'd hafta ask Sonny that, too."

"What a dumbass honyocker."

Buddy looked kinda hurt. "Him or me?"

"Both of you. Why the hell would he think I had a clue? I haven't seen your sister for maybe eight years."

"'Cause something went wrong. He was supposed to be able to get his hands on the codes. Now he can't."

"But why me?"

"You had a kinda high profile since you came back. Now you got that nice new cabin on the meadow where there wasn't jack shit a year ago. Your wife's a deputy. You're pals with the FBI. Shit, I don't know. Ask Sonny."

I really wanted to strangle him right then.

"Anyway, you gonna cover me if I can get into that account?"

"So you're a slick cyberthief, now?"

"I said I could get it," he said. "I can get it."

"What do I get?"

"Half?" he said.

"You're ready to cross VanOwen. You'll cross me if you get the chance. Besides, the FBI will be on the trail of whoever gets into that account."

"That mean you don't want half her money, then?"

"It's not her money, dumbass. Or yours either."

"But I can *get* it," he said. "She told me *how*. How to get it so nobody knows."

I looked past him to the rental boats tied under the dock lights and watched the little quiver the breeze made on the surface and how the lapping water rocked the empty skiffs just so, then looked beyond to the patch of moon on the black water out in the middle of the lake and beyond that to the shape of the ridge under the peaks. I never knew a thing about boats, but I always liked the feel of walking on a dock and stepping into one, and the gasoline smell from the outboard.

"It was you."

"Whaddya mean?" He sounded scared. He knew what I meant.

"You were the one who told VanOwen I was messing in his plans. Your sister was dead. You say you know how to get the money. You needed somebody to pin it on if you did. You've been setting me up since the day I went looking for that kid."

I knocked him over backwards with a straight-arm to the chest before I even knew what I was doing. He lit on the grass close to the water's edge. It occurred to me I might shoot him right there with his own revolver.

"I figured you could stand up to him." He was on all fours.

"I oughta let VanOwen rip your goddamn colon out."

I had the .38 in his face. "If anything happens to my family because of this . . ."

I went for him again. He scrambled backwards on the grass till he was about to fall into the lake. I stood over him, breathing hard.

"And how could you do that to your own sister? Ruin her life to cover your sorry ass. She worked in a bank in a job she didn't give one shit about to support a ranch you were running into the ground because you're a lazy dumbass daydreaming gunsel who wanted that life but couldn't hack the work it took. You pissed away money the ranch didn't have on motorcycles and whores and you got your sister murdered." I stepped back from him before I actually did kill him.

"It's pretty damn easy to see what your weakness is."

I stepped further back. I opened the cylinder of the Colt again and ejected the six rounds into my hand and backhanded them into the lake. Now the only way I could kill him would be to pistol-whip him in plain sight of my customers in the café. It's those little things that make a new business take off.

"Stolen money's got a life of its own, dipshit. It outsmarts losers like you and VanOwen every time. You think you got a shot, but all you got is a circular firing squad. Whoever stays, dies."

I grabbed his wrist and yanked him close. Then I jammed the Colt into his holster. I should've thrown it into the lake with the cartridges, but it would be a waste of a cool old gun.

"Mind you don't blow your pecker off."

I walked out of the shadows heading for the lights of the café.

"Sonny knows what *your* weakness is, you cocky bastard," he said. "It's that kid."

CHAPTER FIFTEEN

It didn't take me long to figure that the only one I'd chased into a trap was me. I'd done it the day I'd taken Audie from Reno. The customers and my wife were waiting out where the cars were parked.

"All good?" Bill said.

"All good. See you at six?"

Scottie sort of groaned, and her husband, Drew, laughed.

"We'll be there," Drew said.

The four of them piled into the Range Rover and shouted their goodbyes, then drove out around the lake towards their motel in town. I climbed into Sarah's truck on the shotgun side before she noticed, then took off my hat and leaned back against the headrest and closed my eyes.

"You okay, babe?" she said.

"Terrific."

I told her about my little parley with Buddy. What he told VanOwen, and what he wanted from me. Sarah got a scary look on her face—sort of seething rage. She knew how much he'd put us at risk. We talked it out and hoped that with the law finally targeting VanOwen we'd passed the worst of the threat.

"Buddy's such an idiot," she said. "Since we won't be blindsided, I think we'll be okay. But he's going to get himself killed, just like he got his sister killed." She reached across the seat and put her hand on my shoulder. "I'd feel way better if I were going with you tomorrow."

"Me too, babe. But you can't put your job on hold for a 'maybe.' I'll only be gone the three nights."

We kicked around Dan's offer to camp at the pack station and help Harvey keep an eye out for VanOwen. We both thought that safety in numbers was the best of a crappy situation.

"I wish it wasn't coming to this," she said.

We fetched the baby at Becky's, then Sarah had me drive so Lorena could nurse. We were both quiet as I rolled on up the logging road. When we pulled into the pack station, Lorena was asleep. I carried her up the steps of the cabin, holding her close. When she was squared away, I walked back outside into the warm breezy moonlight along the corral fence to the outhouse and reached up for my rifle. I didn't need a light. I knew right where it was.

I'd been aiming for seven and we headed out by seven forty. It would be a long ride into the Wilderness Area and over North Pass to Little Meadows, and I wasn't sure how much horseback time this bunch could take. Harvey and I had been up since four-thirty graining and saddling the mules and getting our loads mantied up. Mom had driven up to see me off, full of worry and bad feeling. Then she and Audie settled in the kitchen to make us all breakfast. Walking up from the corrals, I asked Harvey about Twister Creed. He stopped and made a face.

"His real name is Byron," Harvey said. "You could never tell that guy anything. He knew it all. Shit." He lit a Winston. "We were taking a big party to Boundary Lake early in the season about five years ago when the crick was high. He was ahead of me with three mules in his string. He got to an open spot on the bank about a hundred feet below the regular crossing at the forks. I hollered at him to stay away but he waved me off and jumped his horse into the crick and the mules followed." Harvey looked frosted just thinking about it. "That water was way deeper than it looked. Old Twister got washed off his horse and swept downstream a-ways and almost died. Two of my god-damned mules drowned." He started brushing the horse again. "Good mules that never hurt a soul. Boy was I sorry you were in Iraq *that* morning."

"So it woulda been me leading the string?"

"So you coulda shot the arrogant bastard for me. You ever see Creed, you tell him he still owes me for them mules."

Just after six thirty the customers staggered out of the Range Rover a half hour late and still dragging ass, all except Bill. He was one of those always-cheerful guys, and he looked like he was ready to jog up to the pass on foot. We got their saddles fitted, then packed the mules last. With all their stuff and my bedroll, we were taking four. I could see Audie out in the open meadow rooting around in the blue iris and lupine that grew there. She was wearing new kids' boots and Wranglers my mom had bought her and looked like she'd spent her whole tiny life up here with us.

Mom stepped out of the cabin with her coffee mug as I walked in. I gave her shoulder a squeeze and thanked her for breakfast. I got a lame smile back. In the cabin I buckled on my chinks and double-checked my stuff and talked to Sarah about the details of Dan spending the night in the trees, alternating watches with Harvey. My rifle scabbard and saddle pockets lay on the table. I caught her watching me pull the .270 out while I talked. I loaded five rounds in the magazine, then stowed the box of cartridges in the pockets and slid the rifle back into the scabbard. She tucked one of her sheriff's radios and extra batteries in the saddle pockets as well. She was strong and cheerful like always, but one part of me wished I didn't have to leave her. VanOwen was still out there somewhere. The other part of me was damned if I'd let that guy have any control over what I did or didn't do.

Sarah was watching the four campers out the window.

"Tess is wearing shorts," she said. "Those pretty tanned legs will look like my dad's old chinks if she rides barelegged through the mahogany."

"You want me to tell her to change?"

She laughed. "Heck no. The only legs you get to discuss are mine." She picked up the baby and ran a finger along my neck as she walked towards the door.

I laughed, then she kissed me goodbye while we still had some quiet. I picked up my gear and followed her out. I tried to act nonchalant as I carried the scabbard down to my horse but I could tell all four of the Newport Beachers were watching me. Scottie said something to Tess, and they both laughed. I buckled on the scabbard and laced the saddle pockets behind the cantle, then tied on my jacket. Scottie walked up to me wearing a plastic riding helmet with a foam brim. I thought she looked like some nerdy intergalactic samurai, but I was probably just being a sourass.

"Are you planning on shooting somebody, Tommy?"

"You never know."

I meant it like a joke, but it came out grim as hell.

"Maybe," Tess said, "we'll get to see another of Tommy Smith's High Sierra adventures."

The two women laughed again, but I had no clue about what.

I got Tess mounted up last. She'd put on hiking pants with big pockets, and I caught Sarah kind of smirking at me as I reached under her leg and checked her cinch. I finally bridled my sorrel and stepped up, pissed at myself for not getting new hind shoes on him before the trip but hoping they could last for the next couple of days. Ahead of me at the far corner of the cabin I could see Harvey light up a Winston and buckle on his tool belt, wiggling to fit the rig under his gut and over the Colt Python he wore crossdraw-style that morning.

I watched my family as I rode out, their eyes on me and none of us saying a word. I passed Sarah first, standing on the porch holding Lorena on her hip with one hand, the thumb of her other hand hooked in her jeans. As we rode by, she faked a smile as best she could and blew me a kiss. Mom leaned against the log wall sipping from her coffee mug, trying to look serene like nothing bad could ever happen to her family. Audie sat down on her folded sleeping bag on the edge of the porch, squinting into the sun with her new boots dangling. She gave me a little wave, then a wave to each of the four folks riding behind. They all waved back. Audie jumped off the porch and ran up to my horse and handed me a sprig of lupine she'd yanked from the meadow. I stuck it in my hatband, and she blew me a kiss, too. Then she looked back laughing to see if Sarah'd noticed. In the open front of the cabin, May handed Harvey a carpenter's square, then gave me a sad look and turned away. I pulled even with Harv just as he fired up the music player sitting next to his table saw, and I heard a half-verse of some lonesome Willie Nelson song before it faded off and there was no sound but the hum of the generator. I touched a finger to my hat brim as I pulled ahead of him, and he did the same back at me, just as corny as hell. The last of my travelers cleared the pack station, and we wound our way through the aspen heading for North Pass hearing no sound but the shuffle of hooves until the screech of Harvey's circular saw ripping a pine plank jarred the sun-dappled clearing. I looked back at the four and could almost see them flinch.

Things were fine when the trail was narrow in the shade high above the creek. It's always fine to start out on a new trip with the horses fresh and the loads well packed and lashed snug and the mules stepping out with slack in their leads. I tried to hold on to that. I could hear bits of folks talking amongst themselves but couldn't make out exactly what they said over the breeze and flowing water. I looked back and caught Scottie in her dorky helmet giving me a wave. I lost that fine feeling quick enough and started thinking about VanOwen and the missing money, and how a guy who'd had a wife and a serious law enforcement job ended up as a pimp and killer and low-rent grifter. Of course, there was no good answer.

We came out of the trees into the first meadow. Scottie and Tess flapped their legs against their horses' flanks and trotted up to me off-trail in the grass, bouncing like crazy. They pulled abreast and asked me about the army and packing and how I met Sarah and what kind of wedding we had and such foolishness as that. They said our whole life up here was just so romantic. They wanted to know whose kid Audie was and was Harvey my dad and had I ever shot anybody with the rifle I was packing? Above the row of no-name peaks ahead of us a single cloud formed, small and white and harmless-looking. It moved slow but steady eastward over our heads. After a bit, a second cloud took its place behind the crest.

We stopped for a leg stretch and piss break at the Blue Rock. I tied up the string and loosened the saddlehorse cinches while my folks disappeared into the aspen. Bill and I sat and leaned against rock slabs in the shade, and he asked me about the things I needed to do to get a business like back-country outfitting off the ground. His questions were smart and savvy and gave me a lot to think about. Before I could ask a few questions of my own, Scottie came crashing out of the aspen.

"Tommy," she said. "There's a horse back there in the trees."

I got up, and she pointed into the aspen near the creek.

"Is it running loose?"

"No," she said. "It's got a saddle on but its legs are all tangled up."

I told them to stay put and keep an eye on the stock. Beyond a willow thicket was another patch of grass along the beaver ponds that couldn't be peered into from the trail. A big brown gelding stood alone in a gray stand of beaverkill aspen. He wasn't tangled. He was hobbled by his hackamore rope and packing a beat-up Wade saddle with a rifle scabbard slung under a stirrup leather. The scabbard was empty. You could tell by his mouth he'd been grazing, but his head was up now, alert and watching the trees for the nearby stock that he could hear and smell. I checked the horse close, especially the hooves. I wasn't real surprised to see hand-drawn clips on the front feet, the steel sort of dimpled and home-made looking. This was the horse that left the tracks I'd seen more than once in this canyon, and I'd only noticed the one cowboy on VanOwen's payroll so far. So Twister Creed was one of the watchers. One down and one to go.

I scanned the creek and the timber slopes and bouldery granite chutes of the south wall of the canyon but couldn't see a trace of him. I walked back to my party, wondering if the camo dome tent had been his hideout while he was scoping us out. I told the four that we'd be leaving quick, so not to wander off.

I saw him soon enough. He stood way off on the farthest and highest edge of Blue Rock, outlined against the sky holding a rifle in the crook of his arm, staring out over canyon we'd just passed through, not moving and not watching us. It was like he was posing. I noticed that the sky was clouding up in the west. I walked over to my horse and pulled the Remington. I laid it across the seat of my saddle, squinting through the scope for a closer look. I saw the same wildrag tight under his chin, the same no-expression look on his face. He never turned in my direction, but he had to have seen me pull the rifle and sight in on him. He was just making sure I knew we weren't alone. I slid my rifle back in the scabbard.

"What's going on?" Drew said.

"Just making sure the owner of that horse is close by and not in trouble. Let's mount up."

"Do you know that guy?" Bill said.

"No."

"So, mister packer . . ." Scottie said.

When I turned around, she held up her phone and took a picture of herself with me in the background.

"I needed a selfie with the manly cowboy," she said. "Can you pull your rifle out for another shot?"

I pretended I didn't hear her.

"He looks more like a flower child with that purple weed in his hatband," Drew said.

Scottie walked up close to me. Too close. "We were all wondering," she said. "Is this one of the places where you shot those men?"

"Not sure what you mean." I stepped away from her. "Let's all check our cinches and rattle our hocks. Got a long way to go yet."

I got them mounted and grabbed up my string and headed on up the trail. I was watching the soggy ground for tracks now, and picked up the clipped shoe prints of Creed's horse soon enough. The newer tracks seemed to be coming down-canyon, as if he'd ridden up ahead, then come back and waited for us at Blue Rock. We got to the Roughs, and I gave a little pay-attention talk before we crossed the shale. Bill was the first to ride out behind me. I got distracted by the metal clank a loose shoe makes. When I stopped to wait for the other three he was right with me. I handed him the lead mule's rope and got off to check the sorrel's left hind shoe. It wasn't horrible yet. I figured I could tighten it up with a couple of new nails when we made camp, but it pissed me off whenever my stuff wasn't totally squared away.

"When Scottie made that crack," he said, "you looked like you were about to ride off and leave us to our own devices."

I got back on my horse.

"I think we owe you an explanation," he said.

I let him talk.

"We read about you a couple of years ago when everyone up here was looking for the plane of a missing billionaire. It was in the *LA Times*, and I'm a pilot so I notice things like plane crash stories. That guy vanishing was a big deal for guys that fly. Plus, I knew folks who knew him. The *Times* said the plane was discovered by an Iraq-vet packer, then all hell broke loose. It sounded pretty—"

"Pretty western?"

"That's a good word for it." He took off his tennis visor and wiped his forehead with his sleeve. "The four of us were

176

sailing to Catalina one weekend on my ketch, and we got to talking. Drew's the real backpacker and climber, so his wife and my wife thought it would be fun to try a pack trip vacation, but nothing came of it. Then last year there was another little article in the *Times* about the same guy again. The four of us were sitting at the bar at the Balboa Bay Club joking about how cool it would be to book a trip with you. Hang out with you a few days. And not tell you, of course."

"How swell for me."

He reached into his shirt pocket and pulled out a little piece of newspaper.

"It doesn't mention the billionaire business, but the name of the ex-outfitter was the same. Tommy Smith."

Bill offered me the clipping but I just waved him off.

He unfolded it. "It says a guy kidnapped a rancher and you took out a bunch of guys to get the rancher back."

"Now, that rancher's my father-in-law."

"It says you were in the middle of a running gun battle covering two states with your ex-lover's husband, who's now in Folsom. They quote an FBI man who said the packer 'declined to kill' the psycho husband in a shootout, 'an omission he may come to regret.' The girls loved that. Scottie tried to track you down, but the pack station from the year before was out of business or something, and you were back in the Army." He folded the clipping and put it back in his pocket.

"True enough."

I looked past him to check on the others. They were going real slow and looked tense, but the horses were solid so I didn't worry.

"Then a couple of months ago Scottie found your new website."

"That was all Sarah's idea. She's good at stuff like that."

Bill put his visor back on. "Sorry. I should've told you before we even signed up for the trip. I feel like a stalker."

"It's okay. That whole newspaper and Internet thing never occurred to me, though. It mighta scared some folks off. Not everybody is as crazy as you."

"It was kind of ghoulish," he said. "But fun to read about."

"I did wonder why folks that wanted to camp at Little Meadows would book a trip with me when coming up from the Little Meadows Pack Station is way shorter and less dust."

"And why we wanted you to stay in camp with us a couple of days," he said, "not just drop us off?"

"Yup."

"Now you know."

"Then you should know that the horse you saw back there belongs to somebody who's up to no damn good."

Bill gave a big old smile. "Then the girls'll get their money's worth on this vacation. Damn."

"We can turn back right now if you want."

"Like hell," Bill said. "This is too cool."

You had to like the guy.

Tess came off the shale and stopped her horse close to us.

"Is everything okay?" she said.

"No problem, sugar," Bill said.

The others caught up with only a little slipping from

Drew's horse. Then we headed into the timber and a more narrow and boggy part of the trail.

After a bit we got to the spot where Jack's dog found the body in the bog. I told the customers I had to check something for my wife—some sheriff's business, which was true enough. I stepped down and tied the lead mule and handed my horse to Bill. I walked through the forensic team's campsite, seeing little bits of what happened by the remains that they left. The fire pit, the flattened grass from their bivy sacks, the firewood gathered and not burned, and the chipped granite from wild gunfire. And finally, the spot where agent D'Angelico would have died. A bit further on I walked to the torn-up bog where the woman's body had been hidden. And where Jack had been standing when he was shot.

It was right there in front of me. Right at eye-level. Nothing special, just a Coors can jammed on a stick with a bullet hole smack in the center of the tiny waterfall logo. It obviously just got put there, staged to remind me by somebody who'd been there that day, too. Somebody who was enough of a marksman to just crease the side of Jack's head and nick his ear like VanOwen had threatened to do, but not to kill him. And good enough to drill the second shooter, the fake dad, dead center in the forehead while the jerk was popping off a few rounds just to scare us. The first shooter would be Twister Creed, and he was letting me know that he could've taken me down that day if VanOwen had wanted it. And that he still could—whenever it suited him.

CHAPTER SIXTEEN

We rode on past the trail maintenance camp we'd resupplied a few days before, heading for the Forks of Aspen Creek. A Forest Service sign marking the trail sat in a rocky notch where you could look way out down the canyon and gauge how far you'd come and how high you'd climbed. I looked over the heads of my folks, scanning the bare rock and treetops behind us for a trace of Creed. I thought I saw a flash of his hat against some aspen way below but didn't take the time to scan it with my scope. Whether it was him or not, I knew I'd best keep moving.

"How do you know this guy wasn't trying to kill you?" Bill said.

We sat a ways away from the rest of his party as they ate their lunch by the abandoned snow cabin. He'd asked me to tell him more about the guy dogging our tracks and about the shootout between VanOwen's ginks and the forensic team. The killing of agent D'Angelico had caught his eye in the online edition of the *LA Times* he'd read on his phone early that morning. Though there was no mention of a connection to me or Sarah or the pack station or bank fraud, it set him thinking.

"Since we saw that first thing in the *Times* two years ago," he said, "I've been following you like you'd follow some rookie pitcher, some talented kid on an out-of-town team."

"Things can't be that boring down in La-La Land."

"Don't bet on it," he said.

I looked over at the other folks. Drew was sitting in the shade with his back against the logs of the snow cabin rearranging a fly box. Scottie and Tess sprawled in the sun a dozen feet away from him, taking naps.

"Gonna stretch my legs. Twenty minutes suit you?"

He said they'd be ready. I walked downstream, limbering up the back of my thigh stiff from an old wound. I got to a grassy spot at the water's edge and studied the clear current running smooth and deep along the bank and rippling over the gravely shoal on the opposite shore. The creek was wide here, spreading across the clearing just below the confluence. Crossing here might look like a shortcut to the south fork trail, but close-up you could see there was nothing gradual about the jump-off. The flow had carved a vertical drop well over four feet. Even in an average season like this you could see the sandy creek bottom, and see that it would be dicey to jump stock into that. At full runoff, mules strung together under heavy packs would have a bad time of it in the deep water and swift current. If one went down, they could all go down. It was an arrogant stunt to pull. For Twister Creed to think he could cross at such a spot told me he wanted to be the guy who took heedless chances because he thought that was the cowboy thing to do.

The snow cabin sat at the forks of Aspen Creek. It had been built in the 1920s and abandoned in the 1950s. The Forest Service had torn the roof off of it a year or two before so it would collapse into what they called a state of natural decay. But the cabin fooled them. The logs were well joined and the walls solid, so the place would last longer than the honyocker who decided to speed its destruction.

We mounted up and took the north fork of the creek, climbing the narrow trail west up through tamarack pine and juniper. This trip was always longer but prettier than a person remembered. I told Bill to ride in front so we could shoot the breeze but I really didn't want to talk anymore. I definitely didn't want one of the others trying to take a turn at me.

I let the folks dismount and rest a few minutes when we had one last climb ahead of us. We had come out of a rocky cirque and stopped amongst a scattering of white-bark pine at the bottom of a steep set of switchbacks. At the top of that climb we would be perched on the upper edge of the cirque on a crushed granite bench just below North Pass. I didn't tell them about the place, only saying that we were close to Little Meadows, which would be our camp for three days while they hiked and climbed and fished. I didn't let them dawdle. I wanted them focused.

"Is it much farther?" Tess said.

"It's always farther." I tried to make it sound like a challenge.

"Are you sure we can get up this?" Drew said.

"Just be watchful. Pay attention. Keep your weight forward, keep moving, and trust your horse."

I checked every cinch and every lash rope, and we mounted up. I grabbed the lead of my front mule and started climbing the switchbacks, not looking back. I counted on my horses to keep everyone traveling. The first turn put me above my party heading in the opposite direction, which is why they call them switchbacks. Drew started to say something. When I didn't look at him he shut up. Bill just rode, looking serious and focused but unconcerned.

Even with switchbacks, the trail was steep, cut through rock and gravel and mahogany that I bet made Tess glad she'd changed her pants. The mahogany got thicker as we climbed. Two more sharp turns and we were halfway to the top. I came to a slick rock followed by a washout where the trail had eroded. I let my gelding pick his way until we were over it, then went slow so the mules could find their footing, just calm and steady. Then, against my better judgment, I looked back. Scottie's hands were clamped around her saddle horn, and she was starting to lean back—like that would somehow slow her down. She started to say something I couldn't hear as I was leaning in, goosing the sorrel up around the next turn where he had to climb hard as he reversed his direction. When I looked down again Scottie was directly below me between two of the others. She got to the washout and leaned back, staring down at it.

"Tommy . . ."

Then she just froze.

"Tommy, I can't," she started to babble. "I—"

"Shut up and *ride*."

I didn't tell them I was sorry. I didn't tell them a lot of things. I did let them catch their breath on the gravely bench where three years before, a plane had crashed and a man had died. Then, how a year after that, I found that wreck and the body, and a part of my life crashed right along with them. I didn't mention the rider way below us, following the trail we'd just taken like he had the whole mountain to himself, riding out in the open around the far side of the cirque.

When they'd collected themselves, we climbed up a sandy slope through sparse whitebark and hemlock to North Pass, then started down another narrow, rocky, dicey bit of trail between two sloping ridges that spilled out onto the upper end of Little Meadows. Drew started pointing at the mountains and talking about Hawksbeak Peak that he hoped to climb the next day. I wondered about that. Small, flat, gray, and purple clouds had started to crowd the peaks.

"They look like Frisbees," Tess said.

"No," Scottie said. She'd pulled herself together since the switchbacks. "I think they look like flying saucers."

Tess was smiling until she reached down to a tear in her pants and her hand came back with blood on it.

Little Meadows was a pair of long, grassy open parks circled by thick tamarack and aspen and rimmed by ridges of exposed granite, all tucked under some major peaks like Hawksbeak and Tower Peak. The narrow headwaters of the West Frémont River meander across the meadows where stockmen a hundred years ago ran the cattle that kept the grasslands open and the trees trimmed to the meadow's edge. We found good places to picket the stock and set up a base camp, all within sight of those peaks that Drew meant to climb. The chatty bunch got quiet crossing that open grass, just taking it all in.

Bill helped me string the picket lines and asked questions about knots and weather. Then I tied the stock and rubbed them down. The other three campers followed Bill's lead and helped unpack and unsaddle, which surprised me. It was midafternoon, and the flat clouds were stacking up. Bill caught me scanning the sky.

"Lenticular," he said. "The clouds. That's what they call those funny-looking bastards. From the Latin, *lenticularis*. Lens-shaped."

I must've given him a strange look.

"Hey," he said, "I'm a sailor, remember? Done the Transpac three times. I gotta know that stuff."

"My wife knows the Latin names for every damn tree and animal we passed today. I'm always impressed. But then she went to Cal Poly." I finished coiling up a lash rope, waiting. "Where'd you go?"

Bill just laughed. "Half a semester at a community college in Costa Mesa. I was just itchin' to get to work, so I bailed." He looked sort of cautious. "You?"

"Half a semester less than that."

We laughed, and he pulled out a bottle of Jim Beam Double Oak and we each had a swig.

"Can I ask you something?"

"Sure," he said.

"It ever bother you? The college thing?" I snuck a look at his wife and Drew. "Lawyers must clean up."

He looked over to the others unpacking under the trees. "Never," he said. He laughed. "Drew sails too, but I got a *way* bigger boat."

He followed me around and helped with hobbling the nine head on the meadow and squaring away the equipment for almost another hour. I told him how not to get hurt as he worked close to the hooves, and he told me that Sarah and I would have to come south and sail to Catalina with him one day.

"And the business about the clouds?"

"Yeah?"

"I was just showing off. All the stuff you know about this place puts every one of us to shame."

He pointed to Hawksbeak. A single dark saucer-shaped cloud was hovering just above the peak.

"Think we're in for a squall?"

I just shrugged.

I planned on leaving the hobbled stock out to graze on the meadow until dark. I dug out the sheriff's radio I'd borrowed from Sarah to try to call her, but the Sierra crest was blocking me and all I got was buzz and crackle with some cross-talk—maybe from the Marine base ten miles north. I went to where I'd parked my saddle and pulled the Remington, then walked out into the meadow to scan the ridges. I could feel the folks' eyes on me so I quit and stowed the rifle. They were paying me for a fun trip, not to get scared to death. I was trying to balance wanting to know what VanOwen was going to pull next with the kind of important, making-a-go-of-the-pack-station thing. Folks were depending on me, and I was vain enough to not want them to think I was screwing everything up. I walked back into the meadow to check the hobbles and looked up at Hawksbeak again, but the peak was hidden. The round cloud had settled down over it like a wet hat.

While I still had good light, I took my dad's roll-up canvas shoeing-tool kit out to the meadow where my hobbled sorrel grazed. I never carried much in it—just old nippers and a rasp and my driving hammer, but I liked it because it was Dad's. On multiday climbs, I'd carry a few pre-shaped shoes, too, but I hadn't for this glorified spot-trip. As he grazed, the gelding let me pick up the hind foot with the loose iron, clean it out, and drop three new nails in to snug it up until I could reshoe him back at the pack station. I watched his ears as I set my clinches, using the edge of my rasp as a clinch block to bend the nail stubs as I pounded and listened. The horse had noticed something.

"Still shoeing, I see." It was a woman's voice.

"Still riding the high country, I see." I lowered the hind leg and straightened up.

Sitting a zebra dun not more than thirty feet away was Erika Hornberg.

CHAPTER SEVENTEEN

Except for dyed black hair, she looked pretty much like I remembered.

"You look at me like I'm 'dead woman walking,'" she said.

I looked at the dun. "Well, 'dead woman riding,' anyway."

She turned around, looking back from where she'd come.

"Step down. I can't be rude to these folks. I'll introduce you."

"As what?"

"Old friend and neighbor."

She took a deep breath.

"Or the female desperado who keeps one jump ahead of the sheriff with grit and savvy. They're both true."

She swung down off the dun. "Still Mister Straight Arrow, Mister 'I cannot tell a lie,' Tommy Smith."

"I've lowered my standards considerable in that department since I saw you last."

I was never real close with the woman, so I was surprised when she gave me a quick, rough hug. She was thinner than I remembered, and her hair looked like she cut it with a hatchet. She wore big gypsy earrings—just like I remembered.

"I doubt that," she said. "That's why I'm counting on you."

"Counting on me to do what?"

"To save my life," she said.

We tied the dun and walked over to my party. I introduced Erika. Scottie asked her if she wanted to stay for dinner. Erika thanked her but said she needed to get moving well before sundown to make it back to the Little Meadows trailhead by dark. She asked them if she could borrow me for a bit so we could get reacquainted. We walked off together.

"You're a hard guy to catch up to," she said.

"You got it done pretty easy."

"Do you think I'm a thief?" she said. "Guilty beyond all redemption?"

"I don't know crap about redemption."

I told Erika what I'd suspected and what Aaron had said. That she'd stolen enough money from the bank to dig her ranch out of a hole, then VanOwen leaned on her hard to make a really big steal. She confirmed it all.

"At first Sonny acted like he could be talked out of it," she said, "if I cooperated." All the life drained out of her then. "I just ended up degrading myself. After I stole the million, he hid me out in his Reno strip club for a while. I thought that would be enough for him, but it wasn't. I finally realized he had no intention of ever letting me off the hook—of not making me go ahead with transferring the million to him. I kept thinking, if I could just save the ranch. For my big brother if not for me." She swallowed a sob. "So I started planning a way to maybe save what my family worked so damn, damn hard for since 1919."

We hunkered in some tamarack as the wind picked up. I watched my party setting up their big wall tent for what looked like a storm coming.

"After you transferred the million, where would that leave you?"

"Sonny said he'd let me keep half, but I was just lying to myself. He'll kill me as soon as he gets the money. I've seen him do it before. I had to figure a way out."

"How was the money thing supposed to work?"

"Sonny was worried about drawing attention to himself if we did the bank transfer first thing last fall. Afraid it might lead the FBI straight to him," she said.

She tried leaning on me, and I edged away.

"What was his idea?"

"To wait half a year at least," she said. "Make it look like I'd been dead that whole time. Then when things cooled down and the FBI thought they'd hit a dead end, Sonny would stage the missing kid search."

She told me how VanOwen and her brother had cooked up the idea for the crazy body swap—to plant a corpse similar to her in a place like the bog where it could be found months later. A place where the body would decompose a bit but not totally disfigure—a dummy Erika.

Enough so folks would think, wow, so *that's* what happened to Erika Hornberg.

"She was close to my height and coloration, but different hair and age and body type. The plan was to slap my clothes and earrings on her, then have Buddy identify her as me once she'd . . . withered like a prune." She wiped her eyes. "Once that led to the body being found in the bog, the law would think I was dead."

"And?"

"With the FBI distracted and giving interviews and the whole county obsessed, the money trail would go cold. Everyone would think the story was over. Folks would think it was a mystery that would never be solved. And right *then* I would transfer the million to Sonny's account. Once he was convinced we'd pulled it off, I would transfer half back to me." She looked off into the mountains. "I knew that as soon as the whole amount showed in his account, I'd be dead for real."

"One more question."

"What?"

"Where'd the corpse in the bog come from?"

"A young prostitute who'd worked for Sonny since she was about thirteen. She was maybe in her mid-twenties. Then she crossed him, Sonny said. She was trying to get him arrested, and he wanted her gone. My god, Tommy. He shot that sweet kid right in front of me. To make a point." She locked eyes with me. "He said, 'This is what happens to little girls who don't do like I say,' then *bang*."

"With your granddad's twenty-five."

"Yeah," she said. "He'd taken that from my brother." She got a panicky look. "How did you know?"

"Ballistics. An FBI agent told me."

"Sonny kept the pistol. He told me if I backed out on him, he'd say I shot the girl and he had witnesses." She twisted her hands together. "By New Year's, I went to work doing housekeeping in a low-rent casino in North Reno, but I was always watched by Myrna Jenks."

She was staring at me. I looked away.

"Sonny hoped the law would think they'd found the solution to the case," she said. "Folks like Mitch might believe it was me and stop looking. Everybody would think the story was over."

"Yeah, Mitch wouldn't spend a dime on forensics if he didn't have to."

"Sonny was counting on that," she said. "He thinks we're all rubes. And by waiting months and months, it would make any search by Reno cops for a missing Jane Doe drop from the radar, too. Not that anybody would spend a second looking for a missing hooker. People would think that girl just ran off or OD-ed or something. There'd be zero connection to a body in a bog a hundred miles south. Then once the body was found, bills scattered in the canyon would make it seem to folks around here that I'd cashed out a secret account then somehow lost the money or got murdered for it."

"Still could happen."

She looked like I'd slapped her.

"What if me and Jack never found that body? What would VanOwen do then?"

"The missing little girl would never be found and the body in the bog would just rot where it lay." She rubbed her

192

eyes where the trail dust and tears had made streaks of mud in the corners. "The 'dead Erika' scheme was just another layer of protection after he shot the prostitute. A twofer. He thinks he's too clever by half, so he figured he'd get his hands on the million dollars either way. He'd eventually risk the transfer, even without the fake me. If things got too hot, he could always just disappear. I guess he's done that before, too."

Scottie hollered that dinner was almost ready. I yelled back we'd be right there. Wind was gusting now and the temperature was dropping.

"And the kid? What would happen to Audie?"

"He talked about selling her to a Russian guy he knew out of state."

"Jesus. It was good you looked after her that night in the canyon."

"I gave her my old sleeping bag," she said. "How did you know about that?"

"She told me. She called you the 'spirit lady.'"

Then I saw it all. That day Jack's dog found the body in the bog, I'd had a feeling I couldn't nail down. That I somehow recognized the dead woman. That I'd seen her before. I thought it must be because the body was Erika's. But standing next to Erika now, I knew it wasn't her that I recognized in that pruney face. It was the dead woman's daughter. And I'd seen that girl just the morning before.

"Whose child is Audie?" she said.

"The murdered whore's, I expect."

We stood up. I looked at the sky. I was in a sweat to get this woman off my hands and into Aaron's. He was getting paid to straighten all this out, not me, and she wouldn't be safe till she was in custody. She stood close again and leaned against me.

"What would VanOwen need to make the transfer without you?"

"A set of numbers on two thumb drives, one for me and one for him."

I had a general idea what that was.

"So where is your drive now?"

"Hidden," she said. "in a safe place where I can get it and give it to the FBI—with your help. I can show them how to access the full amount."

"So when you disappeared, he figured you'd cheated him."

"Pretty much."

"It took some nerve to cross Sonny."

"That's why I thought of you. I heard you were back in the valley. I thought you were the one guy who could protect me from him—if only I could catch you alone. Then you could hook me up with the FBI." She looked at me hard. "Can you?"

"So you'll turn over the keys to the million and hope for short time in some federal pen."

"That was the hope," she said. "I had to find a way to contact you without alerting that pretty deputy you married. I didn't know how sympathetic she'd be."

"You don't know how sympathetic I'm gonna be, either."

She let go of my arm.

"Why didn't you just go to Agent Fuchs yourself? He

told me his office hauled you in when the first thirty-eight thousand was stolen. Why didn't you ask him for protection then?"

"It's hard to admit to yourself that you're going to prison. That your whole life is ending. Not to mention your reputation. It's like riding a runaway horse. You know you might break your neck if it stumbles, but you'll for-sure break your neck if you jump." She reached down and put her hand on mine, more timid this time. "I was scared to jump."

"Well, you found me. How'd you keep yourself hid up here?"

"I set up a tent in the canyon the day before the search. I even shouted at you two days later when I saw you leading Jack Harney on a horse by Blue Rock, but you were too far away."

"That about when you hid those bills in my saddle pockets?"

She nodded. "That was my calling card."

"So when he couldn't find you in North Reno, Sonny put the plan in motion anyway?"

"He didn't have any choice," she said. "He thought I must be in league with . . . with a third party."

"If you've been on the dodge, how do you know all this?"

"Buddy told me."

"Your brother is up to his eyeballs in this—you know that."

She nodded, looking beat. "He was the third party. He was helping me."

"Bullshit. He was trying to help himself. Buddy told VanOwen *I* was the third party. He's trying to stiff VanOwen and lay it off on me, but he doesn't have the brains or the *huevos.*"

Erika helped me bring in the stock hobbled out on the meadow and tie them to the picket lines for the night. By now the wind was swirling hard and I felt the first snap of raindrops scattering down from the west.

"Being wanted by the government is pretty intimidating, but I was more afraid of Sonny. He's crazy mean."

"He ain't afraid of burning his bridges, that's for sure. He let a woman fry to death in a shootout at his LA house and made out it was his wife. Then he killed his wife later and buried her in the desert."

"Is that supposed to reassure me?"

"Just making small talk."

"I know that could've happened to me," Erika said. "He shot the prostitute because she tried to go to the police on him."

"For what?"

"For molesting her little girl," she said.

I told her that she should stay in camp that night, and we'd figure the best plan to get her to Aaron in the morning. With no working communication, that probably meant leading the stock all the way back to the pack station, then dragging them back the day after that. No way was I leaving my new mules with a bunch of sailboaters, no matter how well intentioned. So they'd just have to do without my company for a day. When I got service with the sheriff radio, I'd have Aaron meet us at the pack station and take Erika into custody. The rest would be up to federal prosecutors and judges, and how well she played her hand with Aaron. My part would be over by midafternoon.

"Did Dan Tyree haul this dun into the canyon for you?"

"Yeah," she said. She almost smiled. "We were sweethearts once."

"Figured. Is he the only one who knows you were coming up here to find me?"

"Oh, Dan doesn't know. I didn't want to expose him any more than I already have."

"Great."

"I needed to get you alone," she said. "Buddy knew you were taking these people here, so I thought it was a safe place to approach you. A place guys on motorcycles couldn't reach. Buddy talked to one of these lady campers of yours in the General Store yesterday when he heard her talking about the dashing Tommy Smith taking her and her friends to Little Meadows. Then he followed them out to the lake last night. Buddy was just trying to give me a chance to catch up to you."

"Anybody see you?"

"I don't think so," she said. "Buddy was talking to a guy at the pack station about fishing, though. Typical. We've turned ourselves into a family of criminals, and he's yakking about Mepps Spinners."

"Who was the guy?"

"I couldn't tell you," she said. "Just some out-of-shape red-headed city dude in a Hawaiian shirt."

"Well, shit."

The rumbling thunder in the west came pretty much right on cue. The folks hunkered at the flap of the wall tent and ate steaks Drew grilled on the fire and drank a French red that was beyond my pay grade to appreciate. I watched them try to keep windblown ash out of their dinner then cut myself a piece of a steak without sitting down and told them I was riding out that night. They were pretty upset— half worried about me, half sorry I wouldn't be around to entertain them with stories of true-west mayhem. When they asked me why, I made up a story that my new mules would be antsy in the storm.

"They are fine looking animals," Scottie said. I was walking away from them. "Where did they come from?"

"Afghanistan."

Right about then, I was wishing I was back there.

Erika followed me out to the stock. I told her that we were bottled up. That the guy in the Hawaiian shirt was a crooked Reno cop, and he'd be waiting out on the Sonora Pass road with a slick-shoed friend or two to grab her and turn her over to Sonny if she headed back the way she came. I told her that Creed, the horseman she'd spied on in the trees above the pack station, was waiting on the other side of the pass so he could block that route down-canyon.

"How do they know for sure?" she said.

"I wasn't kidding. Buddy sold you out." I told her about his triple-cross offer the night before. "He knows how to get the bank codes 'cause I'm betting you told him. Your brother's sent us both to hell."

She turned away so I couldn't see her face.

"Grab a chunk of beef for the road. We're out of here in twenty."

I walked over to the campfire and made small talk with the folks for two minutes. Drew asked if I'd ever climbed Hawksbeak. I told him I'd climbed it in high school. I told him he could try it the next morning as the storm would've passed by then, but there'd be slick spots and maybe fresh snow, so he needed to be careful and not take chances. He seemed semi-oblivious that something was going on between me and the lady visitor. Bill followed me over to the picket lines.

"Everything okay?" he said.

"No. I gotta take this woman out of here."

"Is she someone close to you?"

"No."

"When do you want to leave?"

"Now."

"Tell me what I can do," he said.

"Help me saddle."

"Whatever you need."

"I should be back with Harvey and the animals late tomorrow. If not me, his wife will help him. I know you paid for me to stay with you guys, but you'll be fine without me."

"Why wouldn't you come back with Harvey?"

I didn't say anything.

"Oh," he said, when he caught my meaning.

I told him the spot I was in. How Erika and I got ourselves boxed in between the crooked cop and the buckaroo we'd passed that morning. I didn't get specific, that if Creed showed up on this side of the pass, it meant I was already dead, but I think he was getting the drift.

"And Bill?"

"Yeah," he said.

"This trip's on me."

The wind like to take my hat off as we saddled. We had them rigged-up fast. I secured my bedroll, the panniers, lash ropes, and bridles against the weather under the tarps and left them in camp. I tied the four mules together, then did the same with the saddle horses. Bill watched me finish up.

"I never meant to put you folks in harm's way."

"No way you could've known, Tommy."

"You'll be safer without me."

"What else can I do?"

"You might want to try a 911 call now and then to see if you got service, and to fill Sarah in if you get through. Tell her 'Erika Hornberg is alive' and I've got her." She'll know what to do."

"Glad to," he said. "So what will this badass do if he gets his hands on this woman?"

"Kill her for a million bucks."

"Do you know how puny a million dollars is in the real world?" he said.

"Up here it's a helluva payday, whether you're a horseshoer or a pimp ex-cop. Guys die for a lot less."

"Go do what you have to do, Tommy."

"Thanks."

"Just another average day in the life of an Eastern Sierra mule packer."

"You're pushin' it, Bill."

He laughed.

When I was ready, he pulled his bottle of high-end Jim Beam from his parka. We each took a pull, then we laughed 'cause there was nothing else to do. He nodded down towards his friends about a hundred feet away.

"How much should I tell them?"

"Whatever makes you comfortable. Make sure Drew doesn't break his neck on the mountain tomorrow."

"I will."

"Sure sorry."

"Don't be," he said. "My wife thinks this is our coolest vacation ever."

"If this is your idea of fun I don't know if I want to go sailing with you."

I checked my horse and Erika rode up, dressed for weather. I handed her the string of four mules. They were used to traveling together and would be easier for her to lead.

"Can you handle these?"

"Sure," she said.

I nodded to Bill, swung up, and took the rope of the lead saddle horse and we headed for the pass.

CHAPTER EIGHTEEN

We rode in the moon shadow of the crest, crossing the meadow into the pines just at dark. The trail narrowed in the rocks as we climbed the pass from the west. It was a hard hour later when we topped out at ten thousand feet on the sandy clearing of North Pass and stopped between boulders in bright moonlight to let the stock blow. They were carrying no weight but the saddles, so even with the long climb they'd had that day they were pointing downhill and ready to move.

We paused again at the top of the switchbacks as the storm picked up. In just minutes the moon was only a glow behind black clouds, and the trail had vanished under our feet. I let my red horse pick his way down and kept my rope hand resting on the butt of my .270. One likely spot for Twister Creed was right here, with us exposed on the open slope and him tucked in the rocks to the side of the switchbacks so he could shoot whenever the mood suited. By him not killing us there, I knew he'd been told to bring Erika back alive.

The four mules brought up the rear behind her. They were solid and sensible, just like I knew they'd be. Two of the saddle horses I was leading got antsy coming down that trail in the dark, the mahogany scratching and jabbing, the crushed granite giving way under their hooves, their iron shoes sliding on slick rock at the edge of steep drop-offs. It was another half-hour when we got to the foot of the switchbacks. We kept moving without slowing and without saying a word. My horse followed the trail like a pro, although it was mostly closed-in sky, with moonlight poking through the storm only now and then. We got further down into the trees as time stopped and the night wrapped us right up.

If Creed hadn't shown himself on the switchbacks, the next place he might be waiting was at the forks by the snow cabin. He knew that ground and knew the roofless old relic would give him a place he would think was somehow safe, though it would be the first place I'd guess. After what seemed like another lifetime in the saddle, I pulled up a hundred yards from the forks. I sat still, listening, then got off my horse. I tied him and the saddle horses in the trees, then walked back to Erika and told her to stay mounted and not let go of the mules. Then I told her about Creed.

"This is the kind of place an amateur would think was a great shooting spot. Plus, he knows if he waits farther down-canyon, he won't know if we've taken the South Fork trail and circled around him to come out through the Summers Lake drainage."

"So what do I do?" she said.

"Just follow my lead. You hear shots but don't hear me, slip off your horse and hide in the timber. Keep listening but keep moving. VanOwen probably wants you alive, but if he's given up on getting the money, then revenge'll suit him just dandy."

I slipped my rifle from the scabbard and walked down-trail slow over the uneven ground towards the cabin ruins. I was getting close before its dark shape was outlined by a few seconds of shifting moonlight. A few seconds more and things faded to black again.

"Creed?"

"Who wants to know?" He sounded surprised.

"Tommy Smith."

"Aw-right," he said. "Are you *trying* to get yourself shot, Smith?"

"I'm coming through."

"I got orders not to let you. But to take the woman."

I heard the click of a hammer cock just as clear as if he was standing next to me.

"You can try. Either way, I'm coming."

"Snake's got a couple more friends on the way," Creed said. "They're coming up behind me, so your trail ends here."

Every time he started talking, I moved closer in the shifting dark.

"He wants that Hornberg woman bad, and I'm betting she's right there with you. Carl said this morning she was headed back my direction."

I moved closer.

"Did you hear me?" he said. He asked again louder.

204

I knew that chunk of ground as well or better than he did and was up on him quick.

"You get by me, you still gotta deal with those guys between here and the pack station," he said.

I didn't answer.

I hunkered down and kept quiet, ignoring his crap. He was talking because he was nervous. The creek was far enough away I could just hear the *tink* of plastic or glass. Like the cap of a bottle of whiskey getting screwed on or screwed off.

"You worked for Harvey same as me," he said. "You and me shouldn't . . . well . . . you know."

I heard him rustle in the dark and what might have been the sound of him lowering his hammer then cocking it again with his thumb. It made me think he had a lever action like a Winchester or a Marlin with a round already jacked in the chamber. And that he was more than nervous, he was scared. I heard him puff out his breath just before his first shot. Three more came in short intervals right after. There wasn't much muzzle flash, but I could spot it well enough, and hear the double clack of the lever action and hear one of the rounds ricochet off the granite behind me. Even in the dark he was letting me know exactly where to shoot. I took my time, then fired once.

I hadn't wanted to shoot him but couldn't risk him hitting Erika or my mules.

"Erika?"

"Tommy—are you all right?"

"Yeah. How's the stock?"

"Antsy but okay," she said. "Is it safe?"

"Just sit tight."

By then I'd covered the last few steps and was crouching over Twister Creed inside the walls of the roofless cabin, checking him with a pocket flash. He was still alive with a chest wound from the single round that entered from his left. It didn't look good. I patted him down as easy as I could till I found a phone. I knew it'd be worthless for another couple of miles but pocketed it just the same. Even though he'd been trying to take me out, we'd both come from the same sort of place and done the same sort of work for some of the same people. Just another hard-working, whiskey-drinking wastrel like some more I could name.

In the white light of the pocket flash, I could see his eyes were open and he was watching me. His lips moved, and I saw blood on his teeth. I stayed with him for those few minutes with my hand on his shoulder. I heard Erika calling out in the dark but didn't answer. While I waited, I found his whiskey bottle. I unscrewed the cap and took a pull then spit it out. It tasted like something drained off a corpse. When he was gone, I rolled him just enough to pull his rifle out from under him. It was a Marlin 336 that had seen hard use. A good, no-frills woodland and brush kind of gun. The scope was the same. An old Weaver that probably only cost half a hundred. Creed was a guy that lived close to the margins with no room for error.

I stood up and walked back to where Erika waited with the stock. I thought it best not to disturb another crime scene, even if it meant leaving a semi-loaded .30-30 just lying there. The clouds raced overhead in the moving storm and let the moon show for a minute, higher now than it had before. Sometimes the moon looks yellow. Sometimes white. I got no idea why.

I sheathed my rifle, then went hunting Creed's horse. It wouldn't do to just leave him. I found him tied downstream from the snow cabin, close to the bank where Creed drowned Harvey's mules those years before. I pulled off the saddle and slipped the bosal off his nose and left them in the grass, then turned the horse loose. He just stood there like a good horse for a minute. After another minute I heard him trotting away down the trail. They're sociable buggers and don't easily leave a herd, even if it's not their own.

I walked back to Erika and untied my sorrel.

"You ready to travel?"

"I'm ready," Erika said. "Is that guy the only one?"

"Nope."

I stepped aboard and grabbed up the string of saddle horses, and we headed down-canyon at a fast walk, nothing more. The ground was still rough as hell, and darkness didn't make it any easier. I needed to fix my eyes on the trail ahead and listen for anything that wasn't right. Erika seemed nervous and wanted to talk, but I didn't and I shushed her. We rode like that for half an hour and my eyes adapted to the shifting dark. Finally, I pulled up in a narrow spot where the granite and timber were close on either side.

"Why are we stopping?" she said.

"I thought you might want to see where you were buried."

I pointed her towards the boggy spot where Jack and I had found the young whore's body. It was dark and creepy and hard to see. We didn't linger.

The shale of the Roughs was wet with the rain that came and went with the gusts. There were no trees or cliffs out on that loose rock for shelter. We saw our first lightning then. In a flash I caught sight of Creed's horse, steam rising off his wet back. He was standing on the shale ahead of us like he was waiting, like the dead man's horse was showing us the way if we were crazy enough to take it. There was nothing to do but keep moving and try not to slip. I could hear the constant clack of hooves sliding on rock. We crossed a high spot where we could see down-canyon over the trees. Way out there, down toward the meadows, I saw a quick flash of light. Maybe a headlight. Maybe a busted blood vessel in my brain. More than likely that would be our reception committee, or the next part of it anyway.

We were down-canyon of the Roughs when I pulled up.

"Is everything okay?" Erika said.

"Get off. Check your cinch."

"I think it's okay."

"Check it like your life depended on it."

She got off and so did I. I cinched up my gelding and the other eight head, making sure anything tied to the saddles would stay tied. Then I dropped a fifth round into the magazine to replace the one I'd left in Creed's heart. When I was finished I walked up to the zebra dun.

"I'm going set the stock loose."

She looked at me like I was crazy.

"VanOwen's got more ginks waiting down there in the meadows, and god knows what we'll find at the pack station."

"So?

"We need a diversion. Something to run interference for us. The stock'll run and keep running. We'll follow and sneak along behind them best we can."

"Won't they just scatter?"

"They know where home is. The steepest part's behind us, so once they get to running we'll have hell's own time trying to stop 'em. Packers in the old days used to do this all the time till scared backpackers complained and the Forest Service told the packers they couldn't do it anymore. I'm thinking the saddle horses'll blast out first and the mules being more sensible will follow. When I turn the first one loose, you be ready to ride, but hold your horse back if you can. Got it?"

"I think so," she said. "Let me help."

I unstrung the four mules and handed her two, their lead ropes tied up to the sawbucks so they wouldn't drag. Erika held them each by the cheek piece, one on either side of her with her reins wrapped around the horn. I untied the riding horses and turned them loose one by one as quiet as I could, as not to start a stampede right away. The first horse ran off down-trail as I loosened the last one. The mules were fidgety. Erika let go of her two, then snatched her reins when the dun bolted after them. I set loose the other pair, and they all followed the horses. We were on flat ground, and it didn't take the animals long to know they were all at liberty. The herd busting out got my sorrel amped up and ready to rage. I had to grab a handful of mane and swing up on the fly as he blasted out after the others. I yelled to Erika.

"Take a deep seat."

Then we rattled on down the trail at a dead run.

There was no way to control the horses out in the lead for the first mile or more. As much ground as they'd covered that day, they knew where they were heading and just wanted to fly, so Erika and I had to sit tight and ride. The sky opened up on us with lightning cracking and wind beating the rain into our faces. Moonlight shot in and out of black clouds overhead, and branches jabbed us as we clattered by. We made a wild chase of it like we were riding lightning with hell on our trail. Racing in the dark like that was scary as crap, but except for the possible death and dying part, it was almost fun.

The horses and mules finally settled into a steady pace, single file, following the trail they knew would take them home. I tried to look back from time to time to see how Erika was hanging, but with the rain in my eyes and mud splattered up from the mule in front of me, most of the time I had to depend on just hearing the zebra dun pounding behind. Then for a single moment I saw a huge bolt of fork lightning hitting behind Flatiron Ridge, putting a silver edge around Erika's black shape. I counted the seconds till the thunder came.

Erika had one bad wreck, and I heard her go down as the dun lost his footing, maybe tripping on a root or maybe just hitting a slick spot wrong. She hit so hard I heard the air whoosh out of her in a grunt. I wheeled the sorrel and grabbed the dun without dismounting. The horse didn't look like it'd busted anything. If I'd got off, we both would have ended up afoot. It took Erika a minute to even get on her hands and knees and longer to catch her wind and drag herself back in the saddle. Her right side was dark with mud and her right wrist just hung there. I asked her if it was busted but she shook her head.

"Think I just sprained it," she said. "Did that once—high school basketball."

She said it hurt like crazy, but she hadn't come this far to quit now.

The horses and mules were out of sight by then. Erika got mounted, and we rattled our hocks, still covering the ground way faster than what was safe. My sorrel took a bad stumble in the aspen thickets somewhere below Blue Rock, and I thought I was going to take a header myself, but that boy somehow lurched and scrambled and kept his front feet under him and we never stopped moving.

I thought we were running ahead of the storm, the lightening hitting behind us in the higher country. The stock had settled into an easy trot when the whole canyon lit up bright as noon and you could count every one of the million aspen leaves, a million green shapes all around us. The thunder came right with the lightning, exploding the same instant with no time to count "one-one-thousand." The whole earth shook under us, and my hair stood up under my hat. It hit so hard and so loud it jolted us in our saddles and scattered the stock again. I ducked my head and covered my face as my horse dove off into trees that I couldn't see and blackness closed back over us. The sorrel ran flat out. I was cut on the face and hands, and my jacket pocket was torn off, taking one of my gloves with it.

It was a while before Erika and I reconnected. Our horses stumbled and crashed back to the trail when lightning flashes let us find it. She looked battered and torn, but she had stayed aboard. It was half an hour before we caught sight of the stock ahead of us in the aspen thickets above the first meadow, still goosey and easily spooked. We pushed our horses through the rocks to close the distance, and I saw the leaders lit up in a bit of brightness out ahead. This time what I was seeing wasn't lightning. I guessed this was the headlight I'd spied earlier. Part of the reception committee Creed had mentioned before he died.

I saw glimmers in distant branches, then the beam of light turned toward us, spinning white in the rain swirls in front of our faces. Then I heard shots, flat and heavy like a shotgun. We pushed our horses hard as we dared and were close on the tails of my stock when a man's shape stepped into the glow. He was carrying something long and black. He raised it and fired two times more at intervals and one of the shots ripped into aspen leaves close to my ear. The light wheeled in the shifting dark like it was circling close to the trail, then the man just vanished and all I could see were the wet, slick rumps of my animals running hard before they disappeared into the night. We rode into the white beam. A thin guy in a raggedy-assed parka lay twisted on his back moaning with blood on his face. A horse won't usually run over the top of a human unless it feels scared or confined, and my animals were both. The guy looked like he took a whoopin'. A rifle stock wrapped in electrician's tape poked out of the mud—like it was maybe the same shotgun I'd bent over the bartender's nose in Reno. The guy on the ground could've been the same city guy at the table with VanOwen that day. Or he could've been just another willing casualty. I jumped my horse over him and didn't stop. We were past the man in an instant, then the light ahead of us bobbed across the meadow and stopped hard, pointing into the ground.

I yelled to Erika to pull up and I rode over to a four-wheeler nose down in a cattle wallow half-full of mud and rainwater. The rider'd fallen off the seat into the goop and looked up at me like a crazy person. It was the bartender, the one with the ponytail. In the glare from his headlight, I could see his face was bruised purple under a big bandage that straddled his nose.

"What're you laughing at, you bastard?" he said when he recognized me.

"Old Sonny's brought the A-team, that's for sure."

"You gonna help me?"

"Sure. You got a phone? I'll call you some help."

The guy pulled a flip phone out of his back pocket and held it up to me like it hurt him to move. I could see a pistol Velcro-ed on his belt.

"It might be too wet," he said.

"You're probably right."

I leaned down and grabbed the phone and chucked it as far as I could out into the dark then goosed the sorrel into a lope back to the trail where Erika was waiting. I could hear the gunsel yelling at me and could see the zebra dun just ahead when the next lightning popped. After a few seconds we heard two pistol shots but we were already leaving the guy far behind.

We rode on for a while at a walk. My animals had slowed, and we all needed a breather. Creed's brown horse appeared out of the dark, fastwalking in the lead now like he was part of the band. It started raining again, light but steady. We rode without a word. The full moon was just a glow parked on the top of the clouds. I fiddled with Sarah's radio, trying to keep it dry and make it work. I heard her voice for a second, then nothing but static. Finally, I could hear her—crackly but clear.

"Hey, baby, is everything okay?" she said. "I wasn't expecting to hear from you so soon."

"Erika Hornberg is alive."

"My god. How do you know for sure?"

"She's right here with me."

I gave Sarah a quick rundown how Erika followed my party to Little Meadows but got herself trapped coming-and-going with me trapped right along with her, and how we had to leave my customers and take the stock with us. She and I had both suspected Erika might still be alive, but neither of us had figured how she'd pull it off. I told Sarah about the VanOwen gunsels who'd been laying for us on the trail, and how it was a good bet there'd be more up ahead. She said she'd get hold of Aaron.

"Now you need to radio Mitch, babe."

"I don't think that's such a great idea," she said. "If there's a way to louse this up, he'll find it. He'll want to make the collar himself, then turn her over to those 'incompetent pencil-pushers at the Bureau.'"

"If you don't tell him, he could have your badge."

For a few seconds there was nothing but silence and static on the radio.

"You look damn fine in your uniform. I'd miss that."

I could hear her getting exasperated, even through the crappy connection. She said something garbled that might've been, ". . . you jerk."

"Okay," she said. "I'll tell him. Now, will you be careful? You worry me."

"I will. But if we get Aaron on board, this whole thing could be over quick." I didn't say how exactly it could be over.

"Let's hope," she said.

"Oh, I turned the stock loose. They come rattling in, we'll be right behind them."

"Then you better let me get to work." The radio crackled and went dead.

"You hear that?"

"Yeah," Erika said. "Now what you're doing makes sense," she said. "The way the stock—"

"Let's just keep moving."

We kept to a walk the length of the meadow with me in the lead. The rain had slacked, but we were already wet to the bone. The zebra dun pulled next to me again.

"So this is it?" Erika said.

"This is it. Keep your eyes open. Be ready to bust out if anyone's on the trail. We're gonna blast in behind the herd in the dark and hope nobody sees us."

"What about the FBI?"

"Sarah will've set up a deal with Aaron Fuchs by the

time I get her back on the radio. Your surrender in exchange for the money."

"I was just looking for a way to jump off that runaway horse," she said. She started to blubber.

"Cut it out. You're doing the right thing. The only thing you can do."

I saw her take a deep breath. "Then I hope this works."

Sarah radioed me back about fifteen minutes later.

"Mitch says you have to turn over Erika Hornberg to him." She spoke crisp and loud. "Otherwise he'll consider that you're harboring a fugitive."

"Tell him I'm bringing her in to surrender."

"Is that true?"

"Yeah. Just not to him."

"He can probably hear you," she said. "It's an open frequency."

"Right."

"Anything else?"

"You may want leave the corral gate open and my pickup parked alongside the gate like a wing. You know. For whenever I come in. Probably be hours and hours."

"Okay," she said. "I'll park my Silverado up by the trailhead with the keys under the visor. So it doesn't get dinged up."

"Good move. Where's Mitch now?"

"In his SUV parked by the bridge," she said. "He just pulled in." I could hear Mitch muttering for a second, trying to shush Sarah. He sounded good and mad, but semi-confused. Sarah didn't say anything more about a meet with Aaron, which was just as well.

"You know I'll be thinking of you, honey," she said.

The radio buzzed and clicked off.

I looked at Erika.

"Let's go."

She nodded, and we stirred up the stock. The animals ahead of us perked up and took off at a trot. The pack station was less than a mile ahead. They knew they were almost home and there was the chance of hay in the mangers. I hissed and slapped my wet romal on my wet chinks. We could hear the horses and mules grunting and blowing, their hooves fading off, then speeding up as something spooked them, just the rush of a herd on the move. Ahead we could see the first glow of the yard lights in the tops of the trees. We'd hit an easy lope by the time we started winding through the Jeffrey pine above the creek. We were half a mile out when the storm opened up on us again, the wind blowing Erika's parka back from her drenched face. Thunder followed lightning, the bare ground slick with a layer of mud under soaked pine needles. Then the glow in the treetops ahead of us faded to black. The generator must've shorted out in the storm or somebody shut it off. We kept riding, keeping our eyes focused on the middle distance and the rumps of the running mules.

We were pounding steady as we rounded the last curve through the aspen before the pack station. With the yard lights off, the place went from moonlight to darkness and back again. I could just see deputy Sorenson in a wet Smokey hat and slicker standing on my porch peering out with a Maglite in his hand. I leaned down over the neck of the sorrel to be less visible. I couldn't tell if Erika had done the same.

We rumbled into the sloppy yard as lightning popped, the stock goosey as they got hemmed in by buildings and corral fence and strange vehicles. Another deputy in a yellow rain-suit stood in the middle of the dirt road ahead of the herd, then scrambled backwards and disappeared. Whether he fell or dove I couldn't tell, but you could see where he'd landed because each critter shied at exactly the same spot as they barreled by like one long twisty animal.

The saddle horses ducked through the open gate into the big corral with the mules just behind. Creed's horse overshot the gate in the dark of the unfamiliar place. He spun and slipped when he got to my truck then turned and trotted in after the rest. Somebody stepped from behind the truck and shut the gate after the last horse. It was too shadowy to tell who the somebody was. There were no other animals in the corral, which meant the rest of the stock was out in the pasture. The horses and mules jogged around the perimeter, stirrup leathers flapping as they checked the mangers for hay and found none. We jogged right behind them, our heads down. Erika and I circled along the fence until we came to the pasture gate on the opposite side of the corral. The gate swung open a couple of feet so fast it spooked our tired horses. We ducked right out of the corral past Harvey who was standing behind the gate. He swung it closed quick so the other animals wouldn't run out behind us. I saw him point across the pasture. Nobody said a word.

Erika and I headed toward the creek at a walk so we wouldn't draw attention, the darkness coming and going with the clouds. We stopped short of the crossing to let our horses cool down a minute before we let them drink. Then we rode out of the creek into the timber on the opposite bank. Erika followed me single file to a half-hidden wire gate on the pack station road. We finally saw headlights turning on. One set was down by Harvey's trailer, a second out by the bridge. I figured those last lights to be Mitch's. He must have figured that waiting there where he could block a vehicle was his smartest play. Or maybe he was just taking a snooze. I got off to open the gate, the smell of rain-wet pine all around.

"Did you have all this all planned out?" Erika said.

"Not a bit."

I shushed her and led my horse up the road. I saw the Silverado up by the trailhead gate just where Sarah said it would be. Then I saw Sarah. I was always pretty happy to see her, maybe more right then than normal. We held on to each other for a second, not saying a word.

Finally, Sarah looked over at Erika.

"You two need to get out of here," Sarah said. "Take the truck down to Becky's and wait for Aaron Fuchs there. He and I traded texts, and he said he'd take you into custody, but I haven't been able to speak with him yet."

She watched Erika slide off the zebra dun and almost fall when she touched the ground.

"I didn't recognize you, Erika," she said. "It's been a while."

Erika was half covered with mud, her black-dyed hair pasted over her skull from the rain and her right arm dangling. She kinda looked like she really had spent the winter in a bog. The smile she gave Sarah was lopsided, like something from beyond the grave.

I loosened my cinch and ran my hands over my horse's legs, checking his tendons for bows. Then I felt his face and brisket and flanks for bruises and cuts and found a few. I picked up his left hind foot just to satisfy my vanity. The reset shoe was still snug.

In the canyon, the yard lights flooded on, blazing up to the treetops. Erika flinched like somebody'd called in an airstrike.

"I'll lead these two down to the corral," Sarah said. "Harvey and Dan should be unsaddling the rest."

Erika thanked Sarah for minding her horse, then started to ask something about Dan.

"You've put my husband in jeopardy," Sarah said. "You two are safe now, so let's just get this over with."

Erika nodded.

I felt in my shirt pocket and pulled out my phone. Except it wasn't my phone. I looked down at it. It was the one I took off Twister Creed. I scrolled down, messing with the unfamiliar screen. I got to a list of recently called numbers and found one for "Snake." I pushed the name on the screen and waited.

"You got the woman?" VanOwen said. He'd answered on the third ring. He sounded cranky but relaxed.

"Yup."

"What about the soldier?"

"He's still alive."

"Shit," VanOwen said. "What the hell happened?"

"I guess I wasn't cowboy enough to take him."

By then he'd figured he was talking to me and not Creed. I could hear him breathing. "So," he said after a long minute. "Where's Twister?" he said. "And where's the woman?"

"You'll never see either of them again, so don't bother asking."

He was quiet again except for the breathing, figuring his next move. When he talked, it was slow.

"But you'll see me," he said. "You know what I want. I want into that goddamn account."

"So?"

"I'll leave you alone. I'll leave your family alone. I'll leave the woman alone." Now he was panting into the phone. "But if she don't transfer that money, all bets are off."

"Too late. I'm turning her over to the FBI."

"When?"

"Tonight. You got no play. You never did. Your plan was dumb."

"We'll see, dude."

"You went to a lot of trouble with this bullshit body and bank account crap. You came up with nothin'. It's over."

He laughed then. "Not so fast," he said.

I heard him talking to someone, but I couldn't make out what he was saying. The storm was still gusting, muffling the sound.

"Don't be mad, Tommy," a voice on the phone said just as clear as could be. "Sonny told me he was gonna see the spirit lady, and did I want to come? I did, Tommy. I want her to take me to my mom."

"Jesus, Audie. Where the hell are you?"

CHAPTER NINETEEN

"You're mad at me," Audie said. "I can tell. I'm sorry, Tommy. I'm so damn sorry, but I miss my mom something bad."

"I'm not mad at you, kiddo. Just worried. I thought you were at my mother's, for chrissakes."

"I was," she said, "but I snuck out. She don't know."

"How?" I tried to sound careless. To sound not afraid. To keep her talking.

"I was walkin' Hoot around out by the barn after supper. Hoot was huntin' rabbits. Sonny was parked out on the lane. He waved to me. Waved me to come over. I was scared not to go. He told me he'd seen my mom. If she was dead, I don't know how that could be, but he knew I missed her. When I asked him if he knew the spirit lady, he said sure. He could take me to her. He told me to sneak out after bedtime and not let your mom know. To meet him on the road." I could hear her crying. "Your mom's gonna be pissed at me and make me go back to Sonny for good, and I'll never see Hoot again, neither."

"That's not going to happen. Where are you?"

"I dunno. Another ranch or something. We drove through Paiute Meadows to get here."

I could hear muffled noise and talking.

"Okay, dude," VanOwen said. "Little Audie wanted some quality time with the old Snake, but now it's reckonin' time."

"I'm listening."

"I got something you want," he said, "and you got something I want. We're gonna do a little straight-up trade. You and me, bro."

"Keep talkin'."

"Sweet little Audie for that skanky Erika Hornberg and those bank codes." He sounded like he was enjoying himself. "I know you got her. We'll do a little swap-a-mundo."

"Where are you?"

"At her brother's. Kind of a pretty place with the lights off. Moonlight on the old rancho. It looks like dog-crap in the daytime, though. If it was mine, I'd burn it to the ground and turn it into a truck stop. But stroll by, cowboy. Buddy's here. We all got a lot to talk about."

"Talk fast. Pretty soon that place'll be crawling with deputies."

He laughed. "Ain't they all up your cabin? Waitin' to arrest your ass? Harboring a fugitive and all?"

I just stood there in the dark with Sarah and Erika staring at me. Erika moved close, doing her best to listen. I couldn't help but think it was always the boneheaded bastards who thought they had the world wired. The ones who were still pimping children and calling themselves Snake and peddling stolen chopper parts and setting arson fires for insurance money when they were pushing fifty. And all the time dreaming that outlaw dream of that one last big score. Wasting a single thought on somebody like Sonny VanOwen didn't make me very smart, either.

"I'll meet you at Hornberg's. I'll give you the account codes for Audie."

"And the Hornberg bitch."

I looked Erika straight in the eye. "She's already on her way to the Feds. And they know she's alive and her brother's ID of the body was a lie. So it's Audie for the codes."

There was silence for a minute.

"Then come on down," he said. "Hell, I'll leave a light on for you." The call went dead.

"I should go, too," Erika said.

"You're not going. You don't deal with guys like him. You don't trade."

"You are," she said.

"I got no choice." I stuck my hand out. "Give me the thing with the codes."

"I don't have it."

"Where the hell is it?" Sarah said.

She looked from Sarah to me. "Audie has it," she said. "Audie has my thumb drive."

"The hell?"

"How could you put a child in that position?" Sarah said. I thought she was going to shoot Erika right there.

"She doesn't know it," Erika said. "I hid it in the sleeping bag I gave her the night she was alone in the canyon. I told her—"

"Oh, for shit's sake."

Erika started blubbering.

"It doesn't matter," Sarah said. She gave me a grim look. "You can't go in without that drive, babe."

"I can't just leave the kid."

"How are you going to get the girl if she's with Sonny?" Erika said.

"I got her once before."

A big gust made it hard to hear a thing for a minute. The two of them stared at me in the dark. Erika was impulsive and heedless and could get us all killed if she was along. I wouldn't take her on a bet.

"If I don't have the money," Erika said, "then what do I have to bargain with? What do I tell the FBI?"

"I'll tell Aaron Fuchs everything the FBI needs to know," Sarah said. "That you came to us with the account codes. To turn yourself in."

"If I get a chance at the sleeping bag, what am I looking for?"

Erika described a little plastic deal about the size of a pack of gum with a plug at one end. She said she'd cut a slit at the bottom of the bag on the inside. I asked her where the account was.

"In a bank in Cyprus. All the most discriminating dictators and Russian gangsters use it." She tried a lame laugh and told me the bank's name. "I think at some level Sonny can't grasp that the money only exists electronically. I think he was kind of hoping for a duffle bag full of cash."

"Ain't we all."

Even in the uneven darkness with tree-branch shadows

bouncing all over our faces, I could see Erika worry. Those numbers had been what she'd counted on to keep herself alive for almost a year.

Sarah pulled my rifle out of the scabbard on the sorrel and handed it to me, looking sad. She took a half-full box of Remington .270 soft points out of my saddle pockets and handed them to me as well.

"I guess these are your bargaining chips, now."

"You know I'm not going there to bargain."

"Why the hell do I bother worrying about you?" she said.

I stowed my rifle behind the seat of the Silverado, gave Sarah a long hug and a last kiss goodbye, and told her to have Fuchs meet me at Hornberg's before he went to Becky's. I knew he'd never get there in time, but Sarah might feel better thinking that he would. I told Erika to hide in the trees below the trailhead until Sarah could get word to Dan Tyree to pick her up on his way home, and for the two of them to sit tight there at his mother's ranch until they heard from Sarah, Aaron, or me. And not to budge.

Sarah and I watched Erika shuffle across the clearing by the trailhead and disappear in the dark. Sarah grabbed the front of my coat and buried her face in it.

"Should I be worried?" she said. "I mean . . . more than usual?"

"I think me going in alone will be the best way out of this. What VanOwen wants most is the money. If I can get my hands on that sleeping bag with the thing inside, I can probably get Audie back safe."

"As long as you get back safe, buster."

"I plan on it." I leaned into her to feel her warmth. "I will. I will."

We saw headlights flare up across the meadow and head towards the bridge.

"That should be Dan's truck. I better get moving."

She gave me another kiss, then started walking down the hill leading the two horses towards the bridge.

I stood next to the cab of the Silverado ready to duck or run until Dan's truck passed by. Sarah stopped with the two horses when the headlights hit her. She was keeping the animals to the side of the road against a cutbank so the vehicle could pass, and I thought I saw her look back at me. Then I saw why. It wasn't Dan's truck heading towards her. It was a Frémont County Sheriff's SUV. I ducked behind the Silverado with my back against a rear tire. The SUV passed Sarah and slowed when it hit the trailhead. A spotlight swept the Silverado and the beam paused on the cab. After a minute the light dimmed off and the SUV drove away down the canyon. I couldn't see who was driving, just that two officers were inside.

Dan's dually followed a couple of minutes later. I kept to the shadows and didn't flag him down. It wasn't just that I didn't want any other deputies to notice Dan's truck stopping if anyone was watching from the pack station. I didn't want to talk about Erika Hornberg anymore, and I didn't want to get into it with Dan about what he thought he'd been doing with her.

I waited another few minutes after he passed me to fire up the Silverado. I crept away from the trailhead with lights off till I hit the quarter mile of pavement that marked the Forest Service campground and watched a black bear mosey across the road ignoring my headlights. In fifteen minutes I was rolling off the logging road onto the Summers Lake Road when my phone buzzed. It took me a second to dig it out of my one damp jacket pocket. It was Becky Tyree.

"Hey, Tommy. We've got a problem. Erika just blasted out of here in Dan's truck."

"Shit. Was he with her?"

"No," she said. "They pulled into the yard about five minutes ago. Dan had called, and I was waiting for them. I hadn't seen her since she vanished last year, and I wanted to talk to her. Dan was stowing his bedroll in the saddle house, and she was pretty distraught. That guy VanOwen had called her on Buddy's phone. He said that he had Buddy and would kill him if she ran out on him again. He's holding Buddy at their ranch and said he'll trade Buddy's life for hers. She was talking wild that no matter how she tried to do the right thing, she always ended up putting people's lives in danger. You, the little girl, my son, and now her brother. I went back into the house to put on some coffee and try to talk sense into her. Then I heard the pickup spinning around, and I saw her fly out the lane like a madwoman."

I could tell Becky was really fried. She'd stuck by Erika when half the valley wanted to string her up.

"Damn. All she had to do was not answer that phone."

"Where are you now?" she said.

"On my way to Hornberg's."

"Do you want to wait for the sheriff?"

"I'm meeting my FBI guy there. Can you call Sarah?"

"It'll be light in three more hours. Would it be better if . . . ?" She let it hang.

"In this kind of deal, dark is my friend."

She told me that she'd get Sarah right away, and my mom next to fill her in.

"Becky?"

"Yes?"

"How come it was you called and not Dan?"

"He thinks you're disappointed in him," she said. "For helping Erika when she was hiding from the law. For letting her get away just now."

"Tell him no worries. Ain't none of us fortunetellers."

Then she called me honey like she did when I was a kid and told me to be careful and do what I thought was best.

Halfway towards town, the pavement of the Summers Lake road took a ninety-degree left following the old homestead boundaries through the treeless grazing land. A local would know that turning right instead of left would put you down in front of a wide gate across a fenced dirt lane that was the division between Becky Tyree's land and the Hornberg ranch. On a hunch, I turned right onto the grass and got out. I looked a mile southeast across the pastures to Hornberg's headquarters and saw what looked like a single yard light in the rainy mist. I scanned the grass under my feet with my pocket flash and could see fresh dually tracks in the ground soggy with rain where someone had just pulled up to the gate. Judging by the black spot the exhaust made on the grass, the driver left the diesel idling.

If that someone was Erika, she probably tried to get the gate to budge. It was a stout wooden thing, not locked, but too heavy for a short person with a just-sprained wrist. I could see where the truck had been thrown into reverse, the wheel jerked around and the tires spinning as the driver almost got themselves stuck. The vehicle left mud and grass tracks on the first few feet of blacktop once it climbed back up on the road. All this told me that Erika had been trying to take the old Hornberg Lane, not because it was quicker than circling through town, but because she was hoping to creep up on the ranch unseen. That's the same thing I was hoping when I dragged the gate open and drove down the lane with my lights off.

I drove a quarter-mile south, then the lane turned due east toward the ranch headquarters another mile off. It was slow going between the fences on a cloudy night. Ahead I could see a single light was on but the house was dark, the whole ranch just shapes and shadows. A quarter-mile on, I drove through a gravel crossing of the East Frémont River. The water ran swift to the top of my tires and ripples flashed in spotty moonlight. The far side of the crossing put me in sight of the first outbuildings. The lone light was shining through the open slaughterhouse door, but that was off to the side of the empty feedlot and not in the direction I needed to go.

The headquarters sat on flat ground about fifteen feet below a curve in the Reno Highway, with a steep bluff rising from the opposite side of the pavement. A southbound set of headlights swept into the curve, then slowed to turn sharp and drop down the dirt lane between the corrals and the house. It was a pickup, heading in my direction. For a second the headlights caught Audie standing alone and perfectly still out by the corrals. She was holding her sleeping bag to her chest and blinking into the light. I almost yelled out the window at her but didn't want to expose myself just yet and maybe put her in jeopardy. If I could get her alone, I might be able to get my hands on the dingus Erika hid in the bag. As the headlights swept farther into the yard, Audie disappeared in shadow. The pickup was Dan's dually, which was no surprise. I could see Erika crouched behind the wheel peering into the shadows like she was figuring just where her life would end. The headlights finished their arc and lit up the spot where Audie had been, but by then the kid had vanished. The truck pulled up along the feedlot and stopped. Down the fence line a five-hundred-gallon above-ground fuel tank sat high on angle-iron legs. The truck lights threw the long shadow of the tank fifty feet across the open yard.

I stopped the Silverado behind the empty bunkhouse and slipped out with my rifle, drifting away from my truck as quick as I could. I found shelter in the darkness trying to figure who else was there. The ranch house with its sagging porch sat unlighted under the poplars, looking abandoned and ready to sink into the earth. There was no telling how soon Aaron Fuchs or Mitch's bunch would be pulling in. When they did, things might settle right down. Or all hell could break loose.

I saw Erika kill the headlights and get out of the pickup. She looked around. Standing in the ranchyard where she'd grown up seemed to disorient her, like she could barely keep her feet. Then I heard her shout her brother's name. I caught a movement off to my right, but whatever it was had disappeared into the dark. When I looked back towards the truck, Erika was gone, too.

If what I'd seen was a man, he'd flanked me. I stayed still for a minute just watching, and caught something move at the edge of a cedar postpile by the equipment shed. Sticking up from behind the shed was the white shape of a rental truck box that the dark clouds had kept hidden from view. I wondered if in the middle of all this mess, Buddy Hornberg had decided to just get out of Dodge.

There was no sound. It was like whoever was there wasn't even leaving footprints on the wet ground. What I could hear next was the noise of eighteen tires hissing by out on the wet pavement before the headlights of a semi arced over my head as the road curved north. I used the sound and light to cover distance fast until I was almost on top of whoever was moving in the dark.

I chambered a round as a shape moved in the shadow. Then I pointed the Remington and cleared my throat.

"Step into the light."

"Whoa—easy."

"Jack?"

I moved closer so I could whisper.

"What the hell are you doing here?"

"Sarah radioed me," he said. I could see he was carrying his department 12 gauge. "Told me you was heading here, and could I keep an eye on you? Back you up without gettin' us both shot or tipping off Mitch."

"How long you been here?"

"Not long," he said.

"Think anybody saw you?"

"Nah. I parked way down by the hot springs gate." He swung open the cylinder of his Smith & Wesson and checked his load, then holstered it. "So what's the play?"

I pointed toward Dan's truck with my rifle just as the semi faded away and the ranchyard went dark. Jack started to say something, but I shushed him. We heard Erika shout Buddy's name again, but this time it was more of a shriek. Like she was desperate. A short line of cars shot by, following the semi, their headlights sweeping the damp air above the housetop and throwing the long shadow of the gas tank on its spindly legs clear across the ranchyard again and again, like it was moving right towards us. But now the shadow of a man moved with it, arcing fast across the sheds and dirt and corral boards, the long shadow making the man look forty feet tall. Then, just as quick, the lights were gone. It was way after midnight and another car might not pass again for an hour. I watched disappearing taillights as the darkness settled.

"Buddy, you think?" Jack said.

I shook my head no. "VanOwen."

A bright white LED beam popped on in someone's hand.

"It's him, alright," Jack said.

There was movement to the side of Dan's pickup. VanOwen whipped the light around. The white beam landed right on Erika's face. She flinched like he'd hit her. He wore a camo hoodie against the storm with the hood pushed back from his face. He carried no visible weapon but I wasn't counting on him being unarmed.

He backed her against the truck, jabbing her with the end of his steel cane. From where I hid, I could see them arguing but not hear a word. I set the Remington on the postpile and motioned for Jack to sit tight. He looked at me like I was nuts when I walked out toward VanOwen without the rifle. I covered half the distance then shouted VanOwen's name.

He turned and watched me. The flashlight glare lit up his face from below and I could see him smile.

"Well, well," he said. "Here's the rifleman, right on time." He looked me up and down and laughed. "But still no rifle. Maybe you're a faker."

"Where's the girl?"

"I dunno know, man. Hey, don't stop. Keep on coming." He laughed. "You know kids are damn hard to keep track of."

I circled left so I'd have the corral fence close by.

"I thought you said the Feds had Erika," he said. "But here she is. You lied to me, son."

"I want that kid."

"Sure, Tommy Smith," he said, "sure. And you were gonna trade me that bank code thingy. That was the deal, right?" He laughed. Then he yelled toward the dark shape of the ranch house. "You can come out, now, Li'l Bit. Come say hi."

I took a few more steps toward them and stopped by the fuel tank. I could see Erika looking at me like I was all that was left in the world. When VanOwen pointed his light at me, I could see three red and yellow plastic gas cans sitting in the dirt, and greasy wet spots where fuel had spilled from the big tank. The padlock from the faucet had been pried off the bent steel hasp and lay in one of the wet spots. When I looked up I could see VanOwen studying me, jiggling the flash in my face.

"Going off-roading?"

"Brush clearing," he said. He laughed.

I looked over to Erika. "Shoulda stayed put."

"I know," she said. "But Buddy . . ."

"One of these days you'll have to let big brother sink or swim."

I turned to VanOwen to be sure he was looking me in the eye. "Erika being here doesn't change anything. FBI's on their way."

"They got nothing on me," he said.

"Don't count on it."

I squinted into the dark for Audie as VanOwen called her name. It took a minute before she drifted out of the shadows. She stopped before she got near any of us. I walked towards her kind of sideways, keeping my eye on VanOwen. When I got to her, I took a knee and she put her arms around my neck. I heard VanOwen say, "Awww."

Audie looked over my shoulder at Erika, who stood with VanOwen seventy feet away. He kept a hand tight around her arm.

"That's her again, right?" Audie said. "The spirit lady?"

"I guess so."

The sleeping bag was stained with mud and grease. Old hay and dried leaves stuck to both the outside and the lining. I picked up a corner of it and tried to whisper.

"Is this what the lady asked you to guard?"

"Yeah," Audie said. "How'd you know?" She watched Erika with tears in her eyes. "You think she's mad? I tried to keep it nice but it kinda looks like shit now."

"No. It's just fine. Can I take a peek at it?"

She nodded and handed it to me. I felt around inside, poking and squeezing the fleecy lining. I could feel bits of twig and hay and grit, but nothing like Erika had described to Sarah and me. No computer gizmo. No hardware. Nothing that was the key to a million bucks. I looked up when I heard VanOwen laugh.

"Looking for this, dude?" he said. He held up something small. I guessed it to be Erika's thumb drive, the metal tip of it catching a bit of light from his flash for just an instant. He laughed just as nasty as he could. "Sorry, rifleman, looks like you got nothin' left to trade for."

CHAPTER TWENTY

I stood up and pulled Audie close.

"You get the drive. I get the kid. That's it. That was the deal."

"You were late," he said. "The kid stays." He pulled an automatic from his hoodie pocket and motioned Audie over.

"You guys are all mad at me," Audie said. She was whimpering as she shuffled back to VanOwen. "I never knew nothin' was in the bag, honest, Sonny."

"How did you know where I hid it?" Erika said. Her voice had fear in it. She'd lost her ace in the hole. She turned to me like VanOwen wasn't there. "I . . . I thought it was the perfect hiding place. You know, in plain sight."

"Your brother told me, you dumb bitch," Sonny said. "So you must've told him. Buddy was trying to sell me out. First with you, then with Mister Sniper, here." He laughed. "Buddy even had me thinking that the rifleman was your boy, not him."

"Where is he?" Erika said. She asked it like she was afraid of the answer. He didn't give her one.

"Let her go. You got what you wanted from her."

"Ohhh, not by a long shot," he said.

"What else can she give you?"

"A life," he said.

I caught of glimpse of Jack poking his head up from behind the postpile, then I turned back to VanOwen. "Better just get your ass down the road before more law shows up."

"Oh, I'm goin'. Tiny found out at the FBI camp just what you told me—they'd quit buying Buddy's story that the little trick in the bog was his sister. They were going for a full autopsy, so it was time for me to boogie." He laughed. "I got my bags packed and my boarding pass"—he held up the thumb drive—"so *vaya con dios*, shitkicker."

"One question." I was just stalling for time. "What was your guy Flaco doing with the old pistol?"

VanOwen laughed. "Dumb sonofabitch never fired a gun in his life. He was only up there in case Tiny passed out from the strain. Walkin' that last couple of miles. He wanted to pack a gun like the big boys, so I figured what the hell. Saved me the trouble of getting rid of him later."

I hollered Jack's name and VanOwen pointed his flash in the direction I'd hollered. Jack stood up with his 12 gauge.

"If it ain't the goddamn wagon-burner," VanOwen said. "How's the ear, Tonto?"

Jack was a scary looking guy when he was pissed.

"That Twister Creed was a damn fine shot." VanOwen

tapped his ear, then turned to me. "But not so smart, huh dude?"

"He was a better man than a pimp like you."

"Aaaw. But now he's dead, ain't he." He kind of shrugged. "Well, there's more where he came from," he said. "Hey, *Tiny*. Start the ball." He grinned and pulled Audie close.

We turned towards where VanOwen was watching. There was a flash and the ranch house started to glow from the inside out, first white like headlights, then yellow, then orange. The yard where we were standing began to light up, too. I could see the poplars from below now, branch by branch. I looked at orange flame growing in the downstairs windows. That explained the gas cans over by the fuel tank. The white flash faded, and the yard darkened a bit as the first flames ate across the downstairs. There was another sound besides the rush of oxygen into breaking windows as the house caught. It took me a second. The sound I was hearing was Erika moaning, the air rushing out of her, not in.

"No!" she said. "How *can* you?"

I grabbed her by the arm as she ran by, heading for the house. It was her bad arm and she yelped when I did, so I let go. She stepped next to me just watching the house, the flames lighting her face. I turned back to VanOwen. He was staring at the fire growing, just as excited as a kid. Audie tried to jerk away, but he held on tight. He wasn't even looking at her, but this seemed like a dance the two of them had danced before.

Erika shrieked at him. "Where is my *brother*?"

When VanOwen started taunting Erika, I saw Audie kick him in his gimpy leg and run off into the dark. He hobbled backwards, closer to the fuel tank, and yelled Tiny's name again.

"Get the goddamn Indian."

I heard the double-clack of a pump shotgun in the near shadows and saw Audie running back into the fire-light towards me. I grabbed her and hit the dirt as buckshot ripped into the fence boards just over our heads. Splinters raked across my hat brim and I heard another shell jacked into a chamber, this one like it was right behind me. I tensed as a second round exploded.

Then the house in front of us just erupted. It went from a fire that could be put out to one that couldn't. In front of me flame jumped up past the roof. Then all the light pointed in a single direction, and the bright orange was all you saw. The rest was just black, the man with the shotgun moving between me and the fire, just a silhouette. I turned my back to the flame and got a good look at whatever had been behind me. I could see the fuel tank against the fence and see Jack rising up from the postpile to fire his 12 gauge. The glow from the house shined on his dark face, and I could see the colors of his uniform shirt and jeans clear as day. He ducked and ran past me toward the house as Tiny fired. I held Audie tight, keeping my body between her and the shotgun duel raging just in front of us, two moving silhouettes against the orange, with red and silver flashes of muzzle blast marking their path. Buckshot tore into sheds and corrals and clanged into the flat end of the fuel tank, the sound hollow and echoing. There was a second's pause, then I heard the sound of another shell being chambered. Then the only sounds were the close-by trickling of gasoline from the punctured tank as it dribbled into the dirt, and the farther-away roar of the burning house. Jack rose up, his silhouette still outlined by the flames.

I could hear VanOwen laugh, then saw him step out of the shadows with his flashlight. The beam swung towards where the shots were fired and lit up Tiny stumbling toward us. He took half a dozen steps then hit the dirt beard-first, the shotgun still in one fist, his leathers covered in blood. In the light of the flames I could see that the stock of the shotgun had been sawed off right to the pistol grip, a wanna-be badass modification of a cheap piece that probably looked cool in The Nogales parking lot.

Moving slow, Jack walked out of the blackness to Audie and me, watching Tiny's body, wary and ready to get to it again if he had to.

I stood and pulled Audie up with me. VanOwen was shining his flash into the dark places. I looked around and couldn't see Erika anywhere. I hadn't seen her since before Jack and Tiny started swapping buckshot. VanOwen heaved his body around, pivoting on his cane planted in the mud. He pulled the automatic and pointed it at my head. I pushed Audie behind me. Jack kept the shotgun in his right fist leveled at VanOwen's middle. We each stood about thirty feet apart. A stand-off.

"The girl," VanOwen said. "I'm not leaving without her."

"Where's Erika? Looks like now I got Audie and you got nothin.'"

He looked pissed. He scanned the yard with his light again and called Erika's name. It was another minute till we saw her. She walked to the edge of the firelight and stopped, just a motionless shape. VanOwen called her name a second time, and she came striding into the light towards him. She looked semi-crazed and tried to beat his face with her fists, though she could hardly reach that high. He grabbed both wrists and said something in her ear as she yelped. Then he laughed as she tried to pull away and kick him at the same time. Finally, she stopped trying to punch him and just stared at the house disappearing behind shimmery thirty-foot flames, the pattern of the fire swirling over us all. She walked toward the house and stopped near the porch, taking a step back from the awful heat. She yelled something that might have been her brother's name, then howled.

"What have you *done* to us?"

She turned three-sixty like she was falling through solid ground. Then she ran into the house.

VanOwen didn't try to stop her. I couldn't be sure, but I thought I saw him smile. The rest of us couldn't stop her. She was gone too fast.

There was a last scream from Erika, muffled and faraway as she stumbled deep into the fire and disappeared. In just that instant she was gone. Even a hard guy like VanOwen had to turn to look. A northbound pickup hummed around the bend in the road, its headlights sending his long shadow and the shadow of the fuel tank rippling across the ground one last time. Then darkness swept the shadows away and VanOwen was gone too. Audie put her arms around my neck and squeezed hard. Her crying turned into heaving sobs as she watched the flames.

"How does the spirit lady live in that?"

"I don't know. I don't know."

I saw Jack flinch as a blast of orange sparks poured from a downstairs window. We heard another smash of breaking glass as a window popped out from the heat, followed by the shrieking, tearing sound like an upstairs floor or wall giving way. It could've been a beam pulling apart from the rest of the framing, or Erika dying, or just that whole family and their history and everything they'd built and lived for vanishing in front of us. The heat caused its own currents. Wispy funnels of smoke spun around the edges of the fire, then rose into the hot air like ghosts.

"Holy shit," Jack said. "What the hell—?"

"She thought her brother was inside."

I turned after I said that in time to see Jack drop to the ground. I had to let go of Audie as I ran over to him. When I was still ten feet off I could see his left arm and ribs oozing blood. Tiny must've got off a clear shot after all. Jack opened his eyes as I checked him out.

"Just a few nicks," he said. He squirmed to ease the pain. "I know you didn't want the kid in a crossfire and all, but your dad's Remington might be a good idea now." He said it like we were talking over coffee, but he was panting hard. When he coughed, it looked like it about killed him.

"No shit, pal."

I checked the wounds a second time, then took off my jacket and covered him with it. When I looked to where I'd left Audie, she'd wandered off again. I turned back to Jack.

He was holding his left arm with his right hand and staring at movement by the equipment shed.

"She's over there," he said.

Headlights popped on behind the shed and began to move.

"Can you hang on another minute?"

Jack nodded. "Go," he said.

I ran for the postpile to grab my rifle. Either Fuchs or Sarah had to be close, with medical teams not far behind.

It was a bobtail truck with a rental company logo on the box. The truck revved and lurched towards us. Blinding mist and smoke spun white in the headlights. At first, the windshield was just orange reflection from the fire across the yard. Then the truck cleared the shed. The front wheels turned, and I could see the driver. VanOwen hung on to the steering wheel with his left hand, the automatic in his right resting across his body on the door panel. I could barely make out Audie flattened against the passenger door.

The truck rocked on the uneven ground and picked up speed. Then shots were fired from the driver's open window. I brought up the .270. I could see Audie sit up when I did.

VanOwen flinched when he saw I was finally armed. The engine wound out as he floored it and aimed the truck right at me, his eyes wide and orange in the reflected flame. I set my feet and didn't move. In the next instant I squeezed off my shot and heard the pop of a hole bursting in the windshield, and I saw VanOwen's head jerk sideways. Audie flattened against the door to get away from the blood.

The truck turned up the slope towards the highway,

veering enough to the right so that the cargo box protected the cab from another rifle shot. It swerved toward the feed-lot fence and smashed into the gas tank, taking out the front legs and tilting the tank forward so the remaining gas spurted over the truck grille.

The bobtail came to a stop with one hind wheel still spinning slow, like VanOwen's foot hadn't quite left the pedal. I ran around to the passenger door to yank Audie out before the tank exploded. I gathered her up and squeezed her tight, looking over her head at VanOwen. He leaned back against the headrest bleeding from the neck. I was still watching him when I heard a whimpering, almost human sound like a baby goat makes. VanOwen's eyes sort of flick-ered as I jerked my head toward the sound. He didn't move, but he tried to grin. He was wheezing like a guy who'd just jogged a couple of miles. There was a lot of blood. I set Audie down.

"Now get out of here."

"I wanna stay with you."

"No. Run like hell before this explodes." I pointed over to Jack curled up under my jacket. "Run to Jack and stay with him. He needs you right now."

The bleating sound started again as she ran off. I hus-tled around the cab, jumping over a puddle of gasoline. I hadn't seen a trace of livestock in the barnyard corrals and was clueless where the sound could've come from. I yanked open the driver side door and reached over VanOwen just careful as could be. He was stretching for his flashlight on the dash when I heard a shotgun blast a dozen feet behind me—metallic and echoing and loud as hell, like it came from the cargo box. I stumbled around to the back of the truck. Jack leaned against the roll-up cargo door breathing hard through his nose, his own blood all over his hands. He looked at me, too breathless to talk, and nodded at the lock he'd just mangled with buckshot. Audie got on one side of him and I got on the other and we helped him stumble away from the truck.

"The kid said unlock it," he said.

We all heard the crying baby goat sound then.

"We gotta open it, Tommy," Audie said.

"Then we gotta do it damn quick."

I told Audie to stand back with Jack. I pried off what was left of the padlock and grabbed the handles and hoisted the roll-up door. I peered into the dark until the human stink hit me.

CHAPTER TWENTY-ONE

In front of me sat two nice Harleys and boxes and duffels of all sorts of crap. One of the duffels was spilling out with pistols, rifles, shotguns, and ammo. Another was stuffed with cash. I heard whimpering and goat bleating, then saw the light of the burning house reflected in tiny pairs of eyes. Twelve feet back in the gloom they could've belonged to a den of coyotes or a mess of possum or even puppies. Then a child started weeping and Jack yelled.

"What the hell is it?" he said.

"Kids."

There were four of them. Four girls, three of them not much older than Audie, one of them with duct tape over her mouth and around her wrists. In the dark they whimpered and moaned and generally acted like they'd been drugged. The fourth was about sixteen and all whored up in stripper shoes and skimpy clothes and a ton of makeup. She looked badly used and quivered but didn't speak. She was the high school kid who made malts at the Sno-Cone in Paiute Meadows. The girl I'd seen purring at VanOwen's elbow as he stroked her arm in the bar of the Sierra Peaks. I called Audie over, and we dragged them out of there fast, all of them too weak or stoned not to stumble or fall. We took two each and walked them away from the bobtail and the spurting gas, Audie just as determined as hell. We got them a safe distance, then I circled back to the cab.

VanOwen sat where I'd left him. He kept his eyes on me as I patted him down, looking for the thumb drive. I found it in a pocket of his hoodie. I had to reach across him to grab it, trying to avoid the blood. He laughed, then put his hand to his throat. I stepped back, my .270 in the crook of my arm.

"You're the freakin' rifleman, after all," he said. His voice was weak and raspy.

"Pretty obvious this was your exit plan. How come you didn't take it sooner? You'd be long gone. A clean getaway."

"Damn straight. Got my Reno boy Carl hidin' down the road in the willows in another rental. Once I got the doohickey from Erika, him and Tiny were gonna switch this load into that truck." When he spoke blood pumped from his wound. "He was gonna drive me to a charter plane at the Mammoth airport and meet me later down south."

Blood bubbled from his mouth as he smiled. "I was gonna be *gone*. Fresh start for me. Helluva plan, huh dude?"

"Foolproof. Teenage whores, guns, and a bag stuffed with cash. A total gangster starter kit. Any regrets?"

"Only that I didn't do your wife."

He tried to spit at me. Blood ran out his nose into his mustache.

"Nice. Hard guy to the end."

He grinned and coughed.

"So what went wrong?"

"Jesus, you're slow."

"You weren't leaving Audie behind. I know that much."

"Well . . ." he stopped for air. "Well, pin a rose on your nose. I thought you woulda figured that out by now." He was taking long breaths, and he stopped to gag on a mess of blood. Then his eyes rolled back like he was going to pass out. He recovered and laughed. "She's my kid, dumbshit."

He turned in my direction with the automatic in his fist. it might've been a Walther 9mm. His big hand wrapped around it so it was hard to tell.

"Too slow to live, dude."

His finger barely fit through the trigger guard but I could see it squeeze. I jumped sideways as he fired. I didn't have time to raise the Remington anywhere near my shoulder, but I'd been rehearsing this shot in my head since I first saw the truck. The soft point took off the top of his skull.

I walked back toward where Jack and Audie waited with the four girls. For the first time since that night when Audie staggered into the pack station she wasn't dragging the sleeping bag. She was tending those children with a blanket and water bottle just like Sarah would have. She'd already stripped the tape off the mouth and wrists of the bound girl and held Jack's radio while he guzzled water.

"That was Sarah," Jack said. He slipped the radio back on his belt.

"She said she's five or ten minutes out. Her and Mitch. I told her you and the girl were okay but pretty much everybody else was shot to shit."

"Including you."

"I ain't so bad," he said. "Hey, I didn't say nothin' about these kids. We can show Mitch when he gets here." He started taking long, slow breaths. "Sarah said he's expecting us to turn Erika over, no questions asked."

We both looked at the house falling in on itself into the flames.

"We can tell him where to find her."

"Can we?" Jack said. he looked grim. "Buddy must've been tied up inside or somethin'."

"I guess."

"Erika was brave as they come," Jack said. "She died trying to save that useless bastard."

"Yeah." I looked at Audie with the other girls. That kid had seen some bad stuff in her ten years. She didn't do shit with a doll a stranger gave her because she didn't see the point in make believe, but she hovered around these four girls and Jack and never looked up.

"He done this before," she said out of nowhere. "With other girls."

"If you hadn't told us, the truck might've blown with these four inside. You saved their lives, Audie."

She looked up like there was just no hope for me. "No shit, Sherlock." Then she almost smiled. "Just like you saved mine."

She watched the ranch house when half the roof caved in. Sparks rose a hundred feet. I caught her looking at me.

"It's okay," she said

"So you knew?"

"That he was my dad? Yeah, I knew. From how my

mom acted and things she said, I kinda guessed, but I never wanted to ask."

She watched me pull the gizmo out of my jacket pocket.

"What's that?" she said.

I held out the drive on the flat of my hand. "Trouble."

She reached out and touched it, then yanked her hand back like it was hot.

"I know he shot my mom." She looked up at me like she was wondering what I'd say. There was nothing to say.

"I was in the next room and heard them yelling about him and me. I never said nothin'. I was afraid he'd shoot me, too."

She shielded her eyes with her hand and looked at the ranch house. By now we could feel the heat radiate from the ruins all the way across the yard. One of the girls held out a water bottle when she was done with it. Audie took it and gave it to another girl.

I could see tears now, but they sure didn't seem to be for VanOwen.

"I knew the spirit lady wasn't real," she said, "but it made me happy to think so. I saw that lady and I could pretend I was gonna see my mom again someday." She was silent and more tears came. She wiped them away like they made her mad.

I looked towards town and could see flashing red lights, either sheriff's or fire or EMTs, still just a glow a mile distant.

"So don't worry," she said. "I'm not mad at you or nothin'. Sonny was a douche-nozzle."

"You even know what that means?"

"No," she said. "But it sounds gross and he was gross. I told you up at Sarah's dad's place that if you shot him, I wouldn't mind." She looked over at the truck like she was afraid he'd roar back from the dead. "I don't mind."

I asked her to stay with Jack while we waited for the emergency crews, and I told her Sarah would be there before she knew it. I wondered where the switch to the yard lights might be, but there was no one left alive to ask. Jack and I looked at each other a second, and he laughed. A what-the-hell laugh, like he just couldn't help it. Even in the damp night we were both sweating like a hungover haying crew, with dirt smudges on our faces and clothes, and blood all over.

I walked up to the house and stood as close as I could in the heat. Only part of the walls were left standing. There was no trace of Erika, but then I didn't expect to find any. I walked across the yard back to the truck and poked around through VanOwen's duffles until I found what I was looking for. I pulled out my granddad's old lever-action shotgun and set it on a post away from the truck, then walked down the corral boards of the feedlot. Maybe I could give that shotgun to a grandkid of mine someday—if I lived that long.

Growing up, I'd never spent much time on the Hornberg place, so the layout wasn't really familiar. Not like Becky Tyree's ranch or Harvey's pack station. I rounded the corner of the feedlot to the brick slaughterhouse. The light inside was still the only electric light burning on the ranch.

The glow was coming from the center corridor, a single bulb hanging from a single cord throwing its weak beam on the steel rail that hung from the ceiling and connected the two rooms on either side. The refrigerator door of the meat locker on the left was open just as it had been the week before when I first came to see Buddy, and the random junk and furniture inside looked untouched. I pushed open the door to the slaughter room and looked into the dark.

I could make out Buddy hanging from the gambrel hooks over the killing floor. He was upside down, his head about three feet off the ground, his eyes open, his ankles spread apart by the gambrel and his stiff arms dangling. Long straight bruises covered his face and arms. Other than the blood, the floor was spotless. Something shone in the light for a second. It was like a twisted bit of copper wire or maybe a piece of fishing lure sitting on the concrete next to the iron drain. It was hard to make out in the gloom. I picked it up and put it in my shirt pocket, then got out of that place.

Someone had found the switch to the yard lights and turned them on. The first ambulance crews were already on the job, tending to Jack and the rescued girls. Sarah and Mitch pulled into the yard with firetrucks close behind. Mitch saw me walking across the ranchyard and got out of his SUV to head me off. Sarah moved faster than he did. She put her arms around me, and we ignored him a minute.

"My god, baby," she said. "This is like a war zone." She looked sorry the minute she said it. I held her close and let her wipe the sweat from my face. Audie ran up to Sarah, and we both held her close as she made gasping sobs in

Sarah's arms. Then Sarah saw Jack, his shirt off as an EMT worked on him.

"Oh, god," she said, "is Jack—"

"He's okay," Audie said. She wiped her eyes with the back of her hand. "He's a tough old bird, ya know."

Then Audie told Sarah about the four girls, and we went to where the EMT's were evaluating them. Sarah recognized the girl from the Sno-Cone and called her by name as she hugged her. Then the crews loaded the four into county ambulances.

"I've known that child her whole life," Sarah said.

"Tommy Smith." Mitch said. He was hustling towards us. "You'll turn over that Hornberg woman now."

"Can't do it."

"You *will* do it. I want her in custody when the FBI gets here or there'll be hell to pay for you two sneaking her past us tonight."

"No can do, Mitch."

"She's over there, mister," Audie said.

Mitch looked across the yard where she was pointing. Then Sarah did, too. By now the ranch house had burned down to a raging bonfire, a jumbled red-hot mess of beams and rubble and part of a brick fireplace and some iron pipes that so far had only half melted. The highest point left was a piece of tiled wall behind a bathtub on the second floor.

"The lady just got burned up," Audie said.

Even in the patchy moonlight I could see a tear on Sarah's cheek. "Nobody could survive that," she said.

The piece of wall and the bathtub and the floor underneath them all fell through into the embers with another blast of sparks. The sparks set a poplar next to the house afire, and the flames rushed up the deadwood branches into the new leaves. Now only the front of the ramshackly screened-in porch was left untouched.

Mitch looked around the yard at the rental truck wedged under the gas tank with its driver's side door hanging open, and at Tiny's body sprawled about sixty feet away. An EMT was poking and jabbing Tiny, making preliminary examinations. Sorenson wore latex gloves as he picked up the big guy's chopped 12 gauge then started clearing a path for more Paiute Meadows Volunteer Fire Department trucks.

I led Mitch and Sarah over to the bobtail where a firefighter was spraying the cab with foam so Mitch could see VanOwen's body. Two more volunteers and an EMT followed behind. We watched the volunteers as they tried pulling VanOwen from the cab. He was so big they got him wedged behind the steering wheel. Mitch turned away before he retched.

"How'd the house catch fire?" he said.

"VanOwen's guy torched it."

"Why?" Mitch said.

"I think he wanted to kill Erika Hornberg in the gruesomest way he could and still keep his hands clean."

"How the hell—?"

"He let her think her brother was inside."

"Was he?" Sarah said.

When I didn't answer her right away, Sarah just nodded.

The three county folks kept yanking on VanOwen's stuck body, then quit to catch their breath.

"Well, I'll be damned," Mitch said. "So who shot Sebastian VanOwen?"

"Me."

"Crap, Tom," he said, making a face. "You gave him the full Zapruder."

He walked over to Tiny's body, getting away from the truck as quick as he could. We all followed him.

"And you shot this fat guy, too?"

"That was Jack."

Mitch bent down for a closer look. "Dang it, this guy is shot all to *hell*," he said. "Glad Jack's gonna be okay." He peered around the death scene looking pretty chipper, all things considered. "So, Buddy Hornberg wasn't in the burning house. He's okay, then?"

"Nope." I pointed to the slaughterhouse. "He's down there. Somebody beat him to death with a steel rod. You know, Mitch, like a cane."

Mitch looked at me half pissed, half whipped.

"And there's a couple of fellas up Aspen Canyon who got thrashed by some pack stock tonight, plus the body of a packer called Twister Creed up in the old snow cabin. They're VanOwen's guys, and they'll need to be found."

"Well, holy crap. I'll need a statement from you and Jack both, then." His eyes moved back to the burning house. "Some families—" he started to say.

"We better take a look at Buddy," Sarah said.

"Yeah, okay," Mitch said. "Lead the way, Tommy. Jeezo Christ."

We were almost to the slaughterhouse when the punctured gas tank set off the bobtail truck like a bomb.

CHAPTER TWENTY-TWO

We waited another half hour for Agent Fuchs. He was driving his own Explorer with bike racks and not the usual government sedan. He pulled in as the fire crew was just mopping up the flames from the gas tank and bobtail. Aaron was half-buried in a North Face fleece and a Heavenly Valley ballcap and looked like he just got out of bed, though as it was close to four in the morning, he had to have been up for hours. We sat on the tailgate of the Silverado, the three of us and Audie, just as we had more than once at the pack station. Audie slept on Sarah's lap, and we drank lukewarm Indian Casino coffee from cardboard cups that Aaron had brought us. I told him the story that began the night before at Little Meadows with Erika showing up out of nowhere. I stopped a few times when he asked questions. He basically called me nuts for the dead-run horseback stunt but allowed it had worked pretty well.

The wind picked up and scattered the clouds, letting the setting moon shine. The wind slackened, and we caught the smell of wet sage from across the highway and the rotten burned smell of the old house and the gasoline fumes from the big tank and burnt vinyl and flesh of the bobtail's interior. Fresh gusts stirred up embers from the house. Jack walked over just stiff as hell when the last EMT left. He leaned against the bed of the truck like it hurt. His bloody shirt was gone and he was wearing a red Frémont County Fire jacket. He pulled a pint of Knob Creek from the pocket.

"Compliments of the volunteer fire department," he said. "So where do we go from here?"

"You're going straight to the emergency room in Mammoth," Sarah said.

"I gotta write my report," Jack said. "It's gonna be freaky-deaky."

Sarah started to say something, then just laughed. We passed the Knob Creek around, watching the county medical examiner's crew wheel VanOwen's burned body away. I thought I saw Audie's eyes open for a second to follow the corpse. If she was watching, I didn't try to shield her from it. The kid was tougher than most grownups. Just as tough as a rasp.

"Well," Aaron said, "poetic justice for an arsonist."

"If Erika were still alive," Sarah said, "what would the government have done with her?"

"I learned a long time ago never to count on what should happen," he said, "only what does."

"That's a pretty mealy-mouthed answer."

Aaron almost laughed.

"Well," Sarah said, "she died thinking she was saving her brother's life."

Audie raised her head. "That's pretty brave, ain't it?"
I don't know how long she'd been listening. "She was hella
brave then, right?"

The four of us didn't quite have a grownup comeback
to that.

"Yeah, sweetie," Sarah said. "It was totally brave."

Audie crawled deeper into Sarah's arms and closed
her eyes again. We chased the Knob Creek with the dregs
of our coffee, then emptied what was left of the coffee on
the dirt. Sorenson walked over and told Aaron he'd found
the second rental truck exactly where VanOwen told me it
would be, just off the highway less than a mile south. There
was no trace of Carl. We watched Sorenson walk off.

"So, Tommy," Aaron said, "what about the money?"

I pulled the thumb drive out of my jacket and held it
out to him. He looked down at it a minute before he took it.

"Doesn't exactly look like a million bucks," he said.

"She got killed trying to get it to you."

Aaron took the drive and bounced it on his palm.

Sarah told him what we'd learned from Erika about
the account in the Cyprus bank. He made notes for his
financial crew.

"If she'd survived," Aaron said, "all this would've
helped her."

"That poor dope," Sarah said. "What a waste of a life."

Finally, Sarah, Audie, and I drove out of the yard past
the firetrucks and county law vehicles and the last milling
first responders. Mitch gave us a wave as we drove by.

"What? We're all pals again?"

"No," Sarah said. "But I bet he's relieved. Now he can

close the book on a pretty big crime that's stumped our department for almost a year, plus take part of the blame off somebody who still has a lot of friends in this valley. No matter how tough he talked, Mitch wasn't looking forward to slapping the cuffs on Erika. The downside for him is he has to share the credit with you and Aaron." She put an arm around my shoulders. "You always seem to frost his cookies. One of the many things I like about you."

We picked up Lorena from Becky Tyree and spent a quick fifteen minutes at her kitchen table telling her how her friend died. Becky sat in her bathrobe listening, dry-eyed but drained.

"I've spent all night thinking about how a family that had everything going for it could just fall apart so fast," she said.

After a few more words, she thanked us and we left. We drove out her lane to the Summers Lake Road close to sunup. The dawn glow from the eastern hills was smudged with oily smoke.

I was driving and Sarah was dozing. Audie slept between us, and the baby was secured on the back seat. I remembered the bit of wire in my shirt pocket and rooted around for it long enough to catch Sarah's attention.

"What is it, babe?"

I held it out to her and she took it. She didn't look impressed.

"It's Erika's," she said. "Erika's earring."

"You sure?"

"Sure I'm sure. I saw her wearing them last night. I hadn't seen her for years but she always wore those dangly things."

I crossed the tip of the sagebrush moraine just as the first bit of sunrise hit the timbered ridge up ahead.

"Why?" she said. "Where did you get it?"

"It was on the floor of the slaughterhouse right near the drain. Not three feet from Buddy's body."

Sarah took it all in for a minute.

"Then Erika knew he wasn't in the house," she said. "That he was already dead. My god, Tommy, she *knew.*"

"Yeah. She wasn't trying to save him."

"No. She was trying to join him."

The day after the killings at the Hornberg ranch, Harvey and I got back to work. We saddled up four horses for the Newport Beachers plus the two we would ride and four mules to pack out our party from their camp at Little Meadows. We saddled a fifth mule just for Harvey's bedroll.

I filled him in on what Bill had told me on the ride up. How his wife and Scottie had tracked me down so they could meet the stony-cold cowboy killer from the tiny article in the *Los Angeles Times*, which would be me. I knew I was in for a world of crap from Harv that would only last a year or two, but I wanted him to know why I was planning on being silent about the mess at Hornberg's.

It was a cloudless June morning with only a slight breeze waving through the early summer grass and fluttering the aspen. Bonner and Tyree cows and calves meandered across the meadows and hid in shady thickets and bogs along the creek. Snowmelt was running high, and the water was clear and chest deep on the horses in the crossings. Becky and Dan had packed Twister Creed's body out for the county the day before.

We climbed out of the canyon through the timber into the Wilderness Area, then kept climbing the trail to the pass. We reached the camp at Little Meadows by early afternoon. We hobbled the stock out to graze, then had some pricey IPAs Tess had chilled in the icy creek, and they told us about their adventures. Drew and Scottie climbed Hawksbeak the morning after Erika and I blasted out of their camp. Bill had hiked to Beartrap Lake to fish. Drew told me the morning had been windy and overcast, and they'd hit some snow, ice, and slick rock from the storms just like I said they might, but that with caution, they stayed out of trouble, and by the time they made it to the top the sun was out. He showed me pictures he'd taken from the summit. The country looked huge from that altitude, with no human scar to be seen and no human stain on the landscape.

Bill said he expected Beartrap would be murky from storm runoff. Instead, the sky was breezy but cloudless and the lake was clear. He landed some nice brookies that he cleaned and packed in snow. This morning he and Drew had headed out early and climbed Tower Peak, while later Scottie and Tess hiked to an old Forest Service cabin to explore, then spent the afternoon reading Anne Cleeland mysteries and napping and drinking creek-chilled chardonnay. It was one of those perfectly warm but crisp days, and the four of them said it made the whole trip.

"How about you, Tommy?" Tess said. "Any new adventures for the fearless wilderness guide?"

"Nope."

"We didn't get our extra days with you." She laughed. "You owe us, cowboy."

"Don't I know it."

I felt a little guilty lying to them, especially Bill, but I didn't want to rehash the last couple of days. Harvey pushed the people to get their gear semi-organized for the next morning. Later he cooked us all dinner with Dutch oven biscuits, wild rice in garlic butter, steak tenderloin, then brook trout stuffed with elk sausage, plus cow-camp coffee and a couple kinds of outstanding wine that the folks shared with us poor packers, finished off with a Dutch oven chocolate cake. But not before he gave them a start by hauling out a cloth sack of potatoes and onions plus a can of Folgers.

Riding out the next day we reached the forks by late morning. Though Creed's body was gone, I'd kept a brisk pace as we passed the snow cabin. We took a lunch break at the Blue Rock, then I let Harvey take the lead with his string and had three of the folks follow him close. Coming into the second meadow I asked Bill to drop back to where I was leading the last three mules, and I told him what happened and asked him to keep it to himself. At least until they got back to civilization. He listened without a word. When I finished, I pulled up my horse.

"I don't feel good about any of this, but at least we got those kids out safe."

Bill sat his horse just as still as could be. Then he laughed, his eyes down-trail on his friends skirting the meadow.

"They are just going to flip out—a gunfight with bank robbers and sex traffickers breaking bad just across the valley while we were all so close, but having no damn clue?" he said. "They will be *so* pissed."

CHAPTER TWENTY-THREE

In late June, Paiute Meadows saw two funerals. They happened one week and a hundred fifty feet apart. The first funeral was big. Several hundred people, about half the population of the valley, stood on the bare ground on a slope east of the town. A few dresses, fewer ties, mostly cowboy hats and clean jeans. It was at the old Hornberg plot, the gravestones surrounded by an iron fence. Mourners circled a new chunk of black marble with both Erika's and Buddy's names freshly chiseled on either side of a badly rendered horseman. The birthdates on the stone were four years apart. The dates of the deaths were identical. The marble said that Buddy's given name was Claus Wolfgang Hornberg, but not one in ten of us had known that.

The black monument stood apart from the tilting century-old pink and white angel with engraving worn by wind and sand. And apart from white marble slabs carved to look like axe-hewn tree trunks, stones with old forgotten names and the birthdates rendered in block letters that went back a hundred fifty years, and newer names from early in the last century right up to Erika and Buddy's father, who had died twelve years before. All ranchers, well remembered by old timers in the crowd, their Masonic symbols carved in stone above the men's names. The names were all there were. Hard old-country names with no Beloved Mother or anything else so frivolous or so kind.

The family wasn't the earliest to work the valley, and their ranch wasn't the biggest. Becky's great-grandfather had them beat by fifty years and fifteen hundred acres, and the Allisons, who'd hired my dad before I was born, had a few more years and a thousand acres more than that. Unspoken was the obvious thing. We were seeing the end of a family. The end of a ranch. For a lot of us, this ceremony was a reminder that the life we'd chosen was not forever. There was talk of an older cousin from Evanston, Illinois, who had visited the ranch once forty years before. The woman got sunburned bad enough to never come back, and told her uncle Kurt that his ranch house was a disgusting dump and should be bulldozed and Erika and Buddy sent to boarding school in Santa Barbara or Lake Forest. Now, that woman was the only heir. She had paid for her cousins' headstone but wouldn't pay to embalm a slacker like Buddy. She told the sheriff over the phone that he could be cremated like his sister, which even Mitch thought was a crass thing to say. After hanging up, he sent Sorenson to scoop up ash from the ruin of the ranch-house so there would be something of Erika to bury. It went against his image, but I was glad he did it, though I'd never tell him so. At the Sierra Peaks bar that night, Sorenson talked about gathering the fake ashes, which started the first rumor that Erika might still be alive. The county not paying for a forensic sifting of the ruins after sworn deputy Jack Harney had seen the woman run into the flames and not seen her come out just added to bar-room speculation. Folks remarked that there was no actual grave, just a little round hole in the ground at the foot of the marble where the canisters of ashes would go.

There was talk the Illinois woman would sell out fast. If no ranching interest stepped up to keep the land in cattle, she might sell part of it as a mobile home park. That would be more Sonny VanOwen's style than Erika's. Sarah and I stood with her father and my mom and Mom's boyfriend, Burt, who was fresh from the base in his Marine Utilities. Everyone had known everyone. What we kept hearing in both the testimonials and the whispers was how much they all thought of Erika, even from folks who'd trashed her in life. Of her kindness and forgiveness to her brother and of her hard work, both on the place and in the bank, and her contrariness in taking the risks she took even when those risks were beyond foolish. Becky Tyree spoke last. She wore a dress and talked from the heart about Erika's love of the high country and of her family, and how she gave herself to save her brother and the way of life they were born to. She stood pretty and strong and optimistic, reminding folks that no matter what, the land endures. I heard the word legacy more than once. As was fitting, nobody mentioned VanOwen or the trouble he brought with him.

The hard winters clean this hard country. I don't know what they do down in Southern Cal where VanOwen came from, down where it never freezes and people like him never get a rest from the evil worm inside them. It just feeds and feeds. A Tecate-born medic in my unit in the Hindu Kush called it the *gusanillo*, that worm inside you. That passion. Passion for good or passion for evil. He said it's what makes bullfighters fight bulls, and makes kiddie pool parties turn bloody when drunken dads whip out their pistols.

By the time the last tears dried in the June heat and the last cars pulled out of the cemetery gate toward town, the dead woman had got a share of her reputation back. The idea that Erika might have faked her death a second time hadn't caught on just yet.

There were barely a dozen of us standing around the second grave a week later. Audie, my mom and Burt, Becky Tyree and Dan, Harvey and May, Sarah's dad, Jack Harney, Sarah—just off duty and still in uniform—the baby, and me. That was it. The site was just a hole in the sand at the edge of the paupers' lot. Last stop for the indigent dead. The forsaken prostitute. The markers, where there were any, were white-painted steel crosses welded from sections of highway signposts or snowplow markers provided by the county road crew. Or short pine planks ruined by mountain winters and half-buried in the sand that marked the oldest Paiute graves, those names long gone. My mom and Becky had raised hell to keep the county from cremating the friendless woman, though they had no legal claim on the remains. They thought Audie should have one spot in this world where she could always go to remember her mother, a woman murdered trying to protect her child. We'd all chipped in, and a headstone had been ordered but not yet delivered. Aaron Fuchs rattled some cages at the FBI to track down the woman's birthplace outside of Coeur d'Alene, and her true name, Jennifer Leigh Ravenswood. It was a pretty name. She was just fifteen when Audie was born and twenty-four last fall when Sonny VanOwen, her rapist and her pimp, put a bullet in her brain. Aaron emailed us a juvi court photo of Jenny taken at around sixteen when her motherhood was new to her. She was beautiful. There was no other way to say it. In spite of the life she'd been dealt, she just glowed and had a smile that would break your heart. There was a passing resemblance to Erika in color and frame and bone structure but little resemblance in beauty. Just enough for VanOwen to think he could pull a switch when he had a body to dispose of. And he came close to getting away with it. Sarah said, looking at the picture of Jenny, that we could see what Audie would look like in a few years. Mom printed out the picture on good paper and framed it for Audie, who said it was the only picture of her mother she'd ever even seen.

She wore a dress my mom had bought for her to the cemetery. We carried the coffin to the grave with the marks of backhoe teeth still fresh in the cut. Audie's tears poured out along with the tears from people who'd never known the dead woman. After all the months in the lifeless water of the airless bog, we lowered her down into dry ground. Staring into that sandy hole, I got the idea that we hadn't gone on a false hunt after all. The search for a missing child was real. And we'd found her. We found Audie.

The first handful of dirt hit the coffin lid, and she wailed loud enough to wake the dead Spaniard in his cave.

When it was over and the tears were wiped and the noses blown, we walked back to our pickups for the drive to town. We were heading to the Sno-Cone for bacon cheeseburgers and chocolate malts, which was Audie's choice. I noticed a little German convertible parked under some runty spruce trees along the cemetery chain-link. It was a hot day to leave the top up. I walked next to the car and pulled my skinning knife so the driver couldn't miss it. Holding the knife in my right hand I ran the back of my thumb across the ragtop so it sounded like I was cutting into it. Carl had the door open quick enough.

His hair and Hawaiian shirt were plastered down with sweat. He looked more scared than pissed.

"What?" he said.

"You're the one scopin' us out. That'll stop right now." I sheathed my knife. "You're not in Reno anymore, so you got no jurisdiction and no cause if you did. Plus, your boss is dead."

"I know," he said. "Word gets around." He started to get out of the car.

"Don't."

He stopped. "Look, I don't want any trouble."

"Then what're you doing here?"

"I wanted to pay my respects."

Boy, there was nothing to say to that.

"To Jenny. She was a nice kid. What Snake did was wrong."

"Killing her? Oh, yeah. But you took his money anyway."

"I ain't perfect, okay. Internal Affairs is breaking my

balls. I'll be lucky to keep my badge." He squirmed in the seat. "They might wanna talk to you about . . . you know, stuff."

"Here's what I *know*. You were following me. That's all. I don't have a clue why. A pimp said you were on the take for him, but he's past talking. You just leave it at that. Enough people died here already. I could give a shit if you get to keep your job."

Carl looked through his windshield, past the crappy spruce trees and down the hill over the sagebrush to the Reno Highway heading south to Hornberg's a few miles below town. If you knew what you were looking for, you could see scorched pasture and blackened trees and fences around the foundation of the burned house in the hazy distance. He sort of nodded toward the grave.

"Jenny deserved better," he said. "I knew her ten years."

"What? Sonny give you a discount with her? Great, a sentimental predator."

He started to close the door, but I put my boot on the rocker panel so he couldn't.

"Now, here's what I *think*. I think Audie's mother went to the only cop she knew to say Sonny was molesting her daughter. *Their* daughter. And that cop, being a vice cop as well as a weak-suck chicken-shit scum, told Sonny instead of his superiors. And that's when Sonny blew that poor girl's brains out. That's what started this whole hoo-rah that ended up at Hornberg's last week."

He wiped the sweat from his forehead with the back of his arm.

"Tell the kid—"

271

"I'll tell her nothing." I took my boot off his car. "I better never see you again."

He closed the door and started the engine. I walked back to the rest of my folks.

"Who was that?" Dan said.

"Nobody."

At the Sno-Cone we piled around two picnic tables and waited for our order. Harvey, May, and I stood by the take-out window.

"I'm ready for some ice cream." Harvey said. He was more a bourbon and beer guy, but he had a devilish sweet tooth.

"What's to become of that child?" May said. She spoke soft so Audie couldn't hear. "You think your mom and Burt can get custody?"

"Maybe. Or she might stay with us. That's what Sarah wants. "

May grabbed me and gave me a big smack on the cheek. "Good," she said.

"Sarah and I need to figure it out. She said anything permanent with non-relatives is hard. Then there's the . . . recent violence. I did kill the kid's father."

"I have the feeling that her being with you and Sarah is just meant to be."

"Now you sound like Mom."

I knew nothing was ever meant to be. You either make it happen or you don't.

Audie dozed off on the drive back up to the pack station, whimpering and mumbling in her sleep. When our two trucks pulled into the yard, Harvey strapped on his tool belt to put in a few hours on the cabin before supper and work off his hot fudge sundae.

Sarah put Lorena down for a nap. I went outside and slid Dad's .270 into the outhouse rafters, then saddled up a brown horse that didn't belong to me. Nobody had claimed Twister Creed's body or even knew if he had any family, much less if this horse actually belonged to him. The gelding stood quiet while I rigged him up, but I was quiet, too. He didn't seem like a horse a guy should take for granted. I'd have to put ads in the *Reno Gazette Journal*, the *Copper County News*, and the *Progressive Rancher* and leave notices at feed stores and such to see if anybody claimed him, but if I was going to feed him, I was going to ride him.

He was watchful as I stepped up, and he seemed light and responsive and ready to move. I saw Audie keeping an eye on me from the porch, more serious and sad than ever. I busted the horse out along the fence to see what he'd do, pushing him harder than I ought, to see if he'd bog his head. He did. He was fast and catty and a bit touchy, a cowboy's horse, but honest, and he settled pretty quick. Sarah had gone inside to change, so I hollered for Audie to open the corral gate for me. Sarah heard the gate creak and walked back outside, barefoot and in jeans, buttoning a cowboy shirt. I rode up to the porch. Sarah gave me that look she had.

"I'm going to ride this guy up the trail for half an hour."

"Are you coming back?" Audie said.

"'Course I'm coming back. I live here, remember?"

"Where do I live?"

I circled the brown horse a few more times. Sarah watched to see what I'd say. I answered Audie, but my eye was on my wife. We'd never really come close to settling this.

"Here. You live here. With Sarah and me."

Sarah nodded and gave me a heartbreaking smile. I nodded back.

I loped the horse out the gate, stopped him, and circled him again. "Tell you what. Go get into your jeans."

"How come?" Audie said.

"'Cause you're going with me."

I didn't have to ask her twice. In the couple weeks we'd known her, getting the kid on a horse was never something I had time to think about. I had a solid old mare saddled when Audie came back. I got her mounted and the stirrups shortened.

"You ever been on a horse before?"

"Hell no," she said. "But I bet I'll be damn good at it."

Sarah shaded her eyes with her hand and watched us ride off up the canyon.